J19

Paris In My Springtime

Books by Vernon Coleman

The Medicine Men (1975)
Paper Doctors (1976)
Everything You Want To Know About Ageing (1976)
Stress Control (1978)
The Home Pharmacy (1980)
Aspirin or Ambulance (1980)
Face Values (1981)
Guilt (1982)
The Good Medicine Guide (1982)
Stress And Your Stomach (1983)
Bodypower (1983)
An A to Z Of Women's Problems (1984)
Bodysense (1984)
Taking Care Of Your Skin (1984)
A Guide to Child Health (1984)
Life Without Tranquillisers (1985)
Diabetes (1985)
Arthritis (1985)
Eczema and Dermatitis (1985)
The Story Of Medicine (1985, 1998)
Natural Pain Control (1986)
Mindpower (1986)
Addicts and Addictions (1986)
Dr Vernon Coleman's Guide To Alternative Medicine (1988)
Stress Management Techniques (1988)
Overcoming Stress (1988)
Know Yourself (1988)
The Health Scandal (1988)
The 20 Minute Health Check (1989)
Sex For Everyone (1989)
Mind Over Body (1989)
Eat Green Lose Weight (1990)
Why Animal Experiments Must Stop (1991)
The Drugs Myth (1992)
How To Overcome Toxic Stress (1991)
Why Doctors Do More Harm Than Good (1993)
Stress and Relaxation (1993)
Complete Guide To Sex (1993)
How to Conquer Backache (1993)
How to Conquer Arthritis (1993)
Betrayal of Trust (1994)
Know Your Drugs (1994, 1997)

Food for Thought (1994)
The Traditional Home Doctor (1994)
I Hope Your Penis Shrivels Up (1994)
People Watching (1995)
Relief from IBS (1995)
The Parent's Handbook (1995)
Oral Sex: Bad Taste And Hard To Swallow? (1995)
Why Is Pubic Hair Curly? (1995)
Men in Dresses (1996)
Power over Cancer (1996)
Crossdressing (1996)
How To Get The Best Out Of Prescription Drugs (1996)
How To Get The Best Out of Alternative Medicine (1996)
How To Conquer Arthritis (1996)
High Blood Pressure (1996)
How To Stop Your Doctor Killing You (1996)
Fighting For Animals (1996)
Alice and Other Friends (1996)
Dr Coleman's Fast Action Health Secrets (1997)
Dr Vernon Coleman's Guide to Vitamins and Minerals (1997)
Spiritpower (1997)
Other People's Problems (1998)
How To Publish Your Own Book (1999)
How To Relax and Overcome Stress (1999)
Animal Rights – Human Wrongs (1999)
Superbody (1999)
The 101 Sexiest, Craziest, Most Outrageous Agony Column
    Questions (and Answers) of All Time (1999)
Strange But True (2000)
Food For Thought [revised edition] (2000)
Daily Inspirations (2000)
Stomach Problems: Relief At Last (2001)
How To Overcome Guilt (2001)
How To Live Longer (2001)

novels

The Village Cricket Tour (1990)
The Bilbury Chronicles (1992)
Bilbury Grange (1993)
Mrs Caldicot's Cabbage War (1993)
Bilbury Revels (1994)
Deadline (1994)

The Man Who Inherited a Golf Course (1995)
Bilbury Country (1996)
Second Innings (1999)
Around the Wicket (2000)
It's Never Too Late (2001)

short stories

Bilbury Pie (1995)

on cricket

Thomas Winsden's Cricketing Almanack (1983)
Diary Of A Cricket Lover (1984)

as Edward Vernon

Practice Makes Perfect (1977)
Practise What You Preach (1978)
Getting Into Practice (1979)
Aphrodisiacs – An Owner's Manual (1983)
Aphrodisiacs – An Owner's Manual (Turbo Edition) (1984)
The Complete Guide To Life (1984)

as Marc Charbonnier

Tunnel (novel 1980)

with Alice

Alice's Diary (1989)
Alice's Adventures (1992)

with Dr Alan C Turin

No More Headaches (1981)

Paris In My Springtime

Vernon Coleman

Chilton Designs

Published by Chilton Designs, Publishing House, Trinity Place, Barnstaple, Devon EX32 9HJ, England

ISBN: 1 898146 55 1

Note
If any of the people, places, businesses or organisations in this book are based on real people, places, businesses or organisations, the names and identifying details have all been changed so completely that any resemblance to real people, places, businesses or organisations is purely coincidental.

A catalogue record for this book is available from the British Library.

Printed by J.W. Arrowsmith Ltd, Bristol

Dedication

To Donna Antoinette, my Welsh Princess, a delicate but steadfast butterfly holding course in a stormy world of cross winds. With my thanks and all my love.

Foreword

I love spring-cleaning. You never know what you're going to find in the next trunk or box you open.

A little while ago, while sorting through some boxes I found in the attic, I came across a large red notebook which turned out to be a diary I had kept during a stay in Paris in the last part of 1963 and the first months of 1964.

For the world, those were exciting times. Lyndon Johnson was elected President of the USA; in India, Nehru died and in Russia shoe banging Kruschev lost power. James Bond creator Ian Fleming, Harpo Marx and Cole Porter all died. A 22-year-old Cassius Clay became World Champion heavyweight boxer after knocking out Sonny Liston. 1964 was the year that the film of *My Fair Lady* was released and it was the year Sergio Leone invented the Spaghetti Western, giving the world a moody Clint Eastwood starring in *For A Few Dollars More*.

It was a pretty exciting time for me too.

I was 18 years old and I spent much of the winter which spread across the years of 1963 and 1964 in Paris.

I was an innocent abroad; away from home and out of my depth.

In September of 1963 I had started medical school. But I'd been taken ill and had to abandon my studies for a year. With the best part of a year to kill I was given two choices. I could either stay at home and get a temporary job driving a fish delivery van or I could go to Paris.

After a great deal of thought (which, on reflection, must have taken very nearly a second) I chose to go to Paris.

And this is the story of what happened to me that year.

Or is it?

Just how much of this story is true you will have to decide for yourself.

Vernon Coleman, Devon 2002

Chapter 1

It was November 1963 and I should have been at University studying medicine. Instead I was in Paris, sitting in the Café Napoleon, eating a flaky croissant and drinking black coffee so strong that I could feel my heart kick into a higher gear every time I took a sip. I glanced at the clock above the bar, took some coins out of my pocket and placed them on the table, using them to weigh down *l'addition* which the waiter had left when he had brought me my breakfast. The coins would prevent the ticket from blowing away when I opened the door to leave.

I stood up, wrapped my thick, grey, woollen scarf around my neck and pulled my brand new navy blue beret onto my head. I had come to Paris without a coat so I had compromised by buying myself a scarf and a beret. I looked round the warm and well lit café. It was early and I was the only customer. Philippe, the solitary waiter had disappeared, either into the cellar or into the store room behind the bar. I called out a goodbye which echoed unanswered in the empty café, pulled my jacket collar tight up against my throat, opened the door, lowered my head and headed off into the darkness, the cold and the rain.

Ten minutes later I was standing behind the counter in the pharmacy where I worked, stamping my feet to keep them warm, waiting for the first customer of the day and going over in my head the strange twists of fate which had led me to this unexpected situation.

Back in September, when my parents had taken me (and

my luggage) to start my first term at medical school, I had had little or no idea of what to expect. I had read books and seen films about medical students and hospitals but, callow that I was, I knew enough to know that there are sometimes vast differences between fiction and reality and I knew enough to know that I did not know what to expect.

I had my first cheque book in my pocket. It was as virginal as I was. I had never written a cheque or made love. I was as innocent as only an eighteen-year-old can be.

I spent that first night in a tiny room in a towering hall of residence. It seemed possible that the plans for the building had been appropriated from a manufacturer of accommodation for hens, and then enlarged slightly and turned on its side so as to reach upwards rather than outwards. I shared the room with a youth I'd never met before.

It was the first time I had not slept under the same roof as my mother and father, and the first time I'd shared a bedroom with a stranger.

In practical terms the stranger was possessive, cautious and modest. He did not hang his clothes or other possessions in the tiny wardrobe by his bed but kept them locked, folded and creased, in a set of three expensive looking leather suitcases. The suitcases were polished, like a guardsman's boots and were themselves kept in smart maroon bags. He put a paisley dressing gown around his shoulders while getting undressed and emerged, minutes later, wearing a pair of paisley pyjamas. He then put the clothes he had removed, and the dressing gown, back into one of the suitcases which he then duly locked before kneeling by the side of his bed to say his prayers. Others of my age might have felt contemptuous, or regarded the ritual as a suitable subject for jest, but I felt envious that he had this apparently indestructible faith with which to dilute the loneliness which, I assumed, he too must have felt.

His name, embroidered, painted or embossed on every item of clothing, luggage or stationery he had brought with him, was Bright-Perkins, LFW. The W stood for William which was, I was soon informed, on no account to be shortened to Will, Bill or Willie. I had, and have, no idea what the L or the F stood for.

William Bright-Perkins may have been modest in a physical sense but I do not think that even he would have claimed modesty as one of his most significant spiritual virtues. Within ten minutes of our meeting he had told me that his father was a banker and drove a Jaguar motor car, that his mother was a keen member of the local hunt and, presumably when not riding horses, drove a Rover and that they, he and his three sisters lived in an eight bedroom house that sat in four acres of prime Home Counties pasture land and was equipped with two hard tennis courts and a croquet lawn.

Like the vast majority of the students around me, I was an innocent stranded in the no-man's land between childhood and adulthood. I didn't realise that, of course. I thought I was grown up. I was so young and so innocent that I thought I was old enough and wise enough to have left fear and uncertainty behind. I didn't know it at the time, but we never get younger or more innocent than that. Inevitably, the fact that I was, in reality, almost suffocated by fear simply made me feel grossly inadequate.

I had felt tired for a day or two before I had arrived at medical school and when I awoke on my first morning I felt even worse. I had absolutely no appetite and no interest in breakfast. I hardly had the strength to walk across the campus to the medical school. Once, I had to sit down on a low stone wall. I had, for no good reason, suddenly burst into tears. That afternoon, after I had stumbled and fallen, one of the lecturers insisted on taking me into the teaching hospital where a senior student took a blood sample.

The blood tests had confirmed that I was suffering from infective hepatitis. I had arrived at the university hospital as a putative medical student but within hours I had been transformed into a patient. When William Bright-Perkins came to visit me (more, I suspect, out of duty than anything else) he stood in the doorway to my hospital room and spoke through a surgical mask. I found it exceedingly difficult to understand anything he said. He brought me a Get Well card upon which he had scrawled: 'It's hard work and you're well out of it. I assume you won't be returning to the Hall of Residence so I've had your things packed and your luggage put into the porter's store. I can spread about a bit now. So, thanks for that.'

They kept me in hospital for three weeks and then sent me home to convalesce. Less than a month after my arrival at medical school I was on my way back home, sitting in the front seat of my father's car, slumped down, wrapped in a thick coat and an even thicker scarf. My luggage, retrieved from the porter's store, filled the boot and two thirds of the back seat of the car. My mother was squashed into the remaining third of the back seat. Every time the car went round a corner she had to work hard to protect herself from cardboard boxes full of books.

After a month's convalescence I received a formal note from the Assistant Dean telling me that they had decided to defer my place. I remembered the Assistant Dean from my interview. He was plump and had been surprisingly friendly. The members of the interview panel had been formal and rather cold. I remembered him because he had smiled just like a human being.

'There is now little point in you trying to catch up your contemporaries,' the Assistant Dean had written. 'Your delayed start would put you under quite unreasonable pressure. I recommend that you take the year off and re-enrol next September. The University will keep your place open. I will telephone you in a few days to make suggestions as to how you might best use your free year in a way of which the university might approve.'

And so had ended my first year at medical school. It was something of an anticlimax. I felt disappointed and frustrated.

'Have you got any idea how you're going to spend your enforced holiday?' the Assistant Dean asked when he'd called.

'I need to find a job,' I said. 'My parents will keep me but I'd rather stand on my own feet. I don't really want them to feed me.'

'Splendid,' said the Assistant Dean. 'Any ideas?'

'Nothing very exciting,' I confessed. I had already checked with the local labour exchange. 'A fishmonger in the local town wants a van driver and a private school needs a games assistant.' I wasn't very keen on either of these opportunities. I hated the smell of fish and at school I'd been one of the few students to welcome heavy rain on sports afternoons.

'I don't think the School would be terribly keen on either of those possibilities,' said the Assistant Dean. 'We would like you to keep your brain active before you come back. I know fish is reputed by some to be good food for the brain but I rather suspect that even the most enthusiastic proponents of that theory would admit that it is crucial to consume the stuff rather than simply deliver it to other people in order to benefit from its brain boosting qualities. We would like you to come back to us a wiser person with a broader view of the world in general. If you're interested I may be able to get you a job which might require a little more cerebral activity. The downside is that the job isn't very exciting and the pay is terrible. The upside is that it's in Paris and, if you're frugal, you'll earn enough to live on.'

'Paris?'

'The French capital rather than the small town in Texas,' explained the Assistant Dean, drily. I didn't know what to reply to this so I mumbled something but said nothing audible.

'Beautiful city,' the Assistant Dean went on. 'Set astride the River Seine. Best known for sin, cancan girls and the Eiffel Tower. Have you been there?'

'When I was about twelve,' I said. 'Just for a couple of nights.'

'Do you speak French?'

'No,' I admitted. I hesitated. 'Well, I studied it at school, of course.'

'Of course,' agreed the Assistant Dean.

I remembered more about my first French teacher, Mr Pentecost, than I did about the language he had taught.

Mr Pentecost had been short and fat and had had a large, hairy wart on his left cheek which made it difficult for me to concentrate on anything he said. The wart seemed to have a life and an identity of its own. I was convinced that it was getting bigger and hairier by the day and as I sat and stared at it I had daydreams (they could not really be described as nightmares) in which it took a life of its own and began to overpower the entire school. One day the deputy headmaster came and told us that Mr Pentecost had been called away to attend a family funeral. When Mr Pentecost returned, two days later, the mole had disappeared.

I must have been a slow child for it was not until several years later that it eventually dawned on me that the deputy headmaster had lied and that instead of going to a funeral Mr Pentecost had been to the hospital to have the wart removed. I was a trusting and undoubtedly rather naive teenager. The disappearance of the mole did not make it any easier for me to concentrate on what Mr Pentecost said. Instead of being hypnotised by the mole I was now hypnotised by the space where the mole had been; mesmerised by its absence. It is not, I suppose, particularly surprising that I learned next to nothing from Mr Pentecost.

'I can just about order a loaf of bread,' I told the Assistant Dean.

'And you know where your aunt keeps her pen?'

'Dans le bureau de mon oncle?'

'Fortunately, the job I'm thinking of won't require much knowledge of the language,' said the Assistant Dean. 'Though, if you put in a little work, you ought to come back fairly fluent and although I admit I do rather subscribe to the view that it is the job of foreigners to learn English I suppose a smattering of French might hold you in good stead in the future.'

'What sort of job is it?'

'Assistant in an English pharmacy which is owned by a friend of mine and which caters largely to British and American tourists. That's the other downside, of course. You'll meet a lot of Americans.'

'I don't mind that,' I said quickly.

'Have you met a lot of Americans?'

'No.'

'I didn't think so. Never mind. So, do you want to see if you can find yourself something a little more intellectually stimulating than delivering fish or do you want me to see if my friend in Paris has a vacancy?'

I hesitated. I wasn't used to getting favours – especially from people in authority. To an almost medical student, an Assistant Dean operated at an almost unimaginably elevated level. 'If it isn't too much trouble I'd be grateful if you would find out if your friend has a vacancy in Paris,' I said. Almost instantaneously, and without any thought, I had taken a decision which would change my life. My parents and teachers had always impressed upon me the importance of thinking carefully, and considering all the options, before making even the simplest decision. I did not, even then, realise just how often crucial, fundamental decisions are taken without either thought or consideration.

'I'll ring you back,' promised the Assistant Dean.

I put the telephone receiver back on the rest but didn't move. I just sat there, staring at the telephone, waiting for it to ring. Twenty minutes later the Assistant Dean called back. He told me that his friend would find me a job.

Three days later I was heading for Paris to start a job with someone I'd never met, on the recommendation of someone I hardly knew. I didn't have the faintest idea what I would be doing or where I would be staying. I had with me one fairly small suitcase containing a spare pair of flannels, a few spare shirts, underwear, a wash bag I'd been given for the previous Christmas and which had first travelled with me when I'd gone to medical school, a few English books to read and a large red notebook.

'Keep a sort of diary,' my mother had said, when she'd handed the notebook to me. 'You might find it interesting to look back at it in years to come.'

Chapter 2

Although the pharmacy was owned by an American called John Tennyson, the friend of the Assistant Dean, it was managed by a young man called Sylvestre Baptiste, a dapper, bilingual Frenchman who had, I was quickly to discover, a rather elevated sense of his own importance and almost no sense of humour.

I travelled to Paris on the cross channel ferry, arriving at the Gare du Nord at 3.30 in the afternoon and, following the simple instructions I had been given, and a free map I had picked up at the railway station, walked down towards the Opéra and then down the Avenue de l'Opéra towards the Louvre. I had been advised to take the Metro to the Opéra but the £20 worth of French Francs which my father had given me before I'd left home ('for travelling expenses and emergencies') had been stolen from me on the boat.

The pharmacy had been designed to cater purely for English speaking travellers and the outside of the shop left absolutely nothing to the imagination. Mr Tennyson, I suspected, was not a man who celebrated modesty or had much time for self-effacing minimalism. Only the registered blind could fail to spot the shop once they'd managed to get themselves within fifty or sixty yards. There were three neon signs outside the shop. One said Drug Store. One said Pharmacy. And one said Chemist. The owner was clearly keen to minimise the risk that a traveller might not understand what the shop sold. Above the door a fourth sign, more dignified than the others, simply stated: 'International Supplier of Pharmaceuticals'.

I walked into the shop and with a sigh of relief put my heavy suitcase down on the floor. It was raining and I had no coat. Both my thin, tweed sports jacket, which had, for several years, been rather too tight for me, and my grey flannel trousers were soaked. There were four people in the shop. Two of them were American and expensively dressed in matching Burberry coats. I had no evidence to support this but I suspected that the two Burberry umbrellas resting against the front of the counter probably belonged to them too. The third and fourth persons stood behind the counter, both wearing starched white coats. One was a woman of about thirty, the other a man in his mid-forties. The woman had a pleasant face and a welcoming smile. The man, tall and well-built, had a sour look and no laughter lines. I got the feeling that he was not a man who wasted a lot of energy in smiling. She looked up when I walked in. The man didn't. Neither of them made any effort to move away from their two customers.

On the counter, between the two Americans and the assistants, lay a large selection of patented medicaments. It was clear that the proceedings, which, judging by the number of boxes and bottles which were sitting on the counter had been a lengthy one, were coming to a triumphant, and for the shop, extremely successful conclusion.

'So you think this one is best for the diarrhoea?' said the male American, picking up one of the packets. He spoke in such an exaggerated Southern drawl that I thought at first that he was acting a part.

The female assistant nodded.

'And this for the sore eyes?'

Another nod.

The American placed the selected eye remedy next to the nominated anti-diarrhoeal.

'And this one for the skin rash?'

Again, the female assistant nodded. This time she added a smile.

'Oh I'm not sure,' said the female American. She pointed

to a larger packet. 'I think that one might be more suitable.' She too sounded as though she had come directly from the set of some Southern drama. I looked around, half expecting to see a couple of faithful black retainers standing by, ready to carry the parcels back to the mansion.

The argument which ensued was heated but neither participant seemed in the slightest bit embarrassed.

'Why don't you just have them both?' suggested the male assistant. The male American obediently picked up the product his wife had selected and added it to their chosen pile. His wife thought about this for a few moments before nodding her agreement. 'I guess so, honey!' she drawled.

Five minutes later, and a large traveller's cheque lighter, the two Americans staggered out of the shop, each carrying a huge plastic carrier bag full of pills and potions. I held the door open for them and watched them leave.

'They'll be back tomorrow,' said the male shop assistant, laughing. 'Wanting remedies for ruptures and backache.'

'I expect they will,' said the female assistant.

'Do they come in every day?' I asked.

The female assistant smiled. 'They've been in Paris for two weeks and so far they've been in here every single day except Sundays.'

'Maybe they go to church and pray on Sundays,' suggested the male assistant. He shrugged to let it be clear that he neither knew nor cared. 'If they come here they won't see me anyway,' he said rather sourly. 'I don't work Sundays.'

'Can I help you, sir?' the female assistant asked me suddenly.

'I'm here about the job,' I said.

They both looked at me rather blankly.

'The job as an assistant,' I explained. 'It was arranged through Mr Tennyson.' I rummaged in my jacket pocket and pulled out my passport, my train ticket, my boarding pass for the cross channel ferry and finally, with some relief, the letter confirming my appointment. I took the letter out of its envelope and handed it across the counter. The male assistant took it, read it and handed it back to me. 'I'll fetch Monsieur Baptiste,' he told me. 'The manager,' he explained. He disappeared through a door at the rear of shop.

'Did you have a good crossing?' asked the female assistant. She spoke excellent English and did not seem to have an accent.

'I wasn't sick,' I replied.

The woman smiled. 'Well, that's a good sign. I am always sick on boats. Even when the sea is calm. Are you English?'

'Yes. Are you?'

The woman laughed. 'No. I'm French. My name is Sylvie Roland. And that was Pierre,' she added, nodding in the direction that the male assistant had disappeared.

'Your English is very good.'

'Thank you. Mr Tennyson only employs people who speak good English. His shops are designed to cater for English people and for Americans – particularly the ones who don't speak any French.' There was no criticism or accusation in what she said, or the way she said it, but nevertheless I felt guilty at the fact that I was one of the travelling English citizens who did not speak French.

It occurred to me for the first time that this might not be Mr Tennyson's only shop. 'Does Mr Tennyson have other pharmacies?'

'Oh yes. He has a chain of them. I think there are over thirty now. Rome, Madrid, Amsterdam, Nice, Athens – all the cities favoured by tourists. I think he plans to have one in every city in Europe which is regularly visited by British and American travellers. Did you apply for this job in England?'

'I was a medical student,' I explained. 'But I fell ill and have had to take a year off. The Assistant Dean at the medical school arranged this for me. He's a friend of Mr Tennyson's.'

'I'm sorry to hear you have been ill.'

'Everything is pretty much OK now, thanks. I had hepatitis.'

'That can be very debilitating.'

'It was. Horrible.' I shrugged. 'But at least I now get to spend some time in Paris.'

Just then the male assistant returned with a short, thin man beside him.

'I hope you will enjoy your stay here,' said the woman, before moving away.

The thin man was not wearing a white coat. He wore a neat pinstriped suit, a plain white shirt and a dark blue tie. His neatly cropped hair had been oiled and was brushed straight back from his forehead.

The manager asked me my name and asked to see my passport. I handed it to him. He looked at it, checked the photograph and handed the passport back to me. I slipped it into my inside jacket pocket.

'I am Monsieur Baptise,' he told me. He wore expensive looking tortoiseshell spectacles which were perched on the tip of his nose. He lowered his head and looked over the top of them when he spoke. 'I am the manager of this store. Do you have any retail experience?'

'No.'

'Do you know anything about drugs?'

'No, I'm afraid not.' I admitted. 'I was about to start studying medicine,' I added and regretted it almost immediately.

'I am aware of that. But a few days at medical school do not qualify you to make any decisions or take any responsibility.'

'No, of course not.'

'You are healthy now?'

'Oh yes.'

'You are free of infectious diseases?'

'Yes.'

The manager stared at me over the top of his spectacles as though trying to decide whether or not I was telling the truth. 'Mr Tennyson has asked me to employ you as a favour to a friend of his. This shop is open twelve hours a day and seven days a week. As the most junior assistant you will naturally work on our rota system. By and large you will work the hours that no one else wants. Your job will be to stock shelves, sweep floors and run errands.'

'That's fine,' I said, anxious to please.

'We have arranged a room for you at a tourist hotel,' continued the manager. 'It is very conveniently situated, not far from the shop.' He handed me a small brochure advertising the hotel. 'You will find a map showing the location of your hotel on this brochure. We will pay the hotel direct for your room.'

Chapter 3

The drugstore manager had been honest when he had told me that the hotel he'd booked me in was convenient. It was less than three minutes away from the drugstore. That was, however, just about all that could be said in its favour.

The hotel had somehow acquired and kept rosettes certifying that it had satisfied certain basic requirements of the tourist industry. But once I'd seen inside the hotel I couldn't help wondering what a hotel without rosettes would look like.

The reception area was bleak and badly lit. I put my suitcase down beside me and for a few moments I stood in the murk, waiting for my eyes to become accustomed to the dim light. A balding man in his late sixties sat on a stool in a cramped space behind a scarred wooden counter. With the aid of a small unshaded bulb above him he was reading a newspaper. Judging by the title of the newspaper and the photographs visible on the front page, the newspaper's main, and possibly only content was horse racing. My entrance was clearly not sufficiently engaging to persuade him to put down his newspaper. Generally speaking, he did not give the impression of being excited to be in Paris in 1963.

'Good evening,' I said, hesitantly when I felt that my eyes had adjusted to the light as well as they were going to.

The receptionist continued to ignore me. I did not have enough experience of hotels in general, let alone French hotels, to know whether or not this was normal. For all I knew it was customary for a hotel guest to have to stand and wait for half an hour before being allocated a room. And so I stood and waited. This went on for some time. The man read his paper. I stood and waited. I waited. The man read. I stood. He read. I tried to occupy myself by reading the notices pinned to the wall behind him. But they were faded, handwritten in French and did not seem to include any information about pens, bureaux, uncles or aunts. I looked around the rest of the lobby. There wasn't much to see. A door guarded by thin, colourful plastic strips which had been tied back out of the way, led into a grubby little dining room furnished with scuffed pine tables and old chairs which did not seem in any way to be related to one another.

This was all something of a shock to me. I had not long left school and there is no more structured, close knit world than a school – particularly one geared towards propelling its students along the educational shuffle board, as mine had been. When I left school I had still not been prepared to spread my wings but had, instead, been mentally prepared for medical school – another structured, hierarchical world. I was ill-prepared for this new world in which there seemed to be no form, no structure, no predictability, no expectations. I was beginning a period of my life that I would never forget; a time that would change me for ever and which would give me, for the first time in my life, an awareness of the unusual and the exceptional and a preparedness for the unpredictable.

I fear that we might have both still been frozen there if the telephone had not rung. But it did. When he had dealt with the caller the balding newspaper reader looked up at me and spoke. I have no idea what he said.

'I think you have a room booked for me,' I said. I gave him my name and mentioned the name of the drugstore manager.

The newspaper reader said nothing to indicate that he might or might not have understood me but then suddenly reached up, plucked a key from a board to his right and tossed it onto the scarred counter between us.

I picked up the key and studied the tag which was attached to it. The tag suggested to me that a search for a room marked number 12 might prove fruitful. I had already spotted a narrow, uncarpeted staircase. I picked up my suitcase with my other hand and headed towards it.

'Thank you,' I said to the man behind the desk. He was too engrossed in his newspaper to respond. I doubt if he even heard me. He seemed to have an enviable ability to ignore his surroundings.

The stairs were steep, narrow, uneven and twisted and turned as though they had been built for entertainment rather than function. I looked, in vain, on the first floor for room number 12. On the second floor I failed yet again. Eventually I found it on the top floor – I had by this time lost count but rather thought it was the sixth floor.

I tried to use my key but found, to my surprise, that the door didn't seem to be locked. I twisted the handle, opened the door and entered the room that was to be my home in Paris. The room was sparsely furnished. There was a small wardrobe, a dressing table, a chair and a narrow bed. There was a small square of filthy carpet on the floor by the side of the bed.

A pair of trousers and a jacket were draped over the chair. A dress and various items which I recognised as feminine underwear were distributed on the floor around the room. And on the bed, lying on top of the dirty brown coverlet, lay a naked blonde woman of about forty and a rather older bald man. He, too, was naked except for his socks. I remember noticing that there appeared to be a large hole in the heel of his left sock. She was lying on her back and had her eyes closed. He was lying face down on top of her. He was moving, she was pretty well lying still and the bed was protesting loudly. They weren't playing checkers.

I had absolutely no experience of sexual matters but I was not so entirely innocent that I was not able to guess what they were doing. He had, I remember, a very large, white bottom which was decorated with a number of red spots. It was not a pretty sight.

'Er...I'm sorry...,' I said, going very red and backing out of the room.

Neither the woman nor the man looked up or showed any sign of registering my presence.

I closed the door. Still carrying my suitcase I retreated, back down the stairs.

'There's a couple in room 12,' I told the man behind the desk when I had got back down to the ground floor. This time I did not wait for him to notice me before speaking.

The receptionist looked up and stared at me. He said something but I understood as much of what he said as I think he had understood of what I had said. I stared at him and then, in desperation, drew an imaginary bed in the air and, on top of it, drew first a female figure and then another figure on top. The man spat onto the floor, and looked at his watch. He then spat again, cursed, stood up and walked around to my side of the desk. He had clearly understood my mime. I was grateful for this because it saved me adding the sound effects. He then walked slowly but steadily up the stairs. I followed. My suitcase, obeying unnatural laws, now seemed to weigh considerably more than it had weighed when I'd first made this journey.

When he got to the top floor the bald and ill-tempered receptionist opened the door to room 12 and walked inside. He did not knock and nor did he hesitate before entering. The man was no longer lying on top of the woman; he was now lying half off her. He looked up as we walked in and for the first time I could see his face. He was sweating and red from the exertions he had made; his hair was dishevelled and damp. Only afterwards did it occur to me that there was no sign of happiness or contentment in his eyes: merely an emptiness. He looked exhausted and relieved rather than exhilarated or excited. The receptionist turned his wrist so that the man could see his watch and said something I did not understand but which, it was pretty fair to assume, referred to the time. The man grunted and sat up. He reached for his clothes and started to dress. The man getting dressed made no effort to cover those parts of his body which a man might normally regard as private. He left as soon as he was dressed. When he had gone I noticed that he had left his tie lying over the back of the room's solitary chair.

'Your husband has forgotten his tie!' I said to the woman.

She stared at me. 'My husband?' she said. At first she seemed surprised. Then she laughed out loud. I blushed. I was embarrassed then to realise that he was not her husband. It embarrasses me now, though for slightly different reasons.

Embarrassment was not an emotion which troubled the woman. She did not seem in the slightest bit surprised or put out at being naked in the presence of a stranger. But then, on reflection, why should she have been? What was to me very new was to her an oft repeated daily ritual. She very slowly sat up and swung around so that her feet were on the floor. Her breasts hung down to her waist and were heavily veined. Her nipples were as big as thimbles. You can judge my inexperience when I tell you that they were the first female breasts I had ever seen. She stood up, walked around the bed and started to dress. I tried to look away but found it more difficult than I would have imagined. The receptionist turned and left the room.

When the woman had dressed she bent down and smoothed the covers. She smiled at me, patted my cheek and blew me a kiss. I didn't know what to do so I smiled back. She stopped for a moment, thought and then kissed me full on the lips. Shocked, I neither did nor said anything. Her breath smelt of aniseed. She said something in French which I did not understand. 'I'm sorry,' I said, in English. 'I don't understand.'

'You want we make love?' she asked me. She spoke English with a theatrical French accent. I felt myself blushing and beginning to sweat through nervousness. 'No, it's all right, thank you,' I replied. 'But thank you very much.'

'You very young,' she said. 'You pay half normal price.'

'No, really,' I said. 'But thank you. Thank you very much indeed.'

To my relief she did not seem put out by this. She shrugged, left the room and clattered across the landing and down the stairs. She wore absurdly high heels which made a great deal of noise but these did not seem to impede her rate of progress.

I shut the door. My heart was beating so fast I thought it would burst out of my chest. I remembered the words of the Assistant Dean. 'We would like you to come back a wiser person with a broader view of the world.'

I looked around. It was, without any doubt, the most depressing room I had ever seen in my life. It was cramped, dingy, dirty and poorly furnished. There was not a single redeeming feature. You could not say 'It is a poor room but...'. There was no 'but'. I walked across the room to the window, hoping that there might, perhaps, be a view to make up for the room's other varied shortcomings. I did not expect much and I was not disappointed. When I pulled back the grey net curtains I could see that the room looked out onto a tiny grey courtyard. Across the courtyard there were other windows. They were all covered with dirty white net curtains. Below one window someone had fixed up a washing line. It was empty. The tiny courtyard was full of rubbish. I turned away from the window. It seemed to me to be not so much a room as a cell and I felt very lonely, very young and rather frightened. I was a long way from home and a long way from the world I knew.

Chapter 4

My duties at the pharmacy were uncomplicated. In other circumstances I suppose that I might have been offended, or felt slighted, if I had been asked to sweep floors, clean out cupboards and move packets of pills and creams from a store room to the shelves of an establishment which, although described on the outside as an international supplier of pharmaceuticals was, on the inside, still no more than a well-equipped chemist's shop.

But as a visitor in a strange country, a long way from home and divorced by the English Channel from friends and family, I was grateful to accept the comfort that routine offered me. I found repetitive duties which might have appeared dull and boring in other, more familiar circumstances, to be curiously soothing. Restocking the revolving rack of toothbrushes, checking that the appropriate display cabinets were well stocked with penknives, sunglasses, nail trimmers and eyebrow tweezers and making sure that the drawers in which were stored more personal items (such as condoms and creams for the eradication of rashes of an intimate nature) were all full, required enough concentration to push my fears into the background but did not require enough intellectual activity to add to my stock of anxieties.

In those days the Channel was much more of a physical barrier than it is today. Back in the 1960s there was no Tunnel, carrying rail passengers seamlessly from Waterloo to the Gare du Nord, and air travel was still something of a novelty for such a short journey. Most travellers reached France from Britain via a sea journey and this gave any continental excursion an air of mystery, romance and excitement. Having to embark, disembark and, in between these two rituals, suffer the discomfort and indignities of a journey across a notoriously bumpy stretch of water made even the most undemanding tourist feel that by the time he reached his destination he had earned the right to describe himself as a genuine traveller in the true Victorian tradition.

The pharmacy was patronised by an endless stream of fascinating characters who brought with them sometimes strange and always personal requirements and expectations. In retrospect the work may appear undemanding and tedious. In practice I do not remember boredom being a serious problem during my stay at the pharmacy in Paris.

The pharmacy's patrons invariably came into the shop without a prescription. Many came in hoping that they would be able to purchase a suitable product over the counter without going to the expense and trouble of visiting an English speaking doctor. I soon learned that this meant that they were prepared to bare their souls, and sometimes (to the embarrassment and amusement of other customers) their bodies, to the pharmacy staff in a way that might, in other circumstances, have been considered more appropriate for the traditional privacy of the doctor's surgery than the very public nature of the pharmacy counter.

It was at the pharmacy that I met an American called Archie Trench.

Hugely overweight and with a personality to match Archie 'entered' a room as though intent on conquering both the territory and everyone within it. He was something of a tyrant and the best way I can describe him is to say that when, in later years, I first met the bullying giant publisher Robert Maxwell I was instantly reminded very much of Archie Trent.

'What have you got for piles?' he demanded, making no attempt to modify his booming voice and seeming quite unembarrassed by a request which usually led customers with the same problem to whisper across the counter or even, on more than one occasion, to writing down their ailment on a slip of paper before sliding it across the counter face down.

I looked around and rather to my horror realised that I was the only person in the shop. This was most unusual. Normally, Sylvie, Pierre or Monsieur Baptiste, the shop manager, would be waiting to attend to customers while I got on with my work of sweeping, tidying and stocking shelves. But Sylvie was away for the day, completing some undisclosed family business which required a train journey to Tours, Monsieur Baptise was on the telephone to a supplier and Pierre had disappeared for a moment, probably taking an illicit puff or two at a cigarette in the tiny toilet which we all shared. Monsieur Baptiste strongly disapproved of smoking, not for health reasons but simply because he regarded it as decadent and sinful.

'Do you speak English?' the American demanded.

'I am English,' I replied.

'Aren't there any Americans working here?'

'No. I'm afraid not.'

'Then you'll have to do. I need something for my damned piles. And no continental crap. I want the good stuff.'

I looked around, desperately hoping that Pierre or Monsieur Baptiste might appear. But Pierre was nowhere to be seen and I could still hear Monsieur Baptise talking on the telephone. I couldn't understand what he was saying but from the tone and pitch of his voice I could tell that he was arguing with someone.

'I went to a drug store near to my hotel and they tried to sell me batteries!' complained the customer. He snorted. 'What am I supposed to do with batteries?' He waved a hand. 'Don't even try to answer that.'

'The word 'pile' means battery in French,' I explained. 'Perhaps that was the cause of the confusion.'

'Pile means battery?'

'I think so,' I said.

On my second day in Paris I had purchased a cheap radio so that I would have a little company in my lonely, dingy hotel room. When I got it back to my hotel I found that the assistant in the store had forgotten to remind me to buy batteries for the radio. When I looked up the word battery in the small French-English dictionary I had purchased I found that the word I wanted was 'pile'. I therefore had the excruciatingly embarrassing task of going into a shop and asking a complete stranger (who was, inevitably, a good-looking woman in her early twenties) if she had any piles.

'Only the damned French could do something so damned stupid,' complained the fat American. He seemed annoyed rather than amused and I got the impression that he had a tendency to see the rest of the world as revolving around himself. I suspected that he would regard every insult, every setback as being devised solely to inconvenience him. I had never met a more self-obsessed man. Americans often seem to regard arrogance as a virtue. Archie seemed to regard arrogance as a duty. 'Get me that chair,' he added, nodding towards a chair on the other side of the pharmacy. 'And a cushion.'

I moved quickly around from behind the counter and carried the chair across the pharmacy. 'I'm afraid I don't think we have a cushion,' I said.

'Well a chair with no damned cushion is no damned good to me,' complained the American, staring at the chair malevolently. Having decided that the chair was not going to be intimidated he glowered at me instead. 'Have you any idea how painful piles can be?'

'No, sir.'

Just then Pierre appeared, smelling far too strongly of after-shave and toothpaste.

'Can I help you, sir?' he asked the American. I wondered for a moment whether to move the chair back to its original position, decided against it, and returned behind the counter.

'It's all right, the kid is serving me,' replied Archie.

'I am a senior sales consultant,' explained Pierre. 'Perhaps I might be able to help you more effectively.'

'Are you American?'

'No, sir.'

'English?'

'No, sir. I am French.'

'Then I'll have him. The English one.'

This did not please Pierre and for a moment I thought he was going to succumb to temptation and give the American advice that was neither professional nor, given the problem which had already been declared, particularly appropriate. But he over-rode temptation, bowed slightly and disappeared without a word.

Hoping to finish the transaction as speedily as possible I took tubes of three appropriate ointments from a nearby drawer and put them on the counter, hoping that at least one of them would be of American origin and, therefore, prove satisfactory.

'Marvellous! My favourite brand!' cried the fat American, pouncing on one of the tubes. 'I'll have six of these.'

I returned the unwanted tubes to the drawer and fetched five more tubes of the chosen product.

'Do you sell hot water bottles?'

'Yes, sir.' I hurried to a far corner of the shop and brought back a hot water bottle.

'Have you got a pink one?'

I found a pink one. The American made no attempt to explain his preference but seemed delighted.

'How much?'

I added up the total and told him.

'Do you deliver?'

'Yes, sir. There is a small delivery charge.'

'I'll take one tube of ointment now. Deliver the rest to me at the Excelsior Hotel this evening.'

'I could have them sent to your hotel immediately,' I offered.

'This evening,' said the American firmly. 'You bring them at 7 o'clock. And deliver them direct to my room. I'll give you an extra 50 francs when you deliver them. I don't trust the idiots on the reception desk. They're all foreign.'

I added up the bill, took the money, sorted out the change, wrapped up the single tube of pile ointment and put the other items to one side for delivery later. It was the first time I had ever sold anything.

When the fat American had gone Pierre reappeared. 'I hate Americans,' he muttered, clearly still indignant. 'Loathsome people. I hope he had piles.'

'He did,' I told him.

'He had piles?'

'Yes.'

'Wonderful!' cried Pierre, grinning. 'You see, there is a God.' He paused. 'And he is French.'

Chapter 5

The Excelsior Hotel was, at the time, one of the smartest and most expensive hotels in Paris. It was, almost inevitably, enormously popular with Americans who were just about the only people in the world who could afford it.

At 6.45 pm I arrived at the hotel, clutching a plain paper bag containing five tubes of pile ointment and a pink hot water bottle. Mr Trench, I discovered, had a suite on the third floor.

I knocked on Mr Trench's door at 6.59 pm but it wasn't Mr Trench who answered.

'I'm from the pharmacy, with a package for Mr Trench,' I told a slender redhead who wore a black low neck cocktail dress and a pair of black high heeled shoes. She looked about my own age.

'Who is it?' called a voice I recognised.

'A boy from the pharmacy,' the girl called back.

'Bring him in,' shouted the fat American.

'Come with me,' said the girl, turning and walking away.

I followed her down a short corridor. Behind me the outer door to the suite swung shut with a faint click.

It was the first time I had ever been into a hotel suite and I was deeply impressed even before we reached the sitting room. When the girl in black led me into the sitting room I felt as though I had walked into a scene from a movie. The fat American was sitting in an easy chair. Two other people were sitting on a sofa.

There was a tray of bottles on a sideboard. A door was slightly ajar and through it I could see a spacious bedroom in which there was a huge double bed.

'I've brought your package, sir,' I said, offering the brown paper bag to the fat American. He took it, looked inside and pulled out the various items. When he'd finished he placed the bag on the floor beside his chair.

'Did you know you could get this stuff in Paris?' he asked a slender white man sitting on the sofa, holding up one of the tubes of haemorrhoid ointment. The man was sitting next to a plump black woman who wore a low cut green dress that fitted her like a glove. A very tight glove.

'Certainly do,' agreed the man. 'We stock up our medicine cabinet with stuff whenever we come to Paris.'

'Wanna drink, son?' the fat American asked me, putting his purchases down on the table beside him.

I hesitated. 'Er, no thank you,' I said. I felt uncomfortable amidst so much luxury. I was also rather startled at having seen two men discuss such private matters as haemorrhoids with such a total lack of embarrassment.

'D'ya wanna Coke? Fifi, get the guy a Coke.'

Fifi opened the door to what looked like a cupboard but turned out to be a fridge. She took out a bottle of coke, closed the fridge door, removed the cap with an opener she took from the tray upon which the bottles were standing, poured half the contents of the coke bottle into a glass and handed the glass to me.

'Sit down, son,' said the fat American. 'What's your name?'

I sat down gingerly on a very expensive looking chair and told him.

'Meet my girlfriend Fifi,' he said, pointing to the girl in black. He then pointed to the couple on the sofa. 'And that's Marvin and Sheila Brown. They live in Monaco.'

Marvin, who looked as though he was in his sixties but was well preserved and might well have been older, was short and very neat. He wore a blue double breasted blazer, a pair of grey slacks with a razor sharp crease and a pair of cream loafers. His shirt was cream and had a monogram on the pocket. Around his neck he wore a paisley cravat. A pair of gold *pince-nez* hung from a gold chain around his neck. For a man of his age he had a surprisingly large quantity of straight, jet black hair.

Sheila was at least three times Marvin's size. Even sitting down she looked tall and she looked to me to be as solid and as well-built as an air raid shelter. A few weeks before I had left England I had heard my mother mention that my aunt Thelma had been weighed in at over twenty stone. By the side of Sheila my aunt Thelma was a midget. Sheila was, I thought at the time, probably the biggest woman I had ever seen. Her skin was jet black. Her fingers dripped with gold jewellery, her neck was encircled by more gold necklaces than I could count and she had a gold brooch pinned to her dress which was either an absurd piece of costume jewellery or the most expensive single item I'd ever seen. I wasn't sure which but since she wore a Cartier watch I wasn't prepared to bet against the brooch being genuine.

Sitting together on Archie's sofa they looked for all the world like a large black mother and her small, white, prematurely aged son awaiting an appointment with the headmaster. They looked an unlikely couple. I did not know then that unlikely lovers are often the strongest, for their love has surpassed and overcome the disapproval of others, and has survived the destructive attempts of the sceptics. I was too young to realise that odd couples are either destroyed or strengthened by the pressure and may be pushed closer together by the outside hatred, surviving because their love has to be strong to win through. I knew none of this. I just saw an extremely odd couple.

I had, of course, heard of Monaco but had never met anyone who lived there before. I assumed (and from what I could see it seemed a safe assumption) that Archie's friends must be enormously rich.

'What do you think of the painting, son?' asked the fat American. He waved a hand in the direction of the far side of the room where an oil painting was resting against the wall. I couldn't work out what the painting depicted. I couldn't even tell whether or not it was the right way up.

'It's very colourful,' I said, diplomatically.

Marvin, the man from Monaco, laughed. 'Guess how much it cost.'

I looked at the painting again. 'I have absolutely no idea,' I said. I didn't want to guess, partly through fear of looking foolish and partly through fear of offending the man who had bought the painting.

'One million French francs,' said Marvin. 'He paid one million French francs for that. I could have done better with my eyes shut.' He squinted at the painting. 'Mind you,' he said, 'It's a nice frame.' He looked at the fat American. 'Why did you pay so much for a painting?'

'Because I like it,' said the American. 'And because I'd rather have the painting than the money.' He paused and thought for a moment. 'Besides,' he added. 'It's a good investment. It's going to be the new trend in art.'

'It will only make money if you can find another idiot prepared to buy it at a greater price than you paid,' Marvin pointed out. He wagged a finger at Archie. 'There are two sorts of people in business,' he told him. 'The trendsetters and the trendspotters. If you want to be rich you need to be in the second group. The trendsetters never make any money because most of the time their trends never take off. The trendspotters, on the other hand, make their money simply by going along for the ride.'

Archie scowled. 'If it ain't worth what I paid for it I'll break the guy's legs. Or sue the bastard.'

'Remember Marvin's three laws of business,' Marvin said. 'Never explain, never complain and never, ever go to court.'

'I couldn't lose,' protested Archie.

'Ah, never, ever go to court if you firmly and honestly believe you're in the right,' said Marvin. 'That's a sure-fire way to find real pain.'

Archie didn't seem particularly happy. Marvin didn't seem to have noticed. He didn't seem to care how Archie felt.

'How long have you worked at the pharmacy?' Marvin asked me, obviously suddenly bored with talking about the painting.

I told him.

'How come you speak such good English?'

'I'm English.'

'So how does a young Englishman find himself working at a pharmacy in Paris?'

I explained.

'You want to keep in touch with this guy,' Marvin said to Archie. 'He's going to be a doctor one day.' He turned to me. 'Archie is a gold dealer,' he explained. 'Some of his best customers are doctors.'

'You deal in gold?' I said to Archie. I was impressed. It was not difficult to impress me then. But I was very impressed.

'Show him some of your stuff,' said Sheila.

'Fetch the briefcase, doll,' said Archie to his girlfriend.

Fifi walked into the bedroom, fetched a grey aluminium briefcase, brought it into the living room and handed it to Archie. It was clearly heavy.

Archie fiddled with the combination lock and opened the briefcase so that I could look inside. He lifted out a plastic strip which contained a dozen or so small gold coins in tiny plastic windows.

'Kruggerand, sovereign, French Napoleon, Swiss Napoleon ...' he said, pointing to each coin in turn as he identified it. When he had finished identifying the coins, and had put the plastic strip back into the briefcase, he took out a small red velvet bag. 'Open your hands,' he told me. I did as I was told. 'Hold them together,' he said. He opened the drawstrings which controlled the neck of the bag, turned it upside down and shook the contents, a dozen small chunks of yellow metal, into my outstretched palms. Then he picked up the nuggets one by one and put them back into the red velvet bag. As he did so he told me what each of them was worth. Finally, when my hands were once again empty, he put the red velvet bag back into the briefcase and then took out and opened a blue velvet bag and removed what he clearly, and justifiably, regarded as the *pièce de résistance*: a gleaming slab of gold.

'What do you think of that?' he demanded.

I just stared at it.

'Pure 24 carat gold,' said Archie, proudly. 'You could buy a small house with that.'

Just then the telephone rang.

'Get that, doll,' said Archie.

Fifi answered the telephone and spoke to the caller for a few moments. She then turned to Archie. 'It's the reception desk,' she said. 'Ira and Dorothy are downstairs.'

'Oh damn,' said Archie. He looked at his watch. 'Sorry, kid,' he said to me. 'Got to throw you out now. We've got a dinner date with friends from Vegas. Very boring but very rich.' He levered himself to his feet. I too stood up. We all exchanged goodbyes.

'Why don't you come and have a drink with us one day?' said Marvin, offering me his hand.

'That's very kind of you,' I said.

'Would the morning of the 17th be any good?' suggested Marvin. I said it would.

'Eleven then? On the terrace of the Café de la Paix near the Opéra?' Marvin gave me the telephone number of the apartment they had rented in Paris.

I accepted the invitation and then left to return to my hotel and normality.

I was waiting for the lift when I realised that the fat American hadn't given me the 50 francs he'd promised me for delivering his package.

'Archie asked me to give you this.'

I turned. Fifi was holding out a thin envelope.

'What's that?'

'Fifty francs,' she said. 'Archie remembered he owed it to you.'

I took the envelope and slipped it into my inside jacket pocket. 'Thanks,' I said. The lift arrived and the doors opened.

'Don't mention it,' said Fifi.

She turned and headed back to their suite. I got into the lift.

Chapter 6

I was having a bad day and was feeling very sorry for myself.

Monsieur Baptiste at the pharmacy had discovered that I didn't have a work permit and bureaucrats had decided that this was a serious threat to the economic future of the French Republic. I had spent hours sitting in a dusty corridor waiting for someone to put the requisite stamps into my passport.

I had discovered that the French are probably the most bureaucratic nation in the world. They love forms and bits of paper. Most of them spend eight hours a day, five days a week doing nothing but shuffle bits of paper around from one desk to another. It is a constant mystery to the rest of the world just how the French ever manage to get anything done.

When my passport was finally stamped and the State had been safeguarded by duly authorising my duties with the broom, I escaped and found that the sun was shining, the sky was blue and the world was still going round.

Monsieur Baptiste, knowing something of French bureaucracy, had told me that I was not expected back at the pharmacy that day.

Having crossed the river Seine I stopped to read the headlines of the English newspapers at a kiosk in St. Germain and realised that it was my sister's birthday in three days time. I began to look for a card to send her.

I spotted one on a rack outside a little bookshop on a corner near the Église St. Sulpice. I had just drunk a coffee at a café and was strolling north to the Luxembourg Gardens.

Just before I went into the shop to buy the card a middle aged woman approached me. She was dressed all in black (black bomber jacket, black jumper and black jeans) except for her shoes which were silver. They looked as though they had once been quite fashionable. She was smart and did not have the appearance of a beggar. But she asked me for money. No one who isn't poor begs for money so I suppose she must have had some very bad luck.

Something about her alarmed me. She seemed very stern, frightening almost. Her manner was at once demanding and submissive. She wanted but could not bring herself to expect. Feeling slightly uncomfortable I backed away, mumbled something and went into the shop.

The shop assistant beamed when he saw me. I approached the counter, laid down the card I had chosen and took out some money. He was ready to start keying figures into the till, when the telephone rang.

He answered the telephone, put down my purchases and ignored me.

I still hate it when people do that. Why does a piece of brrring plastic take precedence over a human being? I glowered at him.

Eventually, the shop assistant found the time to deal with my order. Now in an irritable mood, I handed over my money, accepted the paper bag containing the card I had bought and left the shop. I was a little short with him as we completed our transaction and, perhaps aware of his rudeness, he became pathetically anxious to oblige. It was too late.

Outside, on the pavement, the woman in the silver shoes was still begging. She was still without luck. Her demeanour and appearance seemed to frighten everyone off. She did not approach me this time. I walked away, continuing my journey up to the Luxembourg Gardens.

Twenty minutes later, I entered the gardens. There was a little shop there. A pretty, wooden place that looked rather like an English summerhouse. It was very bright and pretty – with coloured balls and other toys hanging up outside.

The shop was shut. I was a little disappointed. I had intended to buy a small bar of chocolate to sustain me on my walk.

As I strolled on into the park I couldn't stop thinking about the woman in the silver shoes. I felt guilty about not having given her any money. I had ignored her the way the man in the shop had ignored me when the telephone had rung. It was, I thought, no wonder that she had looked so tortured, so frightened and so lost. Everyone else had ignored her too. Cities are full of people but they can at the same time be the loneliest places in the world.

I walked on for a while. But I knew it was no good. I had no choice. I had to go back and find her. I took all the change I had in my pockets and held it in my hand. There were quite a few coins and my fist felt full. I don't know why, but I knew I would find her. I retraced my steps and eventually found her just a yard or two from where I had first seen her. She had just lit a cigarette and was standing smoking it. I didn't say anything but just walked up to her, looked into her face, opened my hand into hers and let the coins gush into her palm.

She looked up at me, our eyes met, and in an instant her face changed. The pain all disappeared and she smiled at me. It was a broad, genuine smile. It was, I think, a smile of thanks for recognising her as a human being as much as a smile of thanks for the money I had given her. 'Vous êtes gentil,' she said quietly as I walked away. I wondered what had brought her to begging on the pavement.

When I got back to the entrance to the Luxembourg Gardens the little shop was open. A woman was standing outside the shop door stamping her feet on small lengths of stale baguette; turning the crusty bread into crumbs for the birds. Around a hundred pigeons were gathered around her. I did not say anything but just stood there and waited and watched.

I don't know how long I waited there. Two or three minutes probably. That's quite a long time to stand quite still. But I didn't want to disturb her or the pigeons. I was happy to wait. Eventually the woman sensed my presence. She turned and apologised. I shook my head to make it clear that I hadn't minded waiting.

45

She had a kind, generous face and went into her little shop and found me what I asked for.

'Vous êtes très gentile avec les oiseux,' I said to her, in my fractured French. Pigeon French. I had to give her a twenty franc note for the chocolate. I didn't have any change.

She smiled. It was a glorious smile with nothing held back. Not one of those polite smiles that so often stand in for the real thing. She thanked me for waiting and said she liked the birds. Our souls touched for a moment.

I took the chocolate, and the change, and walked on through the park.

It was a crisp, dry day. The sky was blue. I walked about in the park. I watched men playing chess and a couple playing tennis. I felt good and glad to be living in Paris.

Chapter 7

I needn't have bothered getting the work permit because two days later, less than three weeks after I had started work at the pharmacy, I was fired.

When I arrived at the shop that morning I could tell by the atmosphere that something unusual was happening in the shop. Pierre had the day off and Sylvie, who was in the shop alone when I arrived, took me on one side. 'Monsieur Tennyson is here,' she whispered.

'The owner?'

Sylvie nodded.

'Where is he?'

'In the office. He has Juliette with him.'

'Who is Juliette? His wife?'

'No, no!' said Sylvie, urgently. 'Juliette is Monsieur Tennyson's mistress.'

'Why on earth has he brought her here?' I asked.

'He brings her to pick out new sunglasses and perfume,' explained Sylvie. 'Besides,' she paused, and lowered her voice still further so that I could hardly hear her, 'I think he likes taking risks. His wife is American and if she finds out he'll be in big trouble.'

The manager came into the shop before Sylvie could say any more. 'Re-stock the sunglasses counter and the vitamins shelf,' Monsieur Baptiste told me. He seemed rather tense and edgy. 'And do it quietly!'

I walked through the door at the back of the shop and down to the storeroom where I took off my jacket and replaced it with my white coat. I then went back into the shop to check at the sunglasses counter to see which models I needed to fetch from the storeroom.

The weather had been gloomy and dark for ages but we still managed to sell numerous pairs of absurdly expensive sunglasses every day. On my first day working at the pharmacy Sylvie had explained to me that rich but dull American businessmen and their wives, staying at the Hotels Meurice, Lotti and Intercontinental, bought them so that they would look like film stars when they walked through the lobby to order a taxi. 'They don't care whether they can see anything or not,' she had told me. 'All they care about is that they are wearing expensive designer frames. I think some of them would like to leave the price tags tied onto the frames.'

I was in the storeroom, having selected the sunglasses I needed for the display cabinet, when I heard a commotion in the shop. Carefully carrying several hundred pounds worth of sunglasses I walked back to the shop where I found Sylvie and Monsieur Baptiste attempting to calm a woman whom I naturally assumed to be a customer. She looked to be in her mid to late thirties and was enveloped in a huge and obviously expensive fur coat and a cloud of some obviously expensive perfume. Monsieur Baptiste was normally very good at calming troubled customers but he wasn't getting very far with this one.

'I know he's here and I want to see him,' insisted the woman, as I carefully put my bundle of sunglasses down on a counter. 'His car is parked across the street for God's sake!'

'Perhaps Monsieur Tennyson came in through the back door, madam,' lied Monsieur Baptiste, knowing full well that the shop did not have a back door and that, even if it had, Mr Tennyson would have never used it. The shop owner was not the sort of man to use a back door anywhere. Monsieur Baptise hurried away, through the doorway at the back of the shop, heading for his office wherein, he knew quite well, he would find his employer and some very expensive evidence.

Sylvie came across to where I was standing and produced a

key to the sunglasses cabinet. When she had opened the back of the cabinet I started putting the sunglasses into place. 'That's Mrs Tennyson,' Sylvie whispered.

Less than two minutes later a tall, well-built, bronzed man in a blue, pinstripe suit strolled nonchalantly into the shop as though he owned it, which, of course, he did. His shirt was unbuttoned and he wore no tie. He had amazing presence.

'Harriet, my dear!' he said, addressing the woman in the fur coat. 'Why didn't you say you were coming?'

'Have you got a woman with you?' demanded Harriet, utterly unselfconscious and quite oblivious to the presence of Monsieur Baptiste, Sylvie and myself.

Mr Tennyson looked around. 'The only woman here is Sylvie,' he replied. 'Do you know Sylvie?'

'I know Sylvie,' spat Mrs Tennyson. 'Have you got a woman here?'

Beside me I was conscious of Sylvie bristling. She pushed out her chest as if it to make it clear that she, too, was a woman.

'Of course not,' laughed Mr Tennyson. He was very convincing. I nearly believed him and I knew that he was lying.

'I'm going to look,' said Harriet. She marched around the counter, through the door at the back of the shop and down to the manager's office. Mr Tennyson followed her. Monsieur Baptiste, Sylvie and I stood and waited for the explosion. It took longer to come than any of us had suspected for Mr Tennyson had pushed his mistress into the store room and it was there that Mrs Tennyson found her.

'And just who the hell is this tart?' we heard Mrs Tennyson demand. 'Are you keeping your women in the store room now?'

The door from the street opened and a nervous looking elderly gentleman in a brown overcoat and a rather lopsided wig timidly stepped into the shop.

'Can I help you, sir? asked Monsieur Baptiste, unconsciously clasping his hands together in front of his body and rubbing them together expectantly.

A tall, willowy blonde, of about my own age, dressed in a short, sleeveless, backless and pretty nearly frontless red dress and a pair of red high heeled shoes, came running into the shop. She was closely followed by Mrs Tennyson. Mr Tennyson brought up the rear of this fast moving trio. The blonde skidded to a halt in front of the sunglasses display cabinet, where I was still standing.

'Who is she?' demanded Mrs Tennyson of her husband, pointing to the blonde with a trembling finger.

'I've no idea!' insisted Mr Tennyson. 'I've never seen her before.' He turned to Monsieur Baptiste. 'Is this a new member of staff?' he asked. 'Why isn't she wearing a white coat?'

'She's no pharmacy assistant!' insisted Mrs Tennyson scornfully. 'Just look at her! Does she look like a shop assistant?' She answered her own question with a rather derisive snort. Sylvie, offended again, pushed out her chest still further.

'I think I'll pop back a little later when you aren't quite so occupied,' murmured the elderly gentleman in the brown overcoat. He absent mindedly lifted his wig as though it was a hat and headed for the exit. Monsieur Baptiste, clearly not sure what to do, simpered and held the door open for the departing customer.

'And who is this?' demanded Mrs Tennyson. This time, to my embarrassment and horror I realised that the trembling finger was pointed in my direction. I wanted to run away, or at the very least to duck, but I was frozen to the spot.

'Yes, who the hell are you?' demanded Mr Tennyson.

I told him my name and explained that I was working for him.

'Didn't you tell him that he wasn't allowed to bring girlfriends onto the premises?' Mr Tennyson demanded of Monsieur Baptiste.

'Oh yes, sir,' said Monsieur Baptiste, desperately protecting himself and selling me out at the same time. 'He was quite specifically told that under no circumstances was he to bring girlfriends – or even boyfriends – into the shop.'

I said nothing and just stood there with my mouth wide open.

'What do you have to say for yourself?' demanded the shop owner.

'I didn't...' I began.

'No,' said Mr Tennyson, before I could say anything. 'You

didn't think. You didn't think of the consequences. And you didn't think you would get caught. I gave you a job as a favour to an old friend. And this is the way you repay me.' Before I could say anything in reply to this he turned to the willowy blonde. 'I don't know your name, young woman,' he said. 'But your boyfriend made a big mistake bringing you here. You'd better leave.' He had turned so that he had his back to his wife and only the blonde and I could see the wink he gave her and the kiss he blew her. Loyally, she turned and marched out of the shop without another word.

'You're fired,' said Mr Tennyson to me. 'Just take off your white coat and leave. You aren't working here any longer. Go back to your hotel and I'll bring round whatever I owe you.'

Monsieur Baptiste and Sylvie stared but said nothing. By the way Sylvie looked at me I knew she wanted to speak up for me but she could not find the courage or the words. When I looked at Monsieur Baptiste he looked down and examined his shoes. I took off my white coat, laid it carefully across the counter and walked to the store room where I had left my jacket. Less than a minute later I was on the pavement. I felt numb and didn't know what to do. I felt very alone and rather frightened. I walked aimlessly along the street and as I did so I looked through a café window and saw the willowy blonde sitting, alone, at one of the tables with a cup of coffee in front of her. When she saw me she smiled, gave a little wave and shrugged. I managed a ghost of a smile, waved back and carried on walking. I felt a tear or two rolling down my cheeks and brushed them away angrily.

Chapter 8

'Thanks for keeping quiet,' said Mr Tennyson. He looked around my room. 'God, is this where we put you? It's awful.'

He had arrived at the hotel about an hour after I'd got back. He had apologised and explained that he'd had to find Natalie first. 'It didn't take long,' he said. 'I knew she'd be in a café nearby.'

'Sit down,' I said, offering him the only chair. My suitcase was on the bed. I'd started packing.

'I think I'll stand if you don't mind,' he said, examining the grubby looking chair. 'I was in a bit of a tricky spot there today,' he said. 'My wife has caught me out once or twice before and she's sworn that if she catches me out again she'll go straight to a divorce lawyer she knows in New York. He's a killer.'

I didn't say anything but waited for him to go on.

'I can understand you being angry with me,' said Mr Tennyson. 'I can't give you your job back at the shop but I'll try and help make it up to you.' He took out his wallet. 'Apart from picking up Natalie I also called in at the bank,' he said. 'You were due to work for us for another six months or so, I think?'

'Yes, that's right.'

'And we were paying for your room here?'

'Yes.'

He counted out a thick, impressive looking wad of notes onto the dressing table. 'That's what we would have paid you,' he said. 'And we'll carry on paying your hotel bill.'

I looked at the money. I'd never seen so many bank notes before.

'I'm sorry again about what happened,' he said, putting his now much thinner wallet back into his jacket pocket. 'I don't expect you to forgive me. But I hope you at least understand. Is there anything else I can do for you?'

'My job with you was arranged by the Assistant Dean at the Medical School where I'll be studying,' I told him. 'If he asks...'

'I'll tell him you were the best damned employee I've ever had,' he promised. 'Hard working, punctual, loyal, respectable, intelligent – anything I've missed out?'

I found myself smiling, for the first time in several hours. 'No,' I said. 'That will do very well.'

'Good.' He looked down at my half packed suitcase. 'You're not leaving Paris, are you?'

'I don't know now,' I admitted.

'Do you want to stay here, or do you want me to get someone to find you a room somewhere else?' suggested Mr Tennyson. 'Even staying in this dump, at your age I'd have jumped at the chance to spend a few months in Paris at someone else's expense. Now you don't even have to turn up at the drug store every day.'

'It's a bit gloomy and grubby here,' I said, thinking aloud. 'But it's convenient and surprisingly it's quiet...'

'If you want to stay here I could get them to give you some better furniture. Maybe even a lick of paint.' He looked around my tiny room. 'They could paint this in a day.'

'That would be nice,' I said.

'I'll sort it,' he said. He held out his hand. I took it. We shook.

Despite everything I rather liked him.

Chapter 9

After Mr Tennyson had left I looked at my watch. The banks would still be open. I decided to take the money he'd given me and put it into my account.

As I headed out of the hotel the receptionist called me over and handed me an envelope. I opened it straight away. It contained a note from Sylvie asking me to meet her at a café across the road.

'I'm so sorry about today,' she said. 'I was too frightened of losing my job to speak up. I feel really ashamed of myself. I've been sitting here for half an hour waiting to see you.'

'Please don't feel bad.' I told her about Mr Tennyson's visit.

'So things have not worked out too badly for you?'

'No.' I paused. 'To be honest I was more worried about what the Assistant Dean would say when he found out that I'd been fired so quickly. But Mr Tennyson promised to say I'd been a good employee.' I looked at her. 'Do you think he'll stick to his word?'

'Oh, he'll stick to his promise,' Sylvie assured me. 'He doesn't have much choice, does he?'

I looked at her and frowned. 'Why not?'

'Because if he drops you in it you can do the same to him. All you have to do is make one phone call to his wife.'

I hadn't thought of that. 'I suppose so,' I agreed. I felt much better.

'I'm so relieved that things have worked out not too badly for you,' said Sylvie. 'Apart from coming to apologise I came because I think I may be able to help if you want another job.'

'Really? That would be terrific. What is it?'

'Giving English conversation classes.'

I frowned, puzzled. 'What do I have to do?' I asked.

'Talk to people in English.'

'That's really all I have to do? Talk?' I could hardly believe that anyone would pay me simply to speak to them in English; to gossip, to chat without any purpose to the conversation. It was, after all, something I had been doing all my life without expecting anyone to pay me for it. In Britain millions of people do it all day long and none of them expect to be paid for their idle chatter.

'In English.'

Genuinely puzzled, I scratched my head. 'But who on earth will pay me to do that?'

'A language school. They won't pay you very much, but you will be paid in cash.'

It sounded too good to be true. At school our French classes had sometimes been supplemented with conversation classes conducted by young French women, who were brought over to England for a single term and usually put up in the French master's home, but they had always stuck very firmly to the syllabus.

'The principal is a friend of mine. He needs a new teacher. You will be doing him a favour.'

'I'm not a teacher,' I protested, seriously worried by the sudden escalation. There was, it seemed to me, quite a difference between simply talking to people and teaching them. I was pretty sure I could do the former. But equally sure that I wasn't quite ready for the latter. 'I've only just left school.' I added, probably unnecessarily.

'That doesn't matter,' said Sylvie. 'You won't be expected to teach. They just want you to correct the students' pronunciation and grammar occasionally.'

Chapter 10

The language school was situated in a side street just off the Champs Elysée. Clutching a piece of paper upon which Sylvie had scribbled the name and address of the language school, I walked along that side street at least half a dozen times in an increasingly desperate search for the school's entrance.

When I eventually found what I was looking for I wasn't particularly surprised that it had taken me so long. The school's entrance door was crammed between the service entrance for an Indian restaurant and a small shop which had its front window completely blacked out. Only a large neon sign with the word 'SEXY' on it in red gave any indication as to the type of customers the owner was hoping to attract. A huge, square, open metal dustbin was parked in front of the restaurant's service entrance and the entrance to the language school. The dustbin was piled high with foul smelling refuse. Next to the dustbin, standing in the doorway to the sex shop, and apparently quite oblivious to the stench, stood a statuesque blonde in her twenties, dressed only in flimsy underwear, a suspender belt, stockings and a pair of gold sandals. Her bra was totally inadequate and although it provided a shelf upon which her breasts could be displayed, it did not cover her nipples which were large and erect.

The first time I had walked past her and the restaurant she had mistaken me for a customer and had, with the aid of a crooked index finger, tried to persuade me to follow her into the shop. I had been so embarrassed by this that on each of the subsequent occasions when I had walked past the doorway I had walked slightly faster and tried to show a very concerned interest in what was happening on the pavement on the other side of the street.

'Are you lost, love?' said a voice behind me.

I turned round.

'Lost? Looking for something?' the blonde asked me. She was, I saw now, considerably older than I had originally thought.

I looked at her and felt myself blushing. 'I'm looking for the language school,' I told her. I showed her the piece of paper I was carrying, to confirm that my search was genuine. I pointed to the address. 'Number 24.'

'It's right here,' she said, pointing to a narrow doorway, half hidden behind the dustbin. 'Fifth floor. There's no lift.'

I thanked her and squeezed behind the dustbin, trying not to brush against it. I could see now that there was a small plaque on the wall advertising the existence of the school. As I entered through the doorway I hesitated, then turned. She was standing, hand on one hip, watching me. 'How did you know that I was English?' I asked her.

The blonde laughed. 'You couldn't be anything else,' she told me.

'Your English is very good,' I told her.

'It should be,' she said. 'I was born in Middlesbrough.' She laughed again and then turned away as a group of men in suits approached her.

I climbed the stairs to the fifth floor. These stairs were straighter and slightly wider than the stairs at my hotel, but they were no cleaner. I guessed that they hadn't been swept, let alone polished, for months.

At the top of the stairs, on the fifth floor, there was a short vestibule and then a door with a large frosted glass panel in its upper half. The bottom half of the door had once been painted brown. The glass panel had the name of the language school sten-cilled across it. I knocked and, in response to an invitation from an unseen female voice, entered.

The invitation to enter had come from a woman in her

fifties or sixties who was sitting behind an untidy desk. She wore a mauve cardigan with huge patch pockets, had two curlers in her untidy grey hair, a pair of tortoiseshell spectacles perched on the tip of her nose, a cigarette between two nicotine stained fingers and a bored, quizzical, seen-it-all-before look. Apart from the cigarette and the look she reminded me very much of one of the librarians in my home town public library.

'I'm looking for Mr James Whitechapel,' I told her. I held up the piece of paper with his name written on it.

She nodded towards a door on her right. 'He's in there,' she said.

I hesitated, not sure whether or not I should sit and wait for her to ring through and introduce me.

'Just go on in, love,' she told me. 'He hasn't got anybody with him.'

Chapter 11

The sign on Mr Whitechapel's door announced that he was the Principal of the Whitechapel International School of Languages. It sounded a terribly important establishment.

James Whitechapel was unmistakeably English. I had never been abroad before and I had very little practical experience of foreigners but even I could see that Mr Whitechapel could not have been anything else other than an Englishman.

He had curly, greying hair which had a vaguely reddish tint to it and which was thinning both at the temples and the crown, pale, freckled skin and a gingery moustache which was so thin and indistinct that it was not immediately obvious that it was, indeed, a moustache rather than an upper lip which had received less than its fair share of attention during the morning shaving ritual. (And I quickly realised that for Mr Whitechapel most daily chores would be a ritual.) He wore a tweed sports coat with leather buttons, cuffs, pocket guards and elbow patches, a checked shirt and a silk club tie which I did not recognise.

His office was cramped, and every useable flat surface (including the floor) was piled high with books and papers. A bird cage stood on top of a medium sized bookcase. From inside the cage a bad-tempered looking cockatoo glared at me. I introduced myself to Mr Whitechapel and explained why I was there.

'You're not American are you? You don't sound it but one cannot always tell these days.'

'N-n-n-n-o,' I stuttered, as I attempted to respond to his

simple query. I hadn't stuttered for years. Considering the nature of the job for which I was applying it didn't seem a good start. I concentrated hard and took a deep breath. 'No,' I said. 'I'm not American. I'm English.'

'Say something to me.'

'What would you like me to say?'

'Anything you like.'

'I don't know what to say.'

'What are you doing in Paris?'

I started to explain. I had reached the part in my story where the Assistant Dean had telephoned to tell me that the University would hold my place for a year when Mr Whitechapel held up a hand to stop me.

'That's fine,' he said.

'I'm sorry,' I apologised.

'Sorry for what?'

'I thought that perhaps I was boring you.'

'No, you weren't boring me. I just wanted to know that you can speak English. And to make sure that you don't speak it with an American accent.' He pulled out a pipe and a tobacco pouch. 'I'm afraid that the French do rather l-o-a-t-h-e Americans,' he said. He drew out the word 'loathe' to give it extra emphasis. 'The Americans all think they speak English, of course.' He opened the pouch, took out a chunk of tobacco and with two fingers of his right hand started to roll it on the palm of his left hand. 'I don't know what it is they do speak,' he said. 'But it isn't English.'

'I've never even been to America,' I said.

'What a wise man you are,' he said. 'I gather that some French teenagers are rather taken with what is known as American culture – something of an oxymoron in my view – but my students don't like the Americans at all.' He started stuffing tobacco into the bowl of his pipe.

I said nothing.

'Would you like a cup of tea?' he asked. 'Coffee? Perhaps a glass of wine?' He compressed the tobacco in his pipe with his right index finger and then carefully stowed away the pouch in his jacket pocket.

I started to reply but I was too slow. Mr Whitechapel was already on his feet, moving around the table. I could see now that he wore a pair of cavalry twill trousers and a pair of heavy, well polished brown brogues. He put his pipe into his mouth, took out a box of matches, lit one and held the flame to the bowl of his pipe.'

'Let's pop out, shall we? Get ourselves a spot of elevenses.'

'Back in five minutes, Miss Haversham,' he said to the receptionist. She said something to him but I didn't hear it and I doubt if he did either. 'Did Miss Haversham give you a tour of the School?' he asked me. When I told him that she had not he strode purposefully past her desk towards a door marked 'Seminar Room' and flung open the door. 'Our seminar room,' he told me. I stepped forward and peeped inside. The room, about ten foot square, contained two wooden chairs and an old, rickety looking wooden table. The Whitechapel International School of Languages was clearly not a large establishment.

He led the way down the stairs and went so quickly that I had difficulty keeping up with him. When we reached the street, he shimmied neatly round the dustbin, turned left and headed for the Champs Elysée. I looked around for the half naked woman from Middlesbrough but she had disappeared.

'Do you know Paris well?' he asked.

'No, not really,' I replied, hurrying along behind him. 'Not very well. Well, not at all, actually,' I added, talking inevitably to the back of his head.

In front of us there was a loud crash. It sounded as if someone was crushing tin cans. Two cars had collided at a junction. Both motorists immediately climbed out of their vehicles and started shouting at one another.

'When Parisian motorists see a traffic light that is green they go as fast as they can to make sure that they get through the lights before they change,' explained Mr Whitechapel. 'When they see a light that is red they know that it will soon be green so they do not see any point in slowing down. Sometimes there are accidents.' He paused and watched for a moment. The two men were both shouting loudly. 'The French way of dealing with a crisis is to panic, get excited, shout a lot and then forget all about it,' said Mr Whitechapel. 'That probably explains why, despite their enthusiasm for alcohol, tobacco and rich food, they have such a low incidence of heart disease.' He hurried on. I followed, keeping as close behind him as I could.

Dodging in and out of the foreign tourists, French sightseers, beggars and drunkards left over from the night before, Mr Whitechapel quickly arrived at a café on the Champs Elysée. We were there within three or four minutes of leaving the language school offices. 'French cafés are wonderful places,' said Mr Whitechapel. 'But you have to remember that in a French café you are not buying a drink.'

'No?' I said, puzzled.

'You are renting a front row seat for the greatest show on earth,' said Mr Whitechapel. 'Look around.'

I looked around. The café was half full.

'Many of these people come into this café every day for their morning brandy,' said Mr Whitechapel. 'They are retired. They read the paper – which the café provides – and they chat to the waiter. They have a croissant and they watch the world go by. In England they would be sitting in plastic arm chairs watching rubbish on daytime TV.' He sighed. 'I love England,' he said. 'But there are some things we do not do well. And life is one of those things. What would you like to drink?' he asked me, when he had found a table he liked.

I hesitated and glanced around. The couple at the next table were holding hands and staring into each others eyes.

Mr Whitechapel said something in French to the waiter who had hurried over the moment we'd sat down. 'I've ordered you a lemon tea,' he told me. 'When can you start?' he asked.

'Any time you like,' I replied.

'This evening?'

'Yes, if you like.'

'Splendid.'

The man at the next table had reached across and was unbuttoning his companion's blouse. She made no effort to stop him.

'Your official title will be Senior Lecturer,' said Mr Whitechapel. The waiter arrived, carrying a large tray.

'That sounds rather grand.'

The waiter began to unload pots and cups from his tray.

'Actually,' I said, 'I'm not sure whether or not you know that I don't have any teaching experience.'

The man at the next table had now unbuttoned his partner's blouse. I watched in astonishment as he slid his hand into her blouse, scooped out one of her breasts and laid it on the table between them. The woman smiled at him. The man stroked the woman's breast as though it was a pet animal.

'Oh, don't worry about that,' said Mr Whitechapel, waving a hand airily. 'That doesn't matter. The important thing is that you speak English with a genuine English accent. That's what our students want. The French have a great affection for language though, sadly, I confess that their affection is mainly reserved for their own language. Most French people do not believe in learning foreign languages. You know what Noel Coward said when, after General de Gaulle died he was asked what de Gaulle would find to talk about to God?'

'Er, no, I'm afraid not,' I confessed.

'It depends,' replied Coward, 'On how good God's French is.'

'Ah,' I said, nodding wisely. 'But I'm not sure that I ought to be a senior lecturer,' I said, getting back to what to me seemed to be a crucial issue. 'Not straight away,' I added, lest my modesty be mistaken for self-criticism.

'The students will like it,' said Mr Whitechapel, clearly untroubled by my concern. 'They like to think they're being taught by someone who is a professional; a specialist. Well qualified for the purpose. They progress far more speedily if they have faith in their teacher.' He poured himself a cup of tea, and added a slice of lemon. 'Pour yourself a cup. They do good tea here. This is Earl Grey. And it looks good when you sign their diploma.'

'Diploma?'

'Oh naturally they all want a diploma,' said Mr Whitechapel. 'They get a diploma after twelve lessons and a degree after twenty.'

I poured myself a cup of tea. I didn't have the foggiest idea who Earl Grey was and had never drunk lemon tea before. When I'd filled my cup I added a slice of lemon. The man at the next table was still stroking his partner's breast.

'A degree?' I said.

'It's what we call our degree of certification,' said Mr Whitechapel. 'They get a beautiful certificate on vellum. Very expensively printed and quite reasonable at the price.'

'What's the pass rate?' I asked, innocently.

'The pass rate?'

'How many students pass?' I asked. 'Of the ones who take the examination?'

'Oh we don't agree with examinations,' said Mr Whitechapel. 'Far too divisive and élitist. We favour the continual assessment scheme which is now becoming increasingly popular among progressive educationalists. We leave it to our lecturers to make the decisions. Examinations are far too arbitrary.'

I nodded as though I understood.

The man at the next table put his hand inside his partner's blouse and pulled out her other breast. Paris seemed to be full of naked breasts. The woman saw me looking and smiled. I felt myself blushing and looked away.

'You have to understand that running an educational establishment is very much a passion with me,' Mr Whitechapel continued. He seemed unaware of the gentle striptease which was taking place a few feet away. 'It's more a vocation than a business. It does mean that we can't pay you very well I'm afraid. But I hope that you will think of your title as in some way something of a reward for your efforts.'

'But I will get paid?' I said, rather anxiously.

'Oh dear me, yes,' said Mr Whitechapel. 'The full rate for the job. The school charges students a fee of thirty francs an hour for tuition. You keep half of that.' He sipped some more tea. 'In addition you may find, from time to time, that one or other of your students may feel moved to make you a little present. Only the other month a particularly generous gentleman from Libya presented me with a very fine paperweight which he had purchased, no doubt at considerable expense, from a small establishment in the shadow of Notre Dame Cathedral. It was not, unfortunately, precisely the sort of *objet d'art* which would fit in comfortably with the other little knick-knacks in my apartment but I passed the item on to my mother when her birthday came round and she was utterly delighted with it.'

'How many other lecturers do you have?' I asked him.

'I will not hide from you the fact that we have retrenched somewhat recently,' said Mr Whitechapel. 'We have, by circumstances, been forced to tighten our collective belt. As you've probably read in the broadsheets the world of private education is in something of a recession at the moment. There was an article about the decline and fall of private education in *The Times Educational Supplement* a couple of months ago. Did you see it?'

'Er, no,' I said. 'I'm afraid not. I don't read *The Times* so I suppose I would have missed their supplement.'

'Never mind, never mind,' said Mr Whitechapel. He leant back, folded his arms and surveyed the Champs Elysée. 'Wonderful place isn't it?'

'It is,' I agreed.

'Well,' said Mr Whitechapel, rather sadly. 'I must be getting back to the school. Oh, and don't forget to keep details of all your expenses. You can claim them against your income tax.'

'Expenses?' I said. 'Income tax?'

'When you pay the rapacious man from the Revenue at the end of the year,' explained Mr Whitechapel. 'You do pay taxes I assume? Still, never mind. I have no interest in that. Entirely up to you. You'll be a freelance with us, of course.'

It had not occurred to me that I might be liable to pay income tax on my earnings and while I mulled over this piece of rather worrying information Mr Whitechapel rose, and held out a hand. I took the proffered digits, rather limp, damp examples of the species, and we shook hands to seal our agreement . 'One other thing,' Mr Whitechapel added, still gripping my hand. 'The school has grown in recent years and we're a bit short of lecture theatres and classrooms, not to mention furniture. Have you any idea of the cost of furniture these days?' I had no idea of the cost of furniture and so I shook my head. 'Still, in a way this is an advantage,' continued Mr Whitechapel. 'You'll be taking all your students out into the real world for their classes. Much better for them. Far less formal and more realistic.' He released my hand.

I was puzzled and must have shown it.

'This café is one of my personal favourites,' said Mr Whitechapel. 'But you can take your students wherever you like.' There was a huge crunching sound. We both looked up. A motorist, trying to reverse a Mercedes into a small parking space, had backed into a small Renault. 'Oh dear,' I said. 'Should we do anything?'

'About what?'

'There's been another accident,' I said, pointing to the glass on the pavement.

'Oh don't worry about that,' said Mr Whitechapel. 'That doesn't count as an accident. The Parisians always park their vehicles in spaces which are too short. They do this by shunting all the cars together. It's perfectly normal.' He took a small black notebook out of his pocket and removed a blue rubber band from around it. 'Now let me see,' he said, thoughtfully. 'Ah, yes. Jules de Prony. He would be perfect for you to cut your teeth on.'

I waited, expectantly.

'Mr de Prony is the eldest son of the de Prony family,' explained Mr Whitechapel. 'You have heard of them?'

I thought for a moment. 'No,' I said at last. 'I'm afraid not.'

'The de Pronys are very wealthy. Very wealthy. The great great grandfather started a mineral water business in the 19th century. They have a huge house out near Versailles. Jules is a student at the Sorbonne. His family want him to have good conversational English so they pay extra for him to take lessons with us.'

'Right,' I said. 'When do I start?'

'He's a rather lively young man,' said Mr Whitechapel. 'Very popular, so I gather, with the ladies.'

'Does he speak good English?'

'Not bad,' said Mr Whitechapel. 'Not bad at all. He likes to have his lessons twice a week in a café called La Rhumerie. It's near the church of St. Michel. You can't miss it. I'll telephone him and tell him to expect you this evening at 8 pm. That's his normal time.'

'How will we know each other?' I asked.

'Good question,' said Mr Whitechapel. 'Carry a copy of *The Times*.' He coughed. 'As to the matter of fee,' he said. 'As I have already explained we charge our students thirty francs an hour and we bill them for a minimum of one hour. Mr de Prony will, in addition, pay for any drinks either of you consume. Half the fee you will remit to me at this office. The other half is yours to keep. I usually like my lecturers to remit fees to the office on a weekly basis but since this is your first engagement perhaps you would call at my office tomorrow with the appropriate sum. If the office is closed just place the cash in an envelope and slide it under the door.'

I promised to do as he had requested. He called the waiter over, paid for our tea, took my hand again, shook it, let go of it and left.

I stayed there for a few minutes, watching the world go by.

At the next table the man in the dark blue suit was still stroking the pair of breasts which lay on the table in front of him. The owner of the breasts was staring into his eyes lovingly and I was convinced I could hear her purring.

When I got back to my hotel I discovered to my astonishment and delight that I had been allocated a much bigger room on the second floor. The room had been freshly decorated. The walls were pale blue and there was a dark blue carpet on the floor. The furniture, although fairly cheap, was brand new and spotless. The bed, too, was new and there were even a few pictures hanging on the walls. Best of all the room had its own shower and WC. Compared to the room I'd had before this was five star luxury.

Chapter 12

My first meeting with Jules was complicated by the fact that when I arrived at the rendezvous there were two men in La Rhumerie already sitting reading *The Times* newspaper.

One of the men, sitting right at the back near the bar, was bald and looked like a school-teacher. He wore a very neatly trimmed toothbrush moustache and a slightly shabby blue blazer with brass buttons. The other, much younger, had a full head of flame red hair and wore a well worn and rather badly creased grey suit. He had a black composite briefcase by his chair.

I chose a seat near the window (not difficult since at La Rhumerie there are windows on three sides) removed from my jacket pocket my carefully folded copy of *The Times* (purchased at such considerable expense from a newsagent's in the rue de Rivoli that I had already decided to keep the same newspaper as my identification for future appointments) and started to read it. When the waiter came over I ordered a small black coffee, assuming that coffee would probably be the cheapest item on the menu.

For the first fifteen minutes I kept my eyes firmly on the door, trying to guess whether which, if any, of the customers might be my first student. With three of us reading *The Times* I was worried that my student might approach the wrong one of us. 'What,' I thought to myself, 'if he approaches the man who looks like a real teacher and he turns out to be a real teacher who is short of money and steals my student. How would I ever explain that to Mr Whitechapel?' Eventually, I got fed up of looking around and concentrated instead on reading the newspaper.

'I'm Jules. Are you my English teacher?'

I looked up.

'Jules de Prony,' said a young man in a bottle green corduroy suit. His jet black hair was shoulder length and shiny. He had quite long sideburns and smelt very faintly of something which was probably expensive.

'Sorry I'm late,' he said. 'But I had a terrible job parking the car.'

'You have a car?'

'Of course,' he replied. He called over the waiter and ordered something. I didn't know what. The café was crowded and noisy but somehow Jules had managed to attract the waiter's attention in a moment. 'You haven't paid for that, have you?' he asked, nodding towards my coffee.

'No,' I said. 'Not yet.'

'Good,' he said. 'I will pay the bill when we leave. Would you like a Ricard?'

'I don't know,' I stuttered.

'Have you ever tried one?'

'No,' I said. 'I don't think so.'

'Ah, you should,' he said. He called to the waiter. The waiter turned. Jules held up two fingers and then pointed first at himself and then at me. The waiter nodded. 'If you don't like it, you don't drink it,' Jules told me firmly. 'OK?'

'Thank you,' I said.

'You are fond of my English?'

'It's very good.'

'Thank you. I need to be good English.'

'To speak good English.'

'I need to be good English to speak good English?'

'No.' I started to explain.

'Oh never mind,' said Jules with a wave of his hand. 'You were understanding me?' The waiter brought over two tumblers containing a clear liquid. He also brought a jug of water.

'Yes. I understood you perfectly.'

'That is what the matter is,' said Jules. He poured water into one of the glasses. The clear liquid turned a yellowy, rich, milky white. It reminded me of an experiment in chemistry at school. He held the jug over the other tumbler. 'Shall I do for you?'

'Is that the normal way to drink it?'

'Yes, certainly.'

'Yes, please, then.' I watched, again, as the Ricard magically changed appearance in front of my eyes.

'And I look English, yes?' he said. He looked down at himself, brushing a tiny speck of dust from the lapel of his immaculate jacket.

'Pretty much,' I agreed.

Jules frowned. 'What is 'pretty much'?'

'It means that you do look quite English,' I said.

'But not perfect?'

'No,' I told him. 'Not perfect.'

'So what is wrong? Tell me so that I can put it right.'

I thought for a moment. 'The only creases in your trousers are the ones which are supposed to be there, you have no loose threads poking out from your jacket and you have neither food nor ink stains on your tie.'

'I need food and ink on my tie to be English?'

'Oh yes. I'm afraid so. It's pretty much compulsory.'

'And have creases which should not be there?'

'Absolutely.'

'Then I stay French,' said Jules. He grinned. 'This is the famous English sense of humour, yes?'

'Not entirely,' I confessed.

Jules shook his head in amazement. And then remembered something and put his hand into his jacket pocket. 'Before I forget I must give you this,' he said, pulling out a plain white envelope.

I felt myself blushing with embarrassment.

'For our lesson,' Jules explained. 'I pay you now so we get this out of the way.' He grinned at me. 'So then we can enjoy ourselves. You can peep inside.'

I wasn't sure whether to put the envelope into my pocket or to open it first. In the end I decided to open it and take a peep.

The envelope contained a one hundred franc note.

'I don't have any change,' I told him.

'I don't want any change,' said Jules. 'Take it, please.'

I took the note and slipped it into my pocket. All I could think was that men who go with prostitutes usually pay before they get down to business.

'You do not have a wallet?'

'It was stolen on the boat across the Channel.'

'Tsk. That is terrible.' He shook his head in dismay. 'Have you made an official report?'

'Do you think I should report it to the police?' I asked him.

'I do not think there is much point,' said Jules. 'Because they want you to be happy they will smile and promise faithfully that they will deal with your problem. But, of course, nothing will happen. It is just a game.'

'A game?'

'They know that you will be happy if you believe they are searching for your wallet. Bringing in all the known wallet thieves. That sort of thing. And so they make this promise.'

'Even though they have no intention of keeping their promise?'

'That is a problem for the future,' said Jules. 'Like all English people you think far, far into the future. Here people worry about today and, maybe, a little about tomorrow. But they do not waste energy worrying about the day after tomorrow because that is too far into the future.'

We both sipped our drinks and for a few moments sat and looked around. I decided not to bother reporting my stolen wallet to the police. The peace of the café was interrupted when the doors burst open and two hugely overweight tourists burst in through the door. They were both carrying maps and had cameras slung around their necks. Both wore ugly, ill-fitting, beige trousers, huge, baggy T-shirts and spectacles. Both had baseball caps on their heads. I wasn't entirely sure but I thought that one was male and the other female. Both carried small rucksacks.

'Americans,' muttered Jules. 'They could be nothing else.

Smug, self-satisfied, arrogant and fat. America's problems are...what is the word...end...'

'Endless?'

'No, no.'

'Endemic?'

'Yes! That is it. Endemic. They have bad tastes, bad judgement and they are far too greedy. They are very self-indulgent. They waddle around Europe, filling up all the taxis and bumping into things with the suitcases and the rucksacks. They are patronising and arrogant.' He pulled a face. 'I know that America is a new country, not yet old enough to have culture but they are old enough to know that they do not know. No?' He took a breath for a moment. I thought he had stopped but I was wrong. He was merely getting into his stride. 'I do not wish to be a general,' he went on. 'But the Americans have the minds closed like the shutters. And they have no taste. They make ghastly clothes and inedible food. They have nothing old, nothing original and nothing traditional. Culturally they are hooligans.' He pulled a face.

'Yes,' I agreed. The Lone Ranger, Hopalong Cassidy and the Range Rider were all good men and true but I felt confident that these were not what Jules meant by Americans.

'They refer to Paris as Paris, France,' Jules continued. 'Have you noticed that? And London, England. As though there is another Paris that matters. Or another London.' He sniffed, derisively. 'And so when I speak with Americans I always refer to New York, America or Washington, America.' He paused and a huge smile appeared on his face. 'I have found this is a good way to annoy Americans,' he said.

The two obese Americans marched up to the waiter who was taking an order from a family of four at the next table. 'Where is your bathroom?' demanded one of the tourists, in an unmistakeable and unpleasant American drawl.

Puzzled, the waiter stared at the American.

'Your bathroom,' shouted the American, assuming that since the waiter did not understand English he must be deaf. 'Where is it?'

The waiter clearly didn't have the faintest idea what the American was talking about.

'*La toilette*,' explained Jules to the waiter.

The waiter pointed to the back of the café.

Without a word or gesture of thanks the Americans blundered their way to the back of the café, knocking into tables with their broad hips and sending drinks and ashtrays flying. I noticed that they had American flags sewn onto their rucksacks.

'The Americans are so very, very stupid,' said Jules. 'Why do they wear those little flags to tell the world where they have come from? For the first thing it is not necessary because they are so fat that they are obviously American. And also do they really not realise that everyone hates the Americans? They are so unwise to advertise the fact that they belong to the nation of the stupid and the rude. They could, with some work and a little effort, have perhaps passed themselves off as the English or more likely the Australian.' He paused. Full of indignation. 'There should,' he said, 'be a limit on the number of Americans allowed into Europe at one time.' He turned and looked at me. 'Do you know,' he said, 'that I was once in a lift in Paris where there was the notice: 'Maximum load: 8 people or 2 Americans.'

'Is that true?' I asked him.

He looked at me and grinned. 'Yes,' he said. 'I wrote it. It is a good joke, yes?'

Jules and I sipped at our drinks again.

Aware of the need to earn my money it was me who broke the silence. 'Do you need to speak English for the work you will do later with the family business?'

Jules laughed. 'No, no!' he cried, holding up a hand and shaking his head. 'I do not like to be working. It is boring. There are other people to do that. I need the good English for the girls!'

'For the girls?'

'Of course!' he explained. 'There are some girls who speak French, yes?'

'Yes, of course.'

'And who do not speak English?'

'No.'

'And there are girls who speak English?'

'Yes.'

'But who do not speak French?'

'Of course.'

'So if there are perhaps ten million beautiful girls who speak the French and none of the English,' said Jules, holding up his left hand, 'and there are ten million beautiful girls who speak the English but none of the French,' he paused and put down his left hand and held up his right hand, 'that means that altogether there are twenty million beautiful girls,' he paused again and held up both hands, 'available to the man who can speak the English and the French?'

I looked at both hands. The maths and the logic seemed impeccable. 'Yes, I suppose so.'

At the back of the café there was something of a commotion as the two Americans emerged from the café's *toilettes*. Anxious patrons picked up their drinks as they approached. The Americans blundered through the café again, opened the front door and left. They did not offer to buy anything as payment for the facilities they had used. I felt embarrassed for them. The waiter glared at their backs and shook his head sadly at their rudeness.

Jules, who had watched the Americans leave, put down his hands, grinned and shrugged. 'American tourists conquering the Europe,' he said. 'An invading army in sensibly baggy, elasticated beige, travelling in expectation from the lavatory to the lavatory.'

I stared at him, impressed.

'I learnt all this from my father,' explained Jules. 'He hates the Americans even more than me.' He grinned and shrugged again. 'So, at the age of 15,' he continued, 'I decided that I have to speak the English,' he said. 'I did think about learning the Spanish. There are lots of girls who speak the Spanish and many of them are very beautiful. But the Spanish girls, like the Italian girls, are Catholic. And also there are so many English speaking girls. From England, from Scotland, from Ireland, from Canada, from New Zealand, from Australia.' He waved his hands in the air. 'Even the Dutch girls speak English. And the Swiss. And there are American girls too. I do not have objection to making love to American girls.

In a way I consider it a duty to my country. It is a way of fighting the Americans.'

'You make love to American girls as a way of fighting Americans?'

'Oh yes. But I do not like the American girls to talk. I do not want to pick up the horrid American accent.'

'So how do you keep them quiet?'

'I feed them or I kiss them,' explained Jules. 'American girls are greedy. Whatever you give them they will take from you.'

I nodded and thought carefully about all this. 'You didn't think about learning German?' I asked him.

'Oh no,' said Jules, in dismay. 'The German girls are ugly. And they do not want to play around before they marry. They want only to be the wives, to be fat and to have thousands of children.'

'You are never tempted to learn Spanish or Italian as well as English?'

'No, no,' said Jules. 'I am not greedy. Twenty million girls are quite enough.' He said this with a straight face. I did not think he was joking. He looked at me, and held his head to one side slightly, rather like a sparrow eyeing up a crumb. 'Do you not agree?'

'Oh yes,' I agreed. He was without a doubt the most charming and roguish man I had ever met. I did not know whether to envy him or to be shocked by him. It occurred to me that very few women would be able to resist his charm.

'I love girls,' he sighed. 'From a very tiny age I have loved them. Unwrapping a woman on a first date is to me as exciting as unwrapping a hoped-for Christmas or birthday gift had been when I had been a small boy. I may know what is inside the wrapping but the sense of excitement and anticipation is always there.'

I had never unwrapped a woman but I felt that it would probably not help our developing relationship if I were to admit this so I nodded and muttered my agreement.

'And here in Paris the women package themselves so beautifully, do you not think?' said Jules. 'This is a city where the women still wear the stockings and the...*les jarretières*...what are these in English?'

'Suspenders?' I suggested, on the basis that these went with stockings rather well.

'Thank you. You are teaching me excellent words. They wear the stockings and the suspenders rather than those horrible new all in one tights. The pantry hose. They are impenetrable! Hah. Only the Americans could invent such things. They are for the professional virgins.' He shuddered, emptied his glass and signalled to the waiter, who was on the other side of the café. 'Would you like another Ricard?' he asked me, managing to hold the waiter's attention while he spoke to me.

'I haven't finished this one,' I said, picking up my glass.

'But you like it?'

'Oh yes.'

Jules held up two fingers. The waiter nodded.

'Do you spend a lot of your time with girls?'

'All of it,' said Jules, emphatically.

'But don't you have studies at the university?'

'At the Sorbonne?'

'Yes.'

'Pfui. It is boring stuff. Books and lectures. Who cares about such things.'

'Aren't there exams you have to pass?'

'My father will deal with those,' said Jules. 'He has friends who know how to deal with this sort of stuff.' He waved a hand as though it was all rather beneath him. 'They are happy and impressed that I am taking extra language lessons with Mr Whitechapel's school.'

'And your parents really don't mind if you don't pass any exams by yourself?'

'My father prefers it this way. Every Sunday I have lunch with him and tell him my exploits. He enjoys this very much. He is old now. He is rich but old. He does not have the time or the energy for sex with the girls. So I do it for him.'

'You do it for him? I don't understand.'

'I have a good times and I tell him everything and he enjoys these things again through me,' said Jules.

'Everything? You tell him everything?'

'Oh yes. He enjoys very much the details of my little adventures,' said Jules. 'That is what he wants from me. He wants to know how I am feeling in my head. He wants to know what the girl says. What I say. What we do.' He shrugged. 'Everything.'

He told me this as naturally as if it were quite normal and commonplace for a father to use his son in this way. For all I knew it was normal in France.

'And your mother?' I asked, not at all sure that I could cope with the answer I might receive.

'Oh no,' said Jules. 'That would be absurd.'

I breathed a sigh of relief.

'My mother is not interested in my adventures,' continued Jules. 'She has a lover so she has all the experiences she wishes for.'

I wasn't sure that I had heard him correctly. 'Your mother has a lover?'

'Oh yes, of course.'

'Doesn't your father mind?'

'Mind? I do not understand.'

'Doesn't he object? Doesn't he disapprove?'

'Why should be disapprove?' asked Jules. He seemed genuinely confused by my question. 'It is nothing to do with him. It is my mother who has the lover.'

I drank the rest of my Ricard. Jules signalled to the waiter and ordered two more. I did not object. But I was still sober enough for it to occur to me that Jules was driving.

'Is it safe for you to drink when you are driving?' I asked him. I was beginning to feel distinctly inebriated but since I was officially being hired as his teacher I felt a certain sense of responsibility towards him.

'Oh yes,' said Jules. 'I am the better driver when I have a little alcohol in the blood. It makes me worry less about the accidents.'

'And that makes you a better driver?'

'But certainly,' insisted Jules. 'When the driver is worrying about making the accidents he becomes nervous and the nervous man is not a good driver.'

Once again I found Jules' logic difficult to counter. The waiter arrived with two more glasses of Ricard.

'Alcohol makes me calm and less – how do you say, what is your word for *apprehensif?*'

'Apprehensive,' I guessed.

'Thank you,' said Jules, adding water to the Ricard and handing the now empty jug back to the waiter. 'You see how you are helping me with the English already. 'Less apprehensive,' he said. 'Besides,' he added. 'I read that only four out of every ten accidents on the roads are caused by motorists who are drunk.'

'That's quite a lot,' I said.

'Ah,' said Jules. 'But if only four out of ten accidents are caused by the people who are drunk that means that six out of ten of the accidents must be caused by the people who are sober. Do you not agree?'

'I guess so,' I agreed.

'So more accidents are caused by sober people than by drunks?'

'I suppose that's right.'

'So,' said Jules. 'I always try to have a drink or two when I am driving. It is the safe thing to do.'

'What sort of car do you drive?' I asked him.

'It is the English car,' said Jules proudly. 'A Morgan. A sports car.' He looked out through the window and pointed across the road. 'There!' he said. 'You can see it from here.'

I looked out of the window. A red Morgan sports car was parked partly on the pavement and partly on a pedestrian crossing. It was causing no little inconvenience to motorists and pedestrians alike. I remembered that he'd claimed he'd been late for our rendezvous because he'd had difficulty in parking his car. It was, however, not so much parked as abandoned 'Is that legal?' I asked him.

Jules shrugged. 'My father knows someone very important in the police department,' he said. He drank some of his Ricard. 'Now, that is enough of me,' he said. 'I want to know about you. How long have you been a teacher? Have you always wanted to be a teacher?'

'I'm not really a proper teacher,' I said. I could have bitten off my tongue as soon as the words had escaped from my mouth. 'Well, not that I'm not qualified,' I said, flustered and embarrassed. 'I do speak English. I was born there. It is the tongue of my mother.'

'The tongue of your mother?'

'My mother tongue.'

'So how did you become my teacher?' asked Jules. 'How did you meet our wonderful Mr Whitechapel?'

'A friend found the job,' I explained. I gave Jules a potted account of my recent history.

'So you worked in a pharmacy?'

'Yes.'

'That would have been very useful,' said Jules. 'You had access to antibiotics and contraceptive pills?'

'Well, yes, those things are in the pharmacy,' I agreed.

'Wonderful!' said Jules. 'These are the two things I need most often. Can you not get back your job at the pharmacy?'

'I'm afraid not.'

'Maybe later,' said Jules. He picked up his glass. 'Let us drink to fate and to your new job,' he said. 'Teaching me the English.'

I picked up my glass and we drank to my new job as a language teacher.

Chapter 13

'I have a friend who works behind the counter in a pharmacy,' continued Jules when we had finished our toast. 'She told me a true story about the pharmacy where she works in the 15th *arrondissement*.' He looked around and then leant across the table, beckoning for me to lean towards him. 'The pharmacy is owned by that man over there,' said Jules. 'The bald man in the red jacket.'

'He is a pharmacist?'

'Absolutely. And a very good one,' said Jules. 'So, one day a young man entered the pharmacy,' began Jules. 'He boldly approached the proprietor, my friend's boss, who is a very stern rather dull man in his mid-forties, and asked for a packet of *les preservatifs* – the condoms.'

'"I have a hot date, tonight," the young man told the pharmacist. "How many of the condoms are there in the pack?"'

'The pharmacist tells him that there are three condoms in a pack and the young man says that in that case he will take two packs. The proprietor, who despite being stern and not at all that old, is a little bit of a dirty old man who hasn't seen his wife naked for over a decade and probably wouldn't want to even if she gave him the opportunity, which it is probably safe to say she would not, says that the young man sounds very sure of himself.'

'At this the young man winks and makes all those nudge-nudge signs that young men make when they are boasting to another man about a new conquest. He admits that he has only been out with the girl once before but says that he has no doubts that the girl will go to bed with him. He says that she has been out with several of his friends and that she went to the bed with all of them and that they told him that whatever they had to offer she could not have enough of it. He says she is not the sort of woman that a man thinks of as a future wife – but just a girl for a good time to be had by all. She is, he says, a woman who welcomes everyone with open legs.'

'By this time the pharmacy proprietor is salivating and wondering whether perhaps he himself might not be too old to take advantage of this young woman's generous nature.' Jules looked at me and smiled. 'As your Mr Shakespeare once said: 'Is it not strange that desire should so many years outlive performance?"

I thought about this for a moment. 'I suppose so,' I agreed.

'But,' continued Jules, 'even if he isn't going to get lucky himself he wants to know more about the woman so that he can enjoy himself at the second hand if you understand what I mean.' Jules looked at me and raised an eyebrow.

'So the young man buys his condoms and promises to go back the next day to tell the pharmacist exactly what happened – in short to give him the blow by blow account!' Jules, smiled to make it clear that the *double entendre* was intentional.

'And so at the end of another long dull day spent putting the pills into the little bottles the pharmacist goes to his home very happy and very excited at the thought that he will, the very next day, hear of this young man's exploits with this young woman. This has quite made his day.'

'Is that it?' I asked, slightly puzzled, for Jules appeared to have come to the end of his story. 'Is there really no more to that story of yours? Did the young man go back to see the pharmacist the next day?'

'Oh no,' said Jules. 'The young man did not go back the next day.'

'That's a pity,' I said. I picked up my glass and took a sip.

'No, I am afraid not,' said Jules, shaking his head. 'The young man did not go back to see the pharmacist the next day.' He paused.

'But the young man and the pharmacist did see one another that very same evening.'

'Oh? How come?'

'How come?' Jules wrinkled up his nose and his eyes.

'How did that happen? Where did they meet?'

'They met when the young man went to pick up his hot date,' said Jules. 'The young man rang the door bell and the pharmacist opened the door.'

'The girl who was known as a 'sure thing' among all the young men of the neighbourhood – the 'bit of hot stuff' the young man was picking up – she was the pharmacist's daughter,' explained Jules.

I stared at him. 'Is that true?' I asked him.

Jules gazed back at me. 'Maybe,' he said.

'And that man,' I said, indicating the bald man in the red jacket with a modest inclination of my head. 'Is that man the father?'

Jules looked from one side to another. 'I do not have the faintest idea who is that man,' he whispered. 'I made that up because it makes for a better story.'

'He isn't a pharmacist?'

'I do not know.'

'Is the story true?'

Jules grinned at me. 'That you must decide,' he said, mischievously. 'It might be.' He paused. 'Or, on the other side, it might not be.'

'And now,' he said, 'Tonight I am having a favour for you,' said Jules, suddenly serious.

I wasn't quite sure whether he meant that he wanted me to do a favour for him or that he was going to do me a favour. I waited.

'I have this night a date with a beautiful woman,' he said. He drew a predictable shape in the air with his hands. 'A gorgeous girl. A dreamboat.'

'This evening,' I said. 'You have a date this evening.'

'Evening, night,' shrugged Jules, with a grin. 'What is the difference?' He winked at me and I got the feeling that he knew very well what the difference was. He sighed and pulled a face. 'But my problem is that I already have been made an arrangement to see a very beautiful woman called Heidi.'

I had a suspicion that I could see where this was heading. He held up two fingers. 'I have two dates,' he said. He then held up one finger. 'But I am only one man and there is only the one evening.'

'How did this happen?' I asked him, though I wasn't sure that I wanted to know.

'I meet loads of women through their smalls,' said Jules. He grinned broadly, leant forward across the table and lowered his voice. 'It is a very good way to meet lonely women.'

I frowned. I tried to visualise Jules patrolling the city's launderettes and picking up solitary women as they watched their lingerie go round and round.

'You meet women in launderettes?'

It was Jules' turn to frown. 'In launderettes?' He thought for a moment. 'In launderettes?' He paused. 'The places for washing the clothes?'

I nodded.

'You meet women in launderettes?' he said.

'Me? No, I don't meet women in launderettes. You do.'

'No, of course I do not.' He seemed offended. 'Why would I go to a launderette to meet a woman? Only poor women, fat women, women with dozens of children and old women go to those places. There are no beautiful, sexy women in launderettes.'

'But how then do you meet women?' I asked him, wondering if perhaps his ploy involved standing around in the lingerie sections of department stores and making his move as some young innocent flicked through the silk camisoles.

'Through the newspaper,' explained Jules impatiently. 'The smalls.'

'The smalls?'

'The advertisements. The – what are they called – the classified sector?'

'The classified section? The classified ads?'

'That's it! The smalls!'

At last I understood. 'Oh! The small ads!'

'Yes! This is what I have been telling you all this time,' he said, clearly exasperated at my inability to understand my own language. 'The small ads. That is the place to meet the best women. Have you heard of a magazine called *The Paris Monthly?*'

I admitted that I was not familiar with the publication.

'It is a small magazine for English speaking people living in Paris,' explained Jules. 'Lonely American and English people advertise in it as do French people who want to meet Americans or English people. It is the excellent way for improving the English.'

'Do you put advertisements in yourself?' I asked him.

'No,' said Jules. 'In some ways it is perhaps better to put in your own advertisement. Then you have control of what happens. You get to pick the girl you go out with instead of the other way round.' He smiled at me. 'But I find it exciting to know that I have been picked from a bundle of applications. It is good for the vanity.'

'I can see that.'

'I have a friend who puts in advertisements saying: 'Women: contact me if size matters to you.' He was not well-endowed but he would get them drunk and keep the lights off and they were so excited that they never noticed. Most people who put in the ads, or reply to them, have strict ideas of what they want. But they are so desperate that if they find someone half lovely they will take him.' He laughed. 'Another guy I knew who had the hang-up over the stockings used to send the women who replied a questionnaire asking them the colour of the stockings they wore. Ninety per cent of the girls replied and told him they would wear whatever turned him on. He used to tell them he was the lead singer in a rock group called Tinker Tailor and the Plumstones.'

'You never know what you will get or what lies you will be told,' continued Jules with a laugh. 'I once had a date with a girl who claimed in her letter that she had a bust like Marilyn Monroe. We cannot have been thinking of the same Marilyn Monroe because this girl had absolutely no breasts at all.' He leant across the table and lowered his voice. 'Now, I am not a person to make a big deal about size – there is too much danger that a chicken could come home to roost – but this woman was as flat as *la table à repasser* and looked like a boy. Still, variety is the spice of living and I have had my share of big women. And the flat-chested girl was very good in bed. I'll never forget one thing. On the night we met I asked her if she was sexually active. I wanted to know if we were going to get anywhere before I wasted any more time on her. She didn't even hesitate. Just came straight on with it. "I think you could say I am," she replied. "I'm not one of those girls who just lies there and lets the man do all of the work."'

'Do men ever marry the women they meet through advertisements?'

'Oh yes. At least two other fellows I know married the women they met through the advertisements. I knew one man who fell madly in love with a woman who would have made a lump of ice look cuddly. He had inherited much money from his family and she wanted little from him apart from joint custody of his bank account. She stuck to him like a sticky bandage until his money ran out and his credit was good no more. Then she left. The yelps of pain were like those which are produced when a sticky bandage is ripped from a hairy limb. It was clear from the start that he was heading for pain and poverty but he would not hear one word said against her until it was too late. Even twenty years later he still says she was worth every penny. She must have been very good between the sheets. Another man answered an ad from a girl searching for a tall, dark man aged between 30 and 35. He was 57, short, bald and tubby at the time. Hardly what she'd thought she was looking for. But they met, got on and two months later they were married. That was fifteen years ago. Today they're still deliriously happily married.'

'So how did you come to make two dates for this evening?'

'Last week I made three dates for this week,' he said. He held up three fingers of his left hand. 'On Tuesday I had the first date with Heidi. She is the nurse. Very beautiful.' He raised his eyes heavenwards. 'And hot. Very hot date.' With his right hand he moved one of the fingers to show that it signified Heidi. 'Tonight I have the date with the woman called Claudette Foucault. She is very beautiful.' He moved a second finger – Claudette. 'And on

Friday – that is the tomorrow after tomorrow – I have the date with Flora. She is a housewife and she too is very beautiful. I have seen a photograph of her.' He waved his hands in the air again. 'I think she is in very good shape.'

'A housewife? You mean she is married?'

'She is not very married. Just four months.'

'You're meeting a woman who has been married for just four months?'

'Yes,' grinned Jules. 'I like very much married women. If they become mothers there is always the ready made father to look after the babies.'

I stared at him, horrified. He just grinned. 'You are shocked?'

'Yes.' I admitted. 'I suppose I am.'

'You are English,' he said. He shrugged. 'Everything is different in England. Here a Frenchman considers he is insulting a man if he does not make a pass at his wife. And a husband will feel insulted if a man does not try to seduce his wife.' He shrugged. 'It is our way. A wife belongs to her husband. A man likes other men to admire his car. He also likes other men to admire his wife.'

'But you can't really compare a wife to a motor car,' I protested.

'Why not?' asked Jules.

'Well, wives are human beings,' I said. 'They have rights. They are equal to men.'

'No, they are not,' said Jules.

'They can vote,' I pointed out.

'Ah, yes, that is true,' said Jules. 'In 1945, after the war, women were given the vote. My mother still does not approve. She does not vote.'

'But lots of women have important jobs,' I said.

'Only if their husbands want them to,' said Jules.

'But this is the 1960s!' I told him. 'If a woman wants to work she can.'

'No, no!' said Jules, sternly. 'There has been talk of changing the law but thankfully a man can still forbid his wife to work.'

I tried to take this in. It was not easy.

'But I still don't see your problem with your dates,' I said, putting the housewife to one side for the moment. 'If you saw Heidi on Tuesday and you're seeing Claudette tonight and Flora on Friday then you don't have a problem at all.'

'Ah,' said Jules. 'But I do. Heidi is very romantic. Very sexy woman. At breakfast this morning I promised to see her tonight. She is cooking me the dinner.'

Now I understood.

'Can't you postpone Claudette?'

'Oh no,' said Jules. 'She would be too disappointed. She is looking forward to our date tonight.'

I was by now confused again.

'So this evening you will make her happy,' he said. 'It will not be the same for her, of course. You are not me. But you are better for her than an evening in front of the television. And so this is my gift to you.'

'You want me to see Claudette?'

'Yes! Thank you! She is a favour for you from me.'

'You're putting me on!'

Jules frowned. 'What is this? I am wearing you? How am I wearing you?'

'It's an English idiom,' I explained. 'It means that you're kidding me.'

'Now I am making you a child?' Jules threw his arms into the air. 'Sometimes I don't understand your language any more.'

'I can't believe you are serious,' I said. 'She is expecting to see you. She won't want to see me.' I was torn. I was frightened, nervous and yet I was also excited. I did not tell Jules (I was frightened he would laugh) but I had never had a date before. I was as much a virgin as it is possible for a man to be.

'We have never met. She does not know what I look like. We have not even spoken on the telephone. Everything was done by the letter.'

'Presumably, she would have to call me Jules?'

'Oh no. She will call you Antoine.'

'Antoine? Why on earth would she call me Antoine?'

'It is the name I gave her. I never use my real name with women. It can lead to the complications. It is another reason why

I reply to their advertisements and do not insert my own.'

My head was spinning.

'I don't understand,' I said. 'Why is that a reason not to insert your own advertisement?'

'Because if I insert an advertisement in the magazine I can only be one person,' explained Jules patiently. 'Unless I pay for more than one advertisement, of course, but that would be tedious. If I reply to the advertisements put in by the women I can be as many people as I want to be. And I can be the person I know that woman is looking for.' He paused. 'To a certain extent, of course. I cannot be black or very short or ugly.'

'I see.' I said.

'Good. You see also I am doing you a big, big favour!' said Jules. 'Thanks to me you get a beautiful woman this evening.'

'Thank you,' I said lamely. 'Is she American?'

'Oh no, she is French this one. But she speaks English. You meet her on the terrace of Fouquets on the Champs Elysée,' said Jules, standing up. 'Have a folded copy of *Le Figaro* on the table in front of you and wear a red scarf. Her name is Claudette.' He wagged a finger at me. 'And remember that you are Antoine.'

'I don't have a red scarf,' I protested.

Jules looked at me, raised an eyebrow and sighed. 'Here I am doing you this huge kindness and you insist on finding trivial problems.' He looked around the café for a moment and then walked purposefully across to the other side of the room. It was only when he stopped that I realised that his destination was a girl who was wearing a red scarf. She was sitting with two girlfriends. Jules said something to her. She laughed. Jules took out his wallet and handed something to the girl. She removed the scarf from around her neck and handed it to him. He then walked back across the room and draped the scarf around my neck. 'Now you have a red scarf,' he said. 'Smile and hug me.' I stared at him. He repeated the instruction. I did as I was told. We headed for the door. The three girls were giggling. Jules waved to them. They waved back. 'When you go to the rendezvous you hide the scarf at first,' he said. 'Try to spot the woman first so if she is ugly you can leave.'

Outside we stood on the pavement for a moment.

'How did you do that?' I asked him, fingering the scarf, confused.

'I bought the scarf for you,' said Jules. 'It is a present.'

'But why should a complete stranger sell you her scarf?'

'They are tourists from Denmark. I told the girl that you had fallen in love with her scarf,' said Jules. He shrugged. 'And I told her that I was trying to seduce you and that I thought the scarf would do the trick.'

I stared at him.

'That is right is it not? Do the trick?'

'It's right,' I agreed.

'You look so funny!' he laughed.

'Is that true? You really said that?'

'Of course it is true.'

I looked back through the plate glass window into the café. The three girls were busy talking and no longer seemed interested in us.

'I don't believe you did that,' I whispered.

Jules laughed again. 'You are so English!'

We walked along the street a few paces until we reached a spot directly opposite to Jules' sports car. 'I cannot give you a lift,' Jules apologised. 'I am late for a date. I must rush.'

'That's OK, I need the walk,' I said. 'I feel a little light headed. A walk will do me good.'

'Fine,' said Jules. He smiled and held out his hand. 'Thank you,' he said. 'We do this again in three days?'

'OK, I said. We shook hands.

'Same place. Same time,' said Jules. He stepped out into the road.

'OK,' I agreed, hoping that the three girls would have gone back to Denmark by then.

'Oh. One other thing,' I called.

Jules turned round, dodging through the traffic.

'How will I recognise her?'

'You are looking for a girl who is 21, blonde and beautiful,' shouted Jules gaily. 'Does it matter if you get the wrong one?' He climbed into his car, started it, slipped it into gear and shot out into the traffic without, as far as I could see, bothering to look to see if it was safe to do so. There was much screeching of brakes and tooting of horns and then he was gone.

On the way back to my hotel I bought a thick notebook.

I had decided to write a novel based on my experiences in Paris.

Chapter 14

It was not until I was sitting on the terrace at Fouquet's, with my red scarf wrapped around my neck and a neatly folded copy of *Le Figaro* on the table in front of me, sipping a glass of water and gazing in horror at the bill the waiter had slipped into the saucer that I realised that there was a big problem which both Jules and I had overlooked. Claudette spoke French. There was a reasonable chance that she might expect me to speak French too.

I was wondering why Jules hadn't instructed Claudette to carry some form of identification, and trying to decide whether a tall young woman in a bright blue beret and a black leather coat might be Claudette, when I was suddenly aware of someone collapsing heavily into the seat next to me.

'Antoine?' said a surprisingly deep female voice. 'Je m'appelle Claudette.'

I turned and was slightly startled by what I saw. The woman sitting next to me was considerably older than I had imagined Claudette to be. She was heavily made up, quite short and plump and I guessed that she was in her mid to late forties. I was no expert on these matters but it was clear, even to me, that the blonde hair which she wore was not her own.

'I'm sorry,' I apologised. 'I'm afraid I don't speak French.' I had remembered enough school-boy French to understand the single simple phrase I had heard but I didn't want Claudette making any assumptions about my linguistic skills. On my first day in France I had learned the truth of the adage that a little knowledge can be a very dangerous thing. I had rehearsed a relevant phrase in French, walked confidently into a shop and asked for the item I wanted to buy. The shopkeeper, thoroughly misled into believing that I was fluent in his language, had replied with a torrent of French of which I had understood not one word.

'You do not speak French?' said Claudette, clearly shocked.

'I'm English,' I explained.

'But you did not make mention of this in your letter,' Claudette pointed out. I was too much of a gentleman to suggest that she too had failed to make full disclosure in the correspond-ence she had exchanged with Jules.

'You speak English!' I said. 'That's quite a relief.'

She held her head on one side and looked at me, examining me as a sparrow might check out a piece of bread.

'I like your accent,' she said. 'I love the English.'

I was about to suggest that we went for a walk, hoping that we could then find a rather cheaper café, when she beckoned to a waiter. When he arrived she gave him instructions in rapid French. I recognised only one word: champagne. 'I have ordered a bottle of champagne,' she told me.

Knowing how much a small bottle of water was costing me I knew that I did not have enough money with me to pay for a bottle of champagne. I could feel myself going bright red. I cursed Jules. I didn't have the foggiest idea what to do.

'I love champagne,' she said. 'Don't you?'

'It's very expensive here,' I said, rather bluntly, wondering how many hours I would have to spend washing dishes to pay the bill.

'Oh, do not worry about that,' she said, waving a plump hand around rather airily. She had expensive looking rings on just about every finger. 'I will pay. My husband is very rich. He can afford to buy champagne for us.'

I stared at her. 'Your husband?'

'He is an actor,' she said. She looked at her watch. 'When we have drunk our champagne we must rush. Tonight we are going to see him in his new play.'

Chapter 15

There was a small crowd standing on the pavement outside the theatre but Claudette pushed through the women in fur coats and jewels, and the men in dark overcoats and bow ties, without pausing. Moments later we found ourselves in the foyer. I felt a trifle under-dressed.

'Madame! cried a pale man in his sixties, rushing over towards us. He was wearing a black suit, a dress shirt and a bow tie. He had a small moustache and looked absurdly like Adolf Hitler. He said something. I didn't understand it but it was clearly intended to be ingratiating.

Claudette simply glowered at him and pushed on through the crowd towards the doors leading into the stalls. She had taken two tickets out of her handbag.

Adolf said something else. Claudette, as though for the first time since we had got out of the taxi remembering that I was with her, introduced me to him. 'He has a French name,' she said. 'But he does not speak French, this one.'

Adolf turned to me.

'The manager asked me to tell you that we have a box available for tonight,' he said. He was sweating profusely. He had a white cotton handkerchief tucked into the breast pocket of his jacket but he took a paper tissue from his trouser pocket and mopped at his forehead. There was a lot of sweat and the tissue wasn't very good quality. Little bits of white paper stuck to his skin.

'No, thank you,' said Claudette coldly. 'I will take my usual seats in the stalls.'

'Please, madam,' begged the bald man. 'No trouble tonight.' He looked at me, beseechingly

'You should talk to my husband about trouble,' said Claudette. 'To him and that whore this theatre employs.'

'Please, madame,' implored Adolf, looking around as though worried that someone might have heard.

Claudette was unstoppable. Like a liner that is travelling too fast to deviate from her course she continued on her way towards her designated seats at the front of the stalls. She sat down and indicated that I should sit down on her right. I looked around. Adolf had followed her half way down the theatre aisle. He was now standing in the middle of the aisle tearing his damp paper handkerchief into shreds. I had no idea what was going on but I was certain that I was destined to play no more than fourth spear holder in whatever drama was going to unfold.

Three or four minutes later the house lights went down and then out. The curtains parted, two girls in flimsy summer dresses bounded onto the stage and the play began.

'Put your arm around me.'

I turned my head and looked at Claudette. I wasn't sure I had heard her properly.

'Put your arm around me,' she repeated, slightly louder.

Somewhere behind us an unseen patron make a loud shushing noise.

Frightened that if I didn't do as I was told Claudette might speak again I put my left arm around her shoulders.

A few feet in front of me a tall, handsome looking actor bounded onto the stage. I felt Claudette's body stiffen and it wasn't difficult to work out that the actor on the stage was her husband. 'Fondle my bosom,' she ordered. One of the girls bounded off the stage.

I looked at her in astonishment. I had often fantasised about my first date. Nothing that was happening to me had ever appeared in any of my fantasies.

On stage the actor had his arms around the remaining

actress and was kissing her with extraordinary professional zeal.

'Fondle my bosom,' Claudette repeated.

I reached down with my left hand, the one at the end of the arm which was already draped around her neck and shoulders. Her bosom, although capacious, was rather low slung and my fingers barely scraped the upper slopes of her left breast.

'Use the other hand as well,' she told me. And, as though uncertain of my ability to follow her simple instructions she reached over, took my right hand and placed it onto her chest. She then pushed my fingers down into her dress. The cleavage was vast and the skin warm and slightly moist. My hand disappeared.

I sat there for a few moments, unmoving and, I am sad to have to report, unmoved. I had no idea what was going on but I was glad that the theatre was dark and that Claudette's husband could not see what was going on. My enthusiasm for the moment was not helped when I remembered reading somewhere that in France a murderer might be released by the courts if he had merely killed his wife's lover.

While I sat with one arm around her back and the other hand stuffed down the front of her dress Claudette was not idle. She was rummaging in the black leather handbag which was sitting on her lap. Eventually she found what she was looking for, pulled it out of her bag, turned it so that it stood upright and then pressed something on its side.

The object she had removed from her handbag was a torch and the beam from it lit up the tableau which Claudette had so carefully created.

On stage her husband who had come up for air, stared down at us. I was relieved to see that he looked more contemptuous than indignant. I was far more startled than he was. I speedily removed my left arm from around Claudette's shoulders and my right hand from inside her dress. Unfortunately, I did not do this quite as delicately as I should have done and several buttons at the front of the dress shot off. One landed on the stage just a few feet away from the actor for whom this small show had been created. It skipped and rolled until it was no more than a few inches from his left foot. Still holding the torch so that it shone upon our faces,

Claudette threw her left arm around my neck, pulled my head towards hers and kissed me full on the lips. A few moments later she let me go, turned off the torch and stood up. She did not seem aware of the fact that her dress had lost several essential buttons.

'Let's go to a hotel,' she said loudly, in English.

On stage the actor was very cool. He bent down, picked up the button and moved towards the footlights. 'I think this is yours, madame,' he said, offering Claudette the button.

She looked up at him and snorted. 'I don't want anything from you,' she said.

She walked out of the theatre to tremendous applause. She did not seem to be in the slightest bit troubled by what had occurred.

More embarrassed by this than by anything else that had ever happened to me before I followed a few feet behind her. I had to run to catch up with her.

Chapter 16

'Why on earth did you do that?' I asked Claudette.

We were sitting in a café just a hundred yards away from the theatre. She was drinking vodka. I was drinking black coffee because I wanted to stay sober. I half expected her husband to burst through the front door at any moment brandishing a pistol or a knife. The red flush of embarrassment which had covered my face was just beginning to fade a little.

'He is having an affair with the girl he was kissing on the stage,' said Claudette. 'I do not care about the affair. I do not mind him having affairs. He is a Frenchman and it is his nature. If I try to stop him he will be miserable. But he has to understand that there have to be rules. He has flaunted her around Paris. He takes her to cafés and has his picture taken with her.' Her torn dress was held together with a safety pin she had borrowed from the exceedingly plump woman behind the bar. 'He has publicly humiliated me. So I publicly humiliate him until he stops.' She took a handkerchief out of her bag and blew her nose daintily. 'A watch has two hands but fits upon just one wrist,' she said.

Puzzled, I looked at her.

'It was a saying of my grandfather,' explained Claudette. 'He was a wise man.'

'You've done this before?'

'At the theatre?'

'Yes.'

'Every night for a week.'

'With different men?'

'Twice with one man. A dancer. A gay friend. All the other occasions were with different men.'

'But you're not really having affairs with any of them?'

'Oh, no.'

'What time does the play end?'

'At ten fifteen.'

I looked at the clock on the wall behind the bar. There was three quarters of an hour to go unless the actor decided to leave before the final curtain.

'Why do you ask?'

'If you don't mind I'd like to be a long way from here before the play finishes,' I explained.

'You are afraid?'

'Of course,' I laughed nervously. 'Your husband may decide to kill me.'

'My husband is too much of a coward to kill you. Besides, he wouldn't care if I slept with you. He only cares that he is humiliated. That he does not like. And for that he will blame me not you.'

Slightly reassured, I sipped at my coffee.

'He has always chased the women,' sighed Claudette, sadly. 'I could never trust him. When we were young and had been married for just three months I noticed that at eight forty five every morning he would stand by the window of our apartment. He would get out of bed to do this. And do you know why?'

'Because a beautiful woman walked by at that time every morning?'

Claudette nodded. 'There was a bus stop outside and one particular woman was always late. He would stand and watch her running to catch the bus. She was a thin woman but had big breasts and he liked to see her run because he enjoyed watching her breasts bounce up and down. He laughed when he confessed this to me. He asked me if I knew her name. I was desolated. I ran away. When he telephoned I would not speak to him for two whole days. It nearly broke my heart. Putting the telephone down on him took up all my courage. It would have been easier for me to rescue people from burning buildings or icy rivers.'

'Do you love him?' I asked her.

She looked at me. 'How old are you?' she asked me.

I told her

'Ah,' she said. 'You are so very young.'

'Do you?' I asked.

She smiled at me but did not say anything for quite a while. When she did speak she lowered her voice and leant slightly towards me. 'Of course I love him,' she said. 'He is a bastard. I do not trust him. I do not like him very much. He never touches me in the way a husband should touch his wife. We have not made love for ten years. But...' She reached up and touched my cheek with my hand. 'You are very sweet,' she said to me.

Embarrassed, I looked down at my coffee.

'Would you like to eat?' she asked me.

'Perhaps we could find a smaller café...' I looked around.

She laughed. 'You mean somewhere cheaper?'

'Yes.' I admitted.

'You want to buy me a something?'

I nodded.

'That, for you, is the right way to do things?'

'Yes.'

'You always pay the bill when you take out a lady on a date?'

I did not reply for a moment. This was my first date but I felt embarrassed to admit it.

'You do not?'

Still I did not answer.

'You have had other dates?'

'Oh, of course. Many.'

Claudette leant closer. 'I am your first? Your first date?'

'Of course not.'

'You have gone red.'

'It is very warm in here.'

'You are lying to me.'

'No, no. I'm not.'

'Yes you are. I am your first date. Is that not true?'

For a while neither of us spoke.

'You are my first date,' I admitted. 'It's embarrassing, isn't it?

'Oh my sweet boy,' she said. 'I am so sorry to do this to you on your first date.' She looked at me. She had big brown eyes. 'Has it been a terrible disappointment?'

I looked up.

'This evening has not been quite what you expected?'

'I don't know what I expected.'

'But not this? Not what happened?'

'No. I suppose not.'

'I am sorry I lied in my advertisement.'

'That's OK.'

'But we all lie a little,' she said. 'So, perhaps, we can hardly complain when we are disappointed by the lies of others.'

I blushed.

'Your name is not Antoine, I think?'

'No.' I admitted. 'It's not.'

'And, of course, you are not French.'

'No.'

'Would you like to see me again?'

'I like you very much,' I told her. I was not lying. 'Yes. I would like to see you again.'

'On Saturday, perhaps?'

'To go to the theatre?' I asked, rather hesitantly.

She laughed. 'No. Not the theatre. I am going there with a different man each night this week. But on Saturday we go somewhere else. Paul will be expecting me so it will be as disconcerting for him if I am not there as if I am there.'

'Paul?'

'My husband.' She took out her purse and put some money down on the café table.

'Who are the other men you are taking to the theatre?' I asked her. I tried to make the question sound innocent. But she was much better at interpreting my feelings than I was at disguising them.

'You are jealous?'

I did not say anything.

'You are jealous?' She put her arm around my neck and drew my face closer to hers. 'You are jealous?'

'I expect so,' I admitted. I felt myself blushing. 'A little. Maybe.'

She kissed me on the lips. 'You are so sweet,' she sighed. She kissed me again. 'Do you know how old I am?'

I shook my head.

'Good.'

She picked up her handbag, stood up and held out a hand. 'Come,' she said. 'Take me to a cheap café where you can afford to buy me an ice-cream.'

I stood up.

'You can afford to buy me an ice cream?'

'Definitely.'

'Good. I would not enjoy a date with a man who would not buy me ice cream.'

We went to a small but clean café which Claudette seemed to know well. Claudette ordered a banana split.

'I'll have the sorbet,' I told Claudette who passed this information on to the waitress. The waitress said something. I waited for Claudette to translate. 'How many balls?' she asked, speaking in English. She allowed the word 'balls' to roll around in her mouth before releasing it.

'Three, please.'

'Which balls do you like?'

I looked at the available flavours on the chart in the menu. 'Strawberry, lemon and passion fruit,' I told her, by-passing the language barrier by pointing to the flavours I wanted. The waitress wrote down my order, smiled, said something which I did not understand and hurried off to take an order from a fat American in mauve and yellow checked trousers and a purple T-shirt whose massive family hadn't eaten for twenty minutes and were consequently all suffering from fat deprivation. They were all in desperate need of emergency hot dogs, chips and Cokes.

'What did she say?' I asked Claudette.

'She asked me to congratulate you on your choices,' said

Claudette, without even a hint of a smile. 'She said the colours will look nice together on the plate.'

We stayed there, just talking, until two in the morning.

'I'm afraid I must go,' I said, at last. 'I have to be at work in the morning.'

Claudette opened her handbag and took out some notes. 'Take these,' she said. 'For the taxi.'

'No, no!' I protested.

'Take them,' she insisted. She stuffed them into the breast pocket of my jacket. Then she kissed me, more tenderly and more affectionately than before. I put my arms around her. For a few moments neither of us spoke.

'We will see one another on Saturday? At Fouquet's again?'

'OK,' I said.

'I am 47,' said Claudette.

'That's OK,' I said.

'I lie about many things, but never my age.'

'OK.'

'I look forward very much to Saturday,' whispered Claudette, stroking my hair affectionately.

'So do I,' I said.

'And always remember,' she said. 'A table with five legs can run no faster than one with four legs.'

I looked at her. 'Your grandfather?'

'My grandfather. He was a wise man, no?'

'Absolutely,' I agreed. I had no idea what the saying meant.

We went outside and found two taxis at a rank at the end of the street. I was in bed in my hotel room half an hour later. But I don't think I slept at all that night.

Chapter 17

'Do you mind if I bring Rupert?' asked Mr Whitechapel.

'Er, no, not at all,' I replied, not having the foggiest idea who Rupert was.

'Fine,' said Mr Whitechapel, picking up the cage which contained the cockatoo. He headed for the door and I followed. 'Rupert likes a little sunshine now and then,' Mr Whitechapel explained. 'So, how did you get on with Jules?' he asked, as we headed down the stairs.

'I think it went well,' I told him. 'We just talked for a while.'

'Did he, er, ask you to help him out with any, er, personal problems?' asked Mr Whitechapel.

'He did get me to take a girl out,' I said. 'Actually, she was more of a woman than a girl, though I didn't know that until I met her.'

'He fixed you up with some sort of blind date?'

'I suppose that's what you'd call it,' I agreed. 'He told me he had double booked and needed someone to help him out of a mess.'

'Yes, that is, I gather, the sort of thing that seems to happen to him.' Mr Whitechapel raised an eyebrow. 'How, er, did the arrangement turn out?'

'Fine,' I said.

'No problems there?'

'No, I don't think so, Mr Whitechapel.'

'Please,' he said. 'You should call me Jim.'

I was startled by this. Six months earlier I had still been at school and while Mr Whitechapel had too much of the air of a schoolmaster about him I still had too much of the air of a schoolboy about me. I would have been just as startled if my old headmaster had invited me to address him by his Christian name (I had never even known that he'd had a Christian name – always, until that moment, assuming that even his wife had always addressed him formally) or if the Pope had invited me to call him 'Johnny'.

'I perhaps should have warned you,' sighed Mr Whitechapel.

'He's done that before?'

'Oh dear me, yes. I'm afraid you aren't the first. I, er, hope you didn't mind?' Mr Whitechapel, Jim, looked very miserable. 'I do feel very guilty,' he said. 'I feared that if you knew you might not take the job.'

'No. Not really. Not at all. Did he get you to...'

'...oh yes, oh dear me yes,' admitted Mr Whitechapel. He mopped his brow. He appeared distracted. I turned to see what had caught his eye. A couple on a bicycle were pedalling down the Champs Elysée amidst the swirl of traffic. They were holding hands and there was clearly something odd about them. Mr Whitechapel turned. 'I see them often,' he told me. 'He is blind and works as a presenter at one of the smaller radio stations in Paris. She holds his hand and he just trusts her to steer him through the traffic.'

He sighed and then returned to his previous story. 'It was all a little too exciting for me. The young woman concerned was married but was looking for what is in England these days known as a 'bit on the side'.'

'Ah,' I said, understandingly.

'Not my cup of tea at all,' said Mr Whitechapel with a shiver. 'I am pretty much a confirmed bachelor. I much prefer a quiet evening with a piece of toast and some Marmite and my gramophone records. Do you like Bach?'

'I don't know terribly much about him,' I admitted.

'Wonderful composer,' said Mr Whitechapel. 'Very soothing. I love France but French women are a little racy for me,' he continued. 'I've lived in nine countries and I think this is probably the only country in the world where women get offended if you don't stare at them.'

Just then a woman pedestrian trying to cross the road was knocked over by a motor car. I was impressed to see that several people rushed forward to help her. The last time I had witnessed anything similar in England, I had offered to help and I had found myself quite alone. Everyone else had walked by as if they had suddenly been struck blind.

'It's impressive to see so many people offering to help,' I said. The woman was now sitting up. She appeared to be simply shaken. Someone took her pulse.

'In France it is against the law to ignore someone needing help. If you do not help you can be sent to prison. Failure to offer assistance to a person in distress is a criminal offence under paragraph 2 of article 63 of the French penal code. This applies to everyone not just doctors.'

I expressed surprise but pleasure at this. 'France is a nation of contradictions,' said Mr Whitechapel. 'The French delight in ignoring rules and regulations,' he went on. 'But I am pleased to say that this is one law which they do seem to take seriously. It is that rarity, a civilising piece of legislation.' I thought it was equally contrary that there should be such a law in a country where the motorists seemed to me to spend much of their time trying to knock down as many pedestrians as possible. I had just that morning watched a motorist deliberately accelerate when he saw a workman struggling across the road with a piece of cumbersome and clearly heavy equipment in tow. I watched, relieved, as the woman stood, thanked her rescuers and went on her way, a little more cautiously this time.

'France is the most bureaucratic country in the world but it is also a natural homeland for revolutionaries,' said Mr Whitechapel. 'You will notice that there are always many demonstrations in the streets?'

'Oh yes. There seems to be one most afternoons.'

'Quite,' agreed Mr Whitechapel. 'The fact is that the right to take direct action in France is highly valued. It comes from the revolutionary traditions of 1789 since when the French have had very little faith in parliamentary representation. Their parliament is weak and pretty much ignored by the executive and by the civil service. This is one of the few Western countries where protests in the street can topple Governments.'

We continued our walk.

'Nothing came of your date, then?'

'Oh good heavens no,' said Mr Whitechapel with convincing emphasis. 'Like most Britons I'd be absolutely terrible at adultery.' He shivered. 'I simply wouldn't know what to do. And I'd be terrified of being found out and shot by some jealous husband. The French, on the other hand, are very good at it . If there were Olympic medals for adultery the French would sweep the board. They've even made it legal in a strange sort of way. If a man kills his wife's lover he can get off if he can prove it was a crime of love. It is something that garlic eating Gallic wine lovers practise with an enviably easy charm and an apparently total lack of guilt.' Mr Whitechapel mopped his brow again and leant a little closer. 'Do you know,' he said, 'I do believe that Frenchmen regard marriage as essential only because without it adultery is impossible. Indeed, Frenchwomen are skilled adulterers too. I read recently that most French women happily claim to average one lover for every year of their lives. So, for example, a 40-year-old French woman will have had 40 lovers. By the time she celebrates her 50th birthday she will expect to have had 50 lovers.'

'You are, I fear, having tea with a living example of the unsuitability of the British in general, and the English in particular, for extra marital bedroom sports. We Britons are best if we stick to golf or trainspotting. We must leave it to our Gallic neighbours to keep the European end up in the international 'oo la la' stakes. Hippolyte Taine once wrote that: 'An Englishman in a state of adultery is miserable: even at the supreme moment his conscience torments him.' Do you know Hippolyte Taine?'

'No, I don't think so. Is he a pupil of yours?'

Mr Whitechapel winced. 'Sadly, no,' he said. 'Regrettably Monsieur Taine passed away in 1893, which was a little before my time.'

'He was a writer?'

'Critic, philosopher and historian,' explained Mr Whitechapel. 'I'm a great fan. Though, if I can be critical for a moment I confess that I am just a little sceptical about his *Notes sur l'Angleterre* which I believe he wrote after rather too short a stay in England in the middle of the nineteenth century.'

We had arrived at the café on the Champs Elysée which Mr Whitechapel regarded as an extension of his office.

Mr Whitechapel found a table, gently put Rupert's cage down and then settled himself down. I sat down beside him. A middle-aged couple on the next table stared at Rupert as though they had never seen a customer bring a cockatoo to a café before.

'Did Jules remember to, er, provide you with the agreed compensation?' Mr Whitechapel asked me.

'Oh yes,' I said. I reached into my pocket and took out the one hundred franc note. I handed the note to Mr Whitechapel.

'Ah,' said Mr Whitechapel. 'You were with him for three hours and twenty minutes?'

'No,' I said. 'It was actually an hour and a half.'

'An hour and a half?'

'Yes. I looked at my watch.'

Mr Whitechapel took out an old envelope and a stub of pencil. He scribbled on the envelope for a moment. As he did so the waiter came. 'Would you like tea?' asked Mr Whitechapel. I nodded. 'Tea for two, thank you,' Mr Whitechapel told the waiter politely. He then returned to his envelope. 'You owe me 22.5 francs,' he said, giving me back the note.

Puzzled, I frowned. But I took the note. 'I thought I owed you fifty francs,' I said.

'No, the correct fee for your teaching appointment was forty five francs,' said Mr Whitechapel, patiently and meticulously. He always spoke with precision. Of that I receive one half. And one half of fifty francs is twenty two and a half francs. The other half of the forty five franc fee is yours, as is the tip.'

'The tip?'

'The remaining fifty five francs was clearly intended as some sort of bonus,' said Mr Whitechapel. 'It is a policy of my school that teachers keep all their tips.'

'Are you sure?'

'I am absolutely sure, thank you,' said Mr Whitechapel. 'I strongly believe that one always should be honest and straightforward in one's business dealings.'

Chapter 18

La Rhumerie was crowded and at first I could not see a free table. Eventually, I spotted one, crammed into a corner. I *pardonned* and *excusezmoied* across the room and eventually slid into one of the two chairs at the solitary vacant table. As I sat down I watched as a couple sitting at a table right by the door got up and started to put on their coats.

Behind me were six students sitting around a table discussing something with great vigour and enormous enthusiasm. Every few moments one would raise his voice or pound with his fist upon the table.

To my left there sat a young couple. They were neither talking nor drinking. They were simply staring into one another's eyes.

To my right sat two well dressed and immaculately coiffed women in their thirties who had obviously just been shopping. Despite the noise from the students behind me it was their voices I could hear most clearly for they were speaking English.

'I see you brought a book with you', said the first woman. She said it as though her friend had brought an ironing board or lawnmower with her.

'I like to look at a book occasionally,' said the second woman.

'Hmm,' said the other. 'I don't mind looking at one – just as long as no one expects me to read one!'

Jules slipped silently into the chair next to me.

'I'm going to have a boob job,' said the first woman.

'You're not to have boobs bigger than mine,' said her friend.

'It won't be worth doing if I don't!' retorted the first woman.

'How did you get on with Claudine?' asked Jules.

'Claudette,' I said.

'Claudette. Of course. How did you get on with her? Is she beautiful?'

'She took me to a theatre where her husband was appearing.' I told Jules. 'He is a leading French actor. We sat in the stalls, just a couple of rows back from the stage. At her request I held her breasts. She then shone a torch at us so that her husband and everyone else could see what was happening.'

'You see!' said Jules, delightedly. 'I bring such excitement to your life.' He thumped the table with delight. He stopped and looked at me. 'She really did that?'

'Yes.'

'Wonderful. How wonderful. I wish I had been there.'

'You should have been,' I pointed out. 'She was supposed to have been your date.'

'You did not find the evening amusing?'

I looked at him. 'I suppose I did,' I admitted. 'In a way.'

'You have to grab your life by the scruff of his neck,' insisted Jules. 'Some people have no present time in their lives. They are constantly obsessed with time that has gone and time that is yet to come. They forget about the now. The today. You will help me with my English and I will help you to live your life now and not to waste any moment of it.' He paused and looked around the café. 'Anyway,' he continued, 'now you will be excited to know that I have another good favour for you,' said Jules, with great enthusiasm.

I sighed. 'You've double booked your social life again?'

Jules grinned and shrugged. He looked like a naughty little boy when he grinned, and though he was several years older than me I felt rather staid and mature in his presence. He was the only person who had ever made me feel fatherly.

'Can't you just ring up one of the women and explain that you've made a mistake with the dates?' I suggested.

Jules seemed shocked. 'Oh no, that would be very impolite,' he said. 'Also it was Anne-Marie who suggested this date. She invited me to be with her. Besides, I do not have the number of her telephone.' He shrugged and leant a little closer. 'But I think she is very beautiful this one.'

I held up a hand. 'I'd really rather pass if you don't mind,' I said.

Jules looked puzzled. 'Pass? What is that?'

'No,' I said, shaking my head to make my feelings clear. 'Thanks, but no thanks.'

'Anne-Marie will be very disappointed,' said Jules. 'You will make her cry if you do not meet the appointment.'

'But I didn't make any appointment with her!' I protested.

'I did not think you were such a cruel, hard man,' said Jules, shaking his head sadly. 'She will cry and her tears will be on your conscience.' Behind us someone banged on the table. There was a crash behind us as a glass crashed to the floor and smashed. The students were getting rowdier than ever.

'What on earth are the they discussing?' I asked Jules.

'Who?'

'The students behind us?'

Jules listened for a moment and then grinned.

'What do you think they are talking about?'

'I don't know...Jean-Paul Sartre and existentialism...the meaning of life...the works of Camus perhaps?'

Jules grinned at me and shook his head. 'No,' he said. 'Guess again.'

'The work of Cocteau?'

'No.'

'The meaning of the play *Waiting for Godot*?'

Jules laughed and shook his head again.

'I don't know,' I said.

'You will never guess,' said Jules.

'They are planning a revolution?'

'No.'

'They are arguing about whether last year was a good one for Bordeaux wines?'

'No. Definitely no! Shall I tell you?'

'Yes, please.'

'You really want to know? It will perhaps spoil your regard for the students of the Sorbonne.'

'Tell me!'

'They are arguing about whether the sex that is paid for can ever be as good as the sex that you get for free,' Jules told me.

I stared at him, trying to decide if he was serious or not.

'It is true. I am serious. Now you are disappointed?'

I laughed and shook my head.

'You see the French students are not always revolutionaries,' said Jules, laughing. 'I enjoy listening to other people's conversation. It is a great entertainment to me. Yesterday I sat in a café and overheard a young man tell his friend that he had been feeling lonely and had telephoned an escort agency. They sent round a beautiful, elegantly dressed woman. The trouble was that it was the man's aunt.'

I looked at him. 'Really?'

'Really!' insisted Jules.

'What did he do?'

'He told his friend that he and the aunt talked it over and decided to make love anyway. She gave him a discount because he was a relative.'

Behind us one of the two women who had been talking about boob jobs suddenly laughed loudly. 'If I drank ten pints of water a day I'd spend all my life either drinking or peeing,' she said. 'I might live to be a hundred but at the end of it what would I be able to say I had done with my life? I drank and I peed.' She laughed again.

Jules looked at me and pulled a face. He could see the two women, though I could not. 'You see?' he said. 'Another time I heard two women arguing. I was sitting in Deux Magots café. Do you know it?'

I shook my head.

'It is very well known,' he insisted. 'We will go there another day. The two women were being very catty and were arguing about how much flesh a respectable woman could show. One argued that to show the cleavage and lots of the leg at the same time was to be like the tart. The other woman, who was wearing a low-necked dress and a very short skirt, disagreed. Eventually, one of the women stood up and threw a one hundred franc note down onto the table. 'There,' she said. 'You can pay for my coffee out of that. There should be fifty francs in change. Keep it and buy yourself a new outfit. It is obviously more than you spent on what you are wearing.'

Behind us the two women were now arguing.

'Are you saying that I am mean?' demanded one.

'No,' said the second. 'Not really. It's just that you are more cautious than most people about parting with your money.'

'If you can live with Anne-Marie's unhappiness then that is the way it must be,' said Jules. 'I would not force you to do something you do not want to do.'

I sighed. 'Where do I meet her and what does she look like?' I paused. 'Oh, and what's my name?'

Jules told me.

Behind me the two American women were friends again.

'He's keen on sport and very hunky,' said the one, clearly describing a man she knew. 'But I think he must be gay. I heard someone describe him as a 'tight end receiver'.

'I think that's something to do with football,' said the second rather uncertainly.

Chapter 19

Jules had agreed that he (and therefore, I) would meet Anne-Marie on the terrace of Fouquet's on the Champs Elysée. I had to wear the red scarf and carry a copy of *Le Figaro*. I didn't mind wearing the red scarf (even though the temperature was warm enough to make me feel rather foolish) but I made a mental note to ask him to find somewhere a little cheaper for future meetings. My name, I was pleased to discover, was still Antoine.

Anne-Marie was in her mid-twenties and looked rather boyish. She was petite, had cropped hair and wore tight jeans, plimsolls and a tight, plain white T-shirt which added to her boyish air. She wore a denim jacket over the T-shirt. I stood up and we introduced ourselves. She didn't mind in the slightest that I did not speak French. She did not even seem surprised.

'Do you want a drink?' I asked her.

'Not here,' said Anne-Marie. 'This place is absurdly expensive and far too snooty. Besides, we are going to a wedding.' She looked at her watch. 'We need to be in Montparnasse in fifteen minutes.'

'A wedding? We're going to a wedding?'

'Don't worry, it's not us who are getting married,' said Anne-Marie. 'But I need an escort. Hope you don't mind?'

'Not at all,' I said. 'I just have to pay for my water.'

'Oh don't bother paying,' said Anne-Marie, airily. 'The waiter won't chase you down the Champs Elysée for the price of a glass of water.' She spoke as though she knew what she was talking about.

'It's OK,' I said, rather shocked. 'I've got the right change.' I pulled some coins out of my pocket, selected a few, and left them on the table.

We crossed the Champs Elysée and walked to the George V Metro station. As we crossed Ann-Marie peered carefully at the driver of each car before moving across.

'You should always check the sex of the driver before crossing the road,' she told me.

'Oh?'

'Women drivers are far more ruthless,' she said. 'If they are in a bad mood they will kill you.'

We were standing on a traffic island in the middle of the Champs Elysée at the time. I blanched and carefully examined the cars which were approaching. Most were travelling far too fast for me to identify the sex of the driver.

'Just because the light says that you can go this does not mean that a woman would not kill you,' said Anne-Marie. 'In France, and particularly in Paris, the road signs and the lights simply mean that the motorist should toot the horn. It doesn't mean slow down, give way or stop. It is like a lottery.'

The wide pavements were thronged, as always, with shoppers, window shoppers and pedestrians simply promenading and showing off their new clothes or their hard-won figures.

'Just look at that!' said Anne-Marie, gripping my arm. I looked at her but could not see what had caught her attention.

'What?'

'That luscious bottom in the pink trousers,' replied Anne-Marie.

The bottom belonged to a plump teenage girl who was eating an ice-cream and walking with three or four friends.

'I have a thing about bottoms,' confessed Anne-Marie, as we headed down into the Metro. 'If we did not have to go to this wedding I would have followed that bottom for hours.'

'Really?'

'Oh yes. I once followed an exquisite bottom around Paris

for a whole day. I was in heaven. I ended up lost somewhere in the 17th *arrondissment*. Can you imagine how many different types of bottom there are?'

'I hadn't really thought about it,' I confessed.

'You can tell a lot about a person just by looking at their bottom,' insisted Anne-Marie. 'One day I may write a book about them. Do you have a camera?'

'No, I'm afraid not.'

'That is a pity. I need someone to take the photographs.'

'What photographs?'

'For my book on bottoms, of course. I am addicted to them.'

'To bottoms?'

'Oh yes.'

'I didn't know you could get addicted to bottoms.'

'If you love anything you can get addicted to it,' she insisted. 'Love leads to desire which is itself a self-perpetuating state. The desire leads to anxiety and frustration and dissatisfaction which need constant attention. Et voila!' She stopped by the Metro ticket office. 'Do you have money?'

'A little.'

'Good. I never carry money. It encourages pickpockets. We need tickets. Buy a *carnet*; it is cheaper.'

I bought a *carnet* of Metro tickets and handed one to Anne-Marie. She dived through the barrier and I hurried after her. As we walked she talked.

'Do you believe there is a God?'

'I don't really know.'

'You don't know if there is a God or you don't know if you believe in her?'

'I'm not sure.'

'Have you got a better explanation?'

'What for?'

'For why we are here.'

I stared at her for a moment. 'No. I suppose not. You believe in God?'

'Of course.'

'Do you think there is also a devil?'

'Oh, no. The devil is in man. That is all.'

We arrived at the platform.

'Do you think I talk too much?'

'Oh no. Not at all.'

'I think I do. But I have so much to say. That is the problem.' The Paris Metro is clean, speedy and efficient. Fifteen minutes later we were entering a hotel in Montparnasse. There was a sign directing us to the wedding. Everyone in the reception room was wearing the sort of clothes people normally wear for weddings. There were even top hats. As we walked through the doorway a waiter approached with a tray full of champagne glasses. Anne-Marie took one. I took one too. The waiter said something to me which I did not understand. I looked at Anne-Marie for help. 'Give him five francs,' she said.

'What for?'

'For the drinks?'

'But it's a wedding,' I protested, rather surprised.

'It's a Jewish wedding,' said Anne-Marie. 'And the bride's father is the meanest man in the world.'

'Who is the bride?' I asked.

'My cousin,' replied Anne-Marie. With her free hand she grabbed my arm. 'Come with me,' she said. 'Earn your keep and meet my parents.'

'Shouldn't we be wearing the right sort of clothes?' I whispered.

'Oh don't worry about it,' said Anne-Marie. I met her parents and the bride's parents. They did not seem particularly put out that Anne-Marie had missed the ceremony itself. Nor did they seem to be surprised, or to mind, at the fact that neither of us was dressed appropriately. On the contrary they seemed pleased to see us. They made me feel very welcome and then disappeared and left us alone again.

'Anne-Marie!' cried someone behind us. We both turned. A tall, florid looking man in a rather tight morning suit beamed at us.

'Hello Uncle Félix!' said Anne-Marie. She did not seem particularly pleased to see him.

117

Uncle Félix said something. It clearly concerned me.

'He is English,' Anne-Marie replied. She leant a little closer to her uncle 'And there may be another wedding soon.'

'Zat is woonderful,' said Uncle Félix, nodding rather sagely. 'Ven are you bringing your lover to Dijon?'

'I don't think he would like Dijon, Uncle Félix.'

'Vy not? She is a bootifool city!'

'It's a tip,' said Anne-Marie.

Uncle Félix seemed rather insulted by this. 'Dijon is woonderful!' he insisted. 'There is no crime. No prostitutes.'

'There are no prostitutes there because no man need ever pay for it,' said Anne-Marie. 'And no crime because there is nothing there worth stealing.'

Uncle Félix muttered something in French and stalked off. He seemed very angry.

'I think you've upset him.'

'I hope so.'

'He is clearly very fond of Dijon.'

'He is a policeman. He thinks the town belongs to him.'

'Is that why you don't like him? Because he is a policeman?'

'No. Though it is a good reason. I do not like him because he once saw me kissing a girl at a party. He told my parents I was a lesbian.'

I could not immediately think of anything to say in reply to this revelation. Fortunately, I was saved by the fact that the bride's father chose that moment to stand up and make his speech.

As he spoke Anne-Marie translated for me.

'He says he is delighted that we could all come here today,' said Anne-Marie. The proud father looked around the room and beaming with proprietorial satisfaction at the assembled guests. 'He says that in his position as editor of a prominent newspaper he mixes daily with some of the world's most important, most powerful and most wealthy individuals.'

'I didn't know he was a newspaper editor,' I whispered to Anne-Marie. 'What does he edit?'

'He is Jewish,' Anne-Marie whispered back. 'He edits a Jewish newspaper. Eight pages every month – every one filled with photographs of fat bankers, jewellers and doctor's mothers. Always they are sitting around banquet tables. The subscribers only read it to see themselves in print.'

'He says he mixes with some of the world's most glamorous screen stars,' continued Anne-Marie. 'Huge stars of the silver screen. He says that people like us can only dream of these stars but that he walks with them and sits with them and stands with them. Big, big stars.'

'What he does not say is that he only gets to move in these circles when movies have been produced by Jews and he gets invited to cover the opening nights in Paris so that the producers' wives will see their photographs somewhere,' explained Anne-Marie.

'He says that two weeks ago he was with the President of the United States of America and the President of France,' said Anne-Marie. 'He says that he could have invited all these important people to be here today, to share the precious moment. But, he says, that instead he chose to invite us.'

I looked at Anne-Marie.

She shrugged. 'It is his way,' she said. 'I am simply telling you what he says. I could not make this up.'

I believed her.

At five, Anne-Marie announced that she was leaving. 'I have to go,' she said. 'But you can stay if you wish.'

I said that I too had to go. 'But I have enjoyed being with you very much,' I told her. It was true. I liked her. 'Can I see you again?'

'What for?'

It wasn't quite the answer I had expected. 'I enjoyed being with you,' I told her.

'You are very sweet,' she said, standing on tiptoe and kissing me on the cheek. 'But you don't have a camera and I am a lesbian.'

I stared at her.

'You didn't guess?'

'I knew about the camera...'

She laughed and touched my cheek with her hand. 'I'm so

sorry,' she said. 'I just needed a man for the wedding.' She laughed.
'You look like one of those dogs with the sad eyes,' she told me.
'Please don't be sad,' she begged me.

'You're absolutely sure you're a lesbian?'

'Absolutely sure.'

'You don't even want to think about it?'

'No. But thank you for the opportunity to reconsider my
sexuality.'

I thanked her again. We hugged. We both said goodbye.

And we never saw one another again.

I was broken-hearted for nearly thirty minutes. And then I
remembered that I had another date with Claudette and I felt
much better.

Chapter 20

The Café de la Paix is one of the smartest cafés in Paris. It is invariably packed with shoppers, tourists and Parisians wanting to see and be seen.

Marvin and Sheila were settled at a comfortable table at the back of the café, next to a radiator. They had piled shopping bags onto a third chair and when I approached Sheila removed the bags and stacked them on the floor underneath the table. Judging by the number of bags, they had been doing their part to keep the French economy alive and booming.

'We've been shopping,' said Sheila, unnecessarily, when she had attracted a waiter's attention and ordered me a pot of tea. Marvin was drinking a glass of red wine and Sheila had a small bottle of still mineral water and a glass in front of her.

'The prices here are so cheap!' said Marvin.

'That's only because we live in Monaco, dear,' Sheila pointed out to him.

'I bought two jackets and six pairs of shoes,' said Marvin. 'They cost me nothing. The shoes were less than 200 francs a pair!'

I did some sums in my head and realised that Marvin's cheap shoes had cost considerably more than I had ever paid for footwear.

'We have to go and buy more suitcases this afternoon,' admitted Sheila. She lowered her voice as though embarrassed by their profligacy. 'We couldn't carry everything we bought. Two of the shops are sending our purchases round to the apartment.' She turned to Marvin and raised her voice back to normal. 'I hope the concierge will be in,' she said.

'The concierge is always in,' said Marvin. 'She'd be far too terrified of missing something to go out.'

'She is a bit nosy,' laughed Sheila. 'She just likes to know everybody's business.' Suddenly she stopped and touched Marvin on the arm. 'Don't look now, but do you know who that is?' said Sheila, inclining his head slightly to make it clear that he was referring to someone sitting in the far corner of the café.

Marvin turned round and stared. He was not a tactful person. I got the impression that if he'd been employed as a diplomat his country would have been at war with everyone. 'The woman in the black leather coat?'

'Sshh! She'll hear you,' said Sheila. 'I'm pretty sure it's Marigold Whatshername. She was married to an Austrian banker.'

'I remember her,' agreed Marvin. 'It's her. Definitely. Boy, she was a keen drinker. She'd have got medals for it if they'd been giving them out.'

'It looks as if she's drinking coffee at the moment.'

'Probably got a splash in it. I thought she was in Africa.'

'She was,' said Sheila. She turned to me. 'She's quite famous, poor woman, for something she once said. She wandered into a very stuffy cocktail party at the Italian Embassy in Madrid and announced, rather too loudly, that she desperately needed a stiff one.'

Marvin sniggered, took a drink from his glass and nearly choked.

'Her simple request for a large gin caused her so much embarrassment that she left the country for seven years and lived quietly in Africa,' said Shelia. 'But, of course, people never forget things like that. When she arrived back in London the first person she saw ignored her lengthy absence and said: "Hello, Marigold. Still looking for a stiff one?" She got back on the next plane to Africa. I thought she was still there.'

'Dare you to go over and ask if she fancies a stiff one,' said Marvin with a giggle.

'Sshhh! Don't be awful,' said Sheila.

The waiter arrived with a tray laden with glasses, cups and tea and coffee pots. I was still astonished at the amount French waiters could carry, apparently without ever dropping anything. He put a pot of tea, a pot of hot water, a pot of milk, a cup and a saucer down on the table. There were wrapped cubes of sugar and a spoon in the saucer.

Two plump English women met directly in front of us. Unlike French women they neither hugged nor kissed. Instead they both complained that their feet were hurting. They were both carrying several large carrier bags.

'That pharmacy where you work must be a goldmine,' said Marvin.

'I expect so,' I agreed.

'Bet they don't pay you much, though!' he added.

'Well, no, I suppose not,' I agreed, rather embarrassed. The two women squeezed onto chairs. The waiter appeared. They ordered cakes by pointing at the menu. They were clearly not women for whom the word 'no' was a viable option when food was available. 'But it's not really a career,' I added. 'It's just a job to see me through until I go back to medical school.'

'We went to the pharmacy twice this week,' said Marvin. 'Didn't see you.'

'I left,' I said. I have no idea why but I found myself blushing. 'I was made redundant. The owner decided he didn't need me after all. That's all.'

'Sorry to hear that,' said Marvin.

'I've found a job at a language school.'

There was a long pause.

Sheila leant forward. 'We know what happened,' she said quietly.

'Appreciate your loyalty,' said Marvin. 'But the man deserves a thrashing. What was it those old English dukes of yours used to do to fellows like that? Give them a horse whipping?'

'That's it,' I laughed. 'But I don't have a horse or a whip.'

'I guess you'll be a bit strapped for cash,' said Marvin.

'The owner gave me a lump sum,' I told him. 'He was quite

generous. It should last me quite a few months. Plus I've now got a part time job teaching English.'

'Guilt,' said Sheila. 'That's why he gave you money.'

'And he probably felt grateful,' said Marvin. 'I expect you saved him a fortune. Divorce doesn't come cheap,' explained Marvin. 'He's American isn't he? The French take this sort of thing in their stride. But in America a man can be ruined if he can't keep his trousers on outside the home.'

'I don't think it was the first time,' I said.

'I'm sure it wasn't,' said Sheila.

'Just make sure you look after the money he gave you,' said Marvin.

'You sound like a father!' said Sheila.

'I feel like one,' said Marvin. 'Besides, there's nothing wrong with giving the kid some advice about money. Money has a life of its own. And it has its own needs,' said Marvin. 'Money demands to be looked after. It wants to be mollycoddled and cared for. If you don't look after it then it will leave you.'

'You make money sound like a person,' I said.

'A very selfish, conceited person,' said Marvin. 'You probably won't believe this but rich people worry more about money than the people who don't have any.'

I must have looked as sceptical as I felt.

'It's true,' said Marvin. He looked to Sheila for support. She nodded. 'He's right,' she admitted. 'People who've got money always worry about losing it. Rich people who've never been poor don't worry about money as much as rich people who dragged themselves out of the gutter. If you've never been poor then you don't know what it's like. But if you've been poor, and you're rich, your biggest fear is that one day it will all be taken away from you and you'll have to be poor again.'

I still didn't believe them, but I smiled and shrugged, as though to say: 'If you say so.' I was young. And the young can be very arrogant. 'I've put the money in the bank,' I said.

'Good lad,' said Marvin.

'So what sort of people are you going to teach?' said Sheila.

'French people who want to learn English,' I told her. 'It's only for a few hours a week. And I've only just started.' The waiter brought cakes to the two women in front of us. 'We've got to look after our figures,' laughed one of the women, admiring the gooey confection on her plate. I suspected that cream played a large part in her daily diet.

'I used to know a girl who did a little language teaching,' said Marvin. 'Remarkable woman.' He put a chocolate into his mouth and suddenly smiled. 'Called Edith. She taught me French.'

'But you don't speak French!' protested Sheila.

'I said she taught me, I didn't say I learnt anything,' said Marvin. 'She was a sporting girl – that's what they called them in those days. That or a *fille de joie*. 'Girl of joy.' Nice, eh? Men had more respect for hookers in those days. I was staying at a hotel near here and the night porter found her for me. She did the French lessons on the side.'

'I thought it was usually the other way around,' said Sheila. Marvin looked at her.

'It's usually the French teacher who does a little hooking on the side,' she explained. 'Rather than the other way around.'

Marvin shrugged. 'She only had a few customers,' he said. 'Me, Horace Brompton and Jack Luton. Horace Brompton never married. He always used sporting girls when he wanted a bit of female companionship. He always claimed they were cheaper than wives and that you could have them when you wanted them and send them away when you didn't want them around.'

'And Jack Luton?' said Sheila, not hiding her surprise. 'How long ago was this?'

Marvin thought for a moment. 'Fifty years,' he said. 'Maybe forty five.'

'Jack is a lay preacher. Was he married then?'

'Probably. But I can't remember which wife he was on. It might have been number one but if it was I can't remember her name. She was a tough, skinny girl with no chest but lots of balls. Come to that I doubt if Jack can remember her name either. They were only married for two months. Anyway, are you going to let me tell this story or not?'

'Sorry,' said Sheila, quietly. She leant towards me. 'The

French say that the ideal condition for a woman is to be born a widow,' she whispered. 'Sometimes I think that is one thing that they are absolutely right about.'

Marvin ignored her. 'Well, one Saturday I met an American banker and his wife at a 'do' at the American Embassy. The Embassy used to invite me to their cocktail parties then and I was young enough and flattered enough to go. The banker and his wife had just moved to Paris and they were desperate to find someone to teach them a little French. They were pretty well the most obnoxious people I had ever met but Edith was the only French teacher I knew. I told her they were loaded and she could charge them whatever she liked as long as she didn't put her teaching prices up for me.'

'I don't know what they did to upset her – they may have just patronised her in that awful way moderately rich Americans have – but she got very, very upset with them.'

'They wanted to learn to speak French because the firm he worked for had organised a bit of a 'do' to welcome them to Paris. Actually, of course, it wasn't a bit of a 'do' at all – it was an incredibly grand affair at The Ritz in the Place Vendome. They told Edith that they wanted to be able to make short speeches in French. They didn't want anyone working for the company to know that they were learning these speeches and so they didn't want to ask any of the official translators for help. They thought it would be a great surprise if they just stood up and spoke in fluent French – without notes.'

'A delighted Edith duly taught them French but because she didn't like them the phrases and sentences she taught them didn't quite match the carefully prepared speeches they'd prepared for themselves.'

'She taught the husband a few set sentences in French. He told her what he wanted to say and she taught him what to say in French. But he didn't learn exactly what he thought he was learning. When he thought he was telling the staff how delighted he was to be the new European Director he was actually apologising for the fact that like all Americans he was grossly overweight and had terrible taste in clothes. He ignored the sniggers which this remark gave birth to and went on to apologise in advance for the fact that he had an unpleasant bowel problem which would, he confessed, result in 'the release of a good deal of foul smelling flatus during the years ahead'.' He ended by insulting the French in general and the employees in particular and then, as a sort of postscript, apologised for the fact that his obese wife had terrible breath and was an alcoholic with a taste for methylated spirits and also a nymphomaniac with a penchant for group sex with large black men.'

'Honestly?'

'Yes. It gets worse. When the fat American wife thought she was telling the staff and their collected wives and mistresses how delighted she was to be in Paris with her wonderful and enormously successful husband and how much she looked forward to organising parties in her home and picnics in the Bois de Boulogne for the staff's children she was in fact warning them not to get too close because she was suffering from a highly infectious sexually transmitted disease which doctors had warned her could be passed on not only through any human contact but also through breathing in the same air. And when she gave them her very best and expensively capped smile, and thought she was inviting the collected wives to join the flower arranging class which she planned to give on Saturday mornings, she was actually saying how much she was looking forward to performing oral sex on all male employees between the ages of 18 and 90. She ended by inviting all well-endowed black employees to pop round to their apartment on the Champs Elysée at any time.'

Sheila and I stared at him, incredulously. 'What happened?'

'The fat American and his awful wife were sent back to Philadelphia after two weeks. He found it impossible to maintain any sort of discipline and when she found out what she'd said she shut herself in her bedroom and refused to show her face to anyone.'

'And Edith?'

Marvin shrugged. 'The Americans were far too embarrassed to complain and, even if they had done so, no one would have taken any notice. What could they have done? She was a ten dollar hooker.'

Sheila looked at Marvin and squinted.

'Was that true?'

Marvin lowered his head and looked at her over the top of his spectacles.

'As true as I'm sitting here,' he insisted.

He looked at me and cleared his throat. 'It's a shame to be young in Paris and not have any money.' He paused and thought for a moment. 'Another one of life's little ironies isn't it?'

I looked at him, puzzled. 'I don't understand,' I admitted.

'The old fogies with wallets and purses stuffed with money are too old to have fun. The young folk with plenty of energy and the legs for fun don't have any money.'

The two women had now finished eating their cakes. One of the women called to the waiter. 'The cakes were stale,' she complained, pointing to her plate although there was not even a crumb of cake left on the plate. The waiter looked at her and looked at the plate. 'Stale,' said the woman loudly. 'The cakes were stale.'

'Why did you eat the cake if it was stale?' asked the waiter, politely and logically. 'You have eaten the evidence.' The woman laughed and shrugged. 'It was worth a try,' she said to her friend. She did not appear to be in the slightest bit embarrassed, even though she could see that several people had watched her appalling attempt to wriggle out of paying for the cake she had just eaten.

'Surely you don't really need to have money to have fun,' I argued, though looking back I really didn't know much about either.

Marvin smiled. 'But you can have more fun if you do have money,' he said. 'Though curiously, the other thing I have observed in my life is that most of the people who do have money don't really know how to spend it – probably because they've spent too much of their lives making it, saving it and hoarding it.' He paused and thought for a moment. 'The corollary to that, of course, is that by and large people who don't have money are often pretty good at spending it. Some of them are spectacularly good at spending it. When I first met my third wife she was absolutely stony broke but she could have won medals for shopping and spending.'

I murmured something and nodded.

'I know of what I speak,' said Marvin, firmly. 'When I was your age I had a tiny studio apartment in Montmartre. It was above a small café where the local prostitutes hung out. The studio was freezing cold. I remember taking up the carpet to let the heat come up through the cracks from the café below. They had a stove in the café and with all the people in there it was always much warmer than my studio. Their ceiling was cracked and the plaster had fallen off in many places. The only problem was that the cigarette smoke all came through the cracks too. I had no radio and no gramophone and no television...'

'Television hadn't been invented then!' interrupted Sheila.

'...that's probably why I didn't have one,' continued Marvin. 'I couldn't afford to go downstairs and drink so I used to lie down flat on the floor, peep through the gap between my floorboards and the crack in their ceiling and watch what went on down below. It was the original *cinéma-vérité*.'

'I bet you wished you had a room above one of the girl's rooms!' said Sheila.

Marvin winked at me. 'You see,' he said. 'My problem is that my wife understands me.' He chuckled. 'Two of the girls had rooms on either side of me,' he said. 'I opened up tiny little cracks in the wall. In the afternoons, when they got up, I watched them getting washed and dressed. At night I watched them with their customers.'

'So you were a pervert even back then?' said Sheila, drily.

'Of course,' said Marvin, who, much to my surprise did not seem to be in the slightest bit embarrassed or offended by being described as a pervert. 'I had to live by their hours anyway. They always kept me awake at night. Noisy customers, thin walls and twangy bedsprings.' He thought for a moment and smiled to himself. 'Great days,' he said. 'I seem to remember having to stand in the corridor for half an hour if I wanted to take a bath and the only telephone was always busy but I did get perks. There was an unending supply of hot water in the bathroom. That was my other way of keeping warm. I used to have two or three baths a day in the winter. The girls never used to take a bath in the mornings. And the girls used to let me have a special rate when they were quiet.' He stopped and thought. 'For some reason Wednesday afternoons were always quiet,' he remembered. He drifted for a moment into nostalgia.

I felt myself blushing and felt embarrassed about having gone red.

'You're making him blush,' said Sheila. She turned to Marvin. 'Don't you own that building now?' she asked him.

'I own every building I've ever lived in,' said Marvin. He was proud but not boasting. 'I bought that one when I was 22, with a loan from a pimp who ran most of the girls in the neighbourhood. Most of the rooms are still rented by sporting girls.'

'I didn't know that!' said Sheila.

'They pay well, they pay on time and they pay cash,' said Marvin with a shrug. 'People tell me they make great wives,' he said. 'They know the value of money and they know all the tricks in the bedroom.' Two heavily laden shoppers tried to squeeze between our table and the backs of the seats in front of us. One of the bags rocked our table. I caught the table and managed to stop anything falling. The shopper didn't even turn round.

'Bloody American tourists,' snarled Marvin.

'Ssshhh, dear!' said Sheila. 'They'll hear you.'

'Don't care,' said Marvin, rather like a sulky child. 'I hope they hear us.' He raised his voice. 'Bloody American tourists.' Several people, probably Americans, turned round and looked in our direction.

'You wouldn't think he was American himself, would you?' Sheila asked me.

I smiled at her and shook my head.

'Used to be,' said Marvin. 'Used to be. Boy, that was a long time ago.'

'I think it's a pity, anyway,' said Sheila. 'All those poor girls who have to sell themselves to make a living.'

Marvin looked at her and snorted. 'When I lived in England in the 50s,' he said, 'I knew three sisters. Their parents, with an extraordinary lack of common sense, had called them April, May and June so although their surname was Westacott we knew them as the Spring sisters. April and May were both born in the months which had given them their names. Thanks to the fact that she arrived three weeks early June was also born in May.' He shrugged. 'The English sometimes amaze me. One daughter, April, the oldest, worked in a factory as a secretary. She gave her whole life to her miserable work and a mean and ungrateful boss. One, May, got married at the age of 18 because she was pregnant. She had seven children in quick succession and by the time she was thirty she looked at least fifty. Her husband was a mean, wicked man who used to give her a pittance for housekeeping and spend the rest boozing on Saturday nights. He would come home drunk, beat her, drag her upstairs and then rape her. The third sister, June, became the mistress of a local estate agent. He dumped her and so that she wouldn't have to lose her rented flat she became a whore. Within five years she had bought her own flat and enough property to make her independent for life. She had her own car, a villa in Spain and beautiful clothes. By the age of 30 she was semi-retired. She had six lovers who each visited her one night a week and she had Tuesdays off. Now, you tell me, which of those women was the whore?'

No one spoke.

'Real white slavery is women working in factories, ruining their health and selling their lives for a pittance. Most of those who complain about hookers are flat chested, moustachioed and jealous.'

'Well, I don't care what you say I'd rather starve than sell my body,' said Sheila.

'Have you never been to bed with a man you didn't love?' Marvin asked her.

Sheila didn't reply. The silence seemed to stretch on for ever. I turned to her. 'Are you American, too?' I asked her.

'Good heavens, no!' said Sheila. 'I'm English, can't you tell?'

'No,' I said. 'Sorry. Have you been out of England for long?'

'Twenty three years,' she replied. 'Ever since I met Marvin and moved to Monaco.'

Now that the embarrassing moment had passed she turned to Marvin. 'Who collects the rents?' she asked.

'Mickey,' replied Marvin. He turned to me. 'Sheila always assumes that everyone who works for me is a thief,' he said. 'She's right to be suspicious. But I trust Mickey. He wouldn't cheat me.'

'Only because he's scared of you,' said Sheila.

Marvin shrugged. 'Fear keeps people in line,' he said. 'If you're soft with people they take advantage of you.'

'Oh, that's not always true,' said Sheila.

'In my experience it is,' said Marvin. 'The one thing I have learned in this life is that we are invariably hurt by our kindnesses to others. And, just as important, others are often hurt by our kindnesses to them.'

'That's cynical and rather sad,' said Sheila. She turned to me. 'Don't you listen to him!' she insisted.

Marvin shrugged his shoulders. 'I'm right,' he said. He took a tiny sip of his wine. 'Let me tell you a true story,' he said to me. 'About my Aunt Lisbeth and my Uncle Jack who lived in Colorado. My Aunt Lisbeth worked as a nurse at the local hospital and she had a cat called Blackie. It was a long-haired cat. Very beautiful, very black, very fat and very lazy. It spent most of its time on her lap. My Aunt Lisbeth loved that cat like it was her favourite child.'

'One day she was sitting on the porch stroking the cat when my Uncle Jack came in. It was about nine o'clock in the evening. He'd been on a fishing trip. It was chilly and Uncle Jack asked Aunt Lisbeth if she shouldn't be indoors, out of the cold. He cared a lot for her, worshipped her in his way, and he didn't want her upping and dying on him.'

"I'm fine,' my Aunt Lisbeth told him, stroking the cat as she spoke. 'My Blackie has such warm and beautiful fur. She keeps me really cosy,' she said. 'She would make a wonderful stole."

'The next day Aunt Lisbeth went off to work at the hospital, just the same as usual. And my Uncle Jack went off to do a little shooting, or hunting, or whatever it was that he did in the days. And when Aunt Lisbeth got back from work that evening she couldn't find the cat. She went all around the neighbourhood calling for it but she couldn't find it anywhere.'

'So, a few days later when Uncle Jack came back from his hunting or shooting or fishing trip or whatever and wants to know why there isn't a meal there ready for him, my Aunt Lisbeth tells him, in tears, the cat is missing.'

'And Uncle Jack opens up his game bag and he takes out this beautiful black stole and hands it to Aunt Lisbeth like he's giving her the greatest present a man ever gave a woman and he says: 'Here you are, my sweet wife. I had a couple of the boys make Blackie up into a stole just like you wanted. They killed her and skinned her and there she is. Now you never need be cold again.'

'And my Aunt Lisbeth took the stole and broke down into tears and cried and cried. And my Uncle Jack thought she was crying because she was so happy until she upped and went into the kitchen and came back and stabbed a ten inch kitchen knife into his chest and killed him stone dead.'

Marvin paused and took another sip of his wine. 'So, you see,' he said. 'My Uncle Jack just thought he was being kind and he acted in what he thought were my Aunt Lisbeth's very best interests. But just look at the harm done by that single act of kindness. The cat was killed, he was killed and my Aunt Lisbeth is still in the State Penitentiary and they won't never let her out now because she's as crazy as they come.'

Neither Sheila nor I said anything.

'Is that story true?' asked Sheila eventually.

'Of course it ain't,' snorted Marvin disdainfully. 'But that's not the point is it? The point is that you weren't sure whether or not it was true. And if you aren't sure whether or not a thing is true it might just as well be true.'

Sheila called the waiter over and ordered more tea, more wine and a vodka martini. 'I need something stronger than water,' she explained.

'Have you ever wanted to own your own café?' Marvin suddenly asked the waiter.

The waiter, surprised by the question, looked at Marvin.

'You're a great waiter,' said Marvin. 'You run this place like clockwork. I don't know who the owners are but you're helping them make a fortune. Haven't you ever thought about running your own place?'

The waiter stood for a moment. 'I thought about it,' he confessed at last. 'Many years ago. I think all waiters do. It is a common dream.'

'What made you decide not to try it?'

'I looked at my boss and saw how much he suffered,' replied the waiter. 'He was 45 but he looked 20 years older. He was always worrying. He worried about the supplies. He worried about the insurance, the taxes and the accounts. He worried about upsetting the customers. When it was too hot he worried that his customers would go away to the countryside. When it was too cold he worried that his customers would stay at home.'

'You're a wise man,' said Marvin. 'There would be more happy people in the world if more people thought like you do.'

The waiter shrugged and left.

'Wise man,' said Marvin. 'Ambition is fine and dandy. Without it a man won't achieve much. But ambition won't amount to a hill of beans without talent or hard work. If you don't have talent or aren't prepared to work hard then you're best off not having any ambition.'

When I left an hour later Marvin invited me to have dinner with them at their apartment.

'Archie will be there,' he said. 'He is a client of mine.'

'I thought he sold gold?'

Marvin nodded. 'He's a gold dealer,' he agreed. 'But he's come over to Paris because he's a client of mine.'

I didn't say anything.

'I have a number of American clients,' explained Marvin, lowering his voice. 'All big earners who have tax problems. I act as a consultant to them and send them financial and management advice.' He paused. 'For a fee, of course. I'm very, very expensive.'

'You're a management consultant?' I asked him.

'Not really,' grinned Marvin. 'Though that's what it says on

my visiting card. They send me a huge fee for my advice. I put
85% of the fee into a numbered bank account for them and I keep
15% for myself. I don't pay any tax because I live in Monaco.'

I thought about this for a while. 'I still don't understand,' I
said.

'They ring a telephone number in Monaco to prove that
they're consulting me,' said Marvin. 'The number connects them
to a telephone answering machine in our apartment. Every
couple of months I send them a huge folder filled with management
gibberish.'

'But what do they get out of it?'

'They get tax relief on the money they pay me,' explained
Marvin. 'All they have to pay is my 15% commission. The rest of
their money sits waiting for them in a nice, warm, numbered
account in Monaco. It's pretty well legal. Of course, with Archie
things are a bit more complicated. His clients pay cash for gold
coins – some of them are worth $30,000 or more – which he gives
to me. I sell the coins and put the money into their numbered
account.'

'That I really don't understand,' I admitted.

'They buy the gold coins with cash they haven't declared,'
explained Marvin. 'Archie gets the coins out of the country for
them. It's a lot easier for him to bring a million dollars' worth of
gold coins out of the States than it would be for them to bring a
million dollars in notes. I turn the coins back into cash and put the
cash into the bank – less my commission, of course.'

I stared at him. For a moment I wondered why he was
telling me all this. And then I realised that he was telling me
because he was proud of his own cleverness and he couldn't tell
anyone else.

'Mind you, between you and me I've been worried recently
about Archie. He does rather a lot of business with men who carry
violin cases but can't read a note of music.'

I wasn't sure how to respond to this.

'They want him to do a bit of laundry for them,' explained
Marvin. He pulled a face.

'He seems a nice guy,' I said.

'He is,' said Marvin. 'Don't tell him I told you any of this,' he said. 'He worries a lot.'

'I think I'd probably worry too,' I said. In fact I was already worrying and none of this had anything to do with me.

'People worry too much,' said Marvin. 'Usually about the wrong things and often about things which really aren't a threat to them. The fact is that suspense always beats reason. That's why we worry when we see a star in a movie in danger. Even though all our good sense tells us that the movie star will escape from their dangerous predicament (no studio is going to allow the director to kill the star in the first reel) we still worry. And so it is with our own worries. Even though our reason – our good sense – tells us that the thing we fear isn't going to happen we still fear it.'

'I suppose so,' I agreed. 'Anyway, he and Fifi seem a very nice couple.'

Marvin laughed. 'Fifi won't be having dinner with us,' he said. 'We've got some confidential business to sort out.'

'Fifi hasn't been invited,' explained Sheila.

'Oh,' I said, failing to hide my surprise.

'They're not what you'd call 'an item',' said Sheila, obviously feeling that she needed to explain.

'They're not married?'

Marvin smiled. 'No,' he said. 'They're not married.' A dry, throaty noise came from him. It was, I realised, a laugh. He turned to Sheila. 'Tell him,' he said.

Sheila seemed embarrassed. 'I'm not sure...,' she began.

'Archie don't mind,' said Marvin. 'And Fifi hasn't got no call to mind.'

'No, I suppose not,' agreed Sheila. She swallowed and looked down at the table. 'Fifi isn't Archie's wife or girlfriend,' she explained. 'She's a call girl.'

'She ain't no call girl,' said Marvin. 'Call girls are the top end of the market. Fifi is a street whore.'

I felt myself blushing. Fifi did not seem to match any of the stereotypes I'd seen in films or on television. She certainly bore no resemblance to the untidy looking woman I had found in my room at the hotel. She had looked like a hooker.

'You're embarrassing him,' said Sheila, nodding in my direction.

'No, no!' I protested. I told them about the prostitute I'd found in my room.

'There used to be proper brothels in Paris,' said Marvin. 'Like they have in Amsterdam. The authorities shut them down, hoping that by shutting down the brothels they'd end prostitution. Crazy. All that happened, of course, was that the girls went onto the streets.'

'Well you can't blame them for that,' said Sheila. 'Closing down the brothels.'

'It was crazy!' insisted Marvin. 'In the brothels the girls had regular medical examinations. They had to carry certificates showing that they were healthy. These days there are no medical examinations and no certificates and if you go with a hooker you'll as like as not find yourself pissing blood the next day. The only thing closing down the brothels did was increase the number of men with the clap.'

'Well, whatever, Archie picked this one up on the rue St. Denis,' explained Sheila. 'She was apparently standing on a street corner in a tiny leather skirt and a see-through blouse. Whenever he comes to Paris he goes to the rue St. Denis and picks up a girl – always the cheapest looking whore he can find. He then takes her to a store in the rue St. Honoré where they know him. He buys her half a dozen expensive dresses, plus all the trimmings, and then keeps her with him until he goes home.'

'Oh,' I said. Or at least I rather assumed that it was me who had spoken. If I had not been there I would not have recognised the thin, reedy, high pitched voice as my own.

'She's a nice girl,' said Marvin. 'I've no idea what her real name is. Archie calls her Fifi d'Orsay but I very much doubt if that is her name. Actually I very much doubt if he ever asked her what her real name is. He gets a real kick out of taking her to dinner in the poshest restaurants in Paris. He took her to a reception at the Japanese embassy two nights ago. I'd love to have been there. He loves to see self-important people bowing and scraping to a street whore.'

It was, perhaps, a sign of my innocence that it had never even occurred to me that Fifi might not be the girl's real name. The story rather reminded me of the flower girl in Shaw's *Pygmalion*. The same tale taken to its illogical conclusion.

'Of course, he doesn't take Fifi absolutely everywhere,' said Sheila. 'And we thought it best to leave her out of our little dinner party.'

'Right,' I said, trying to give the impression that all this was nothing out of the ordinary to me. It never occurred to me to ask myself why a rich American, exiled and living in Monaco, would want to invite me to a private dinner at his apartment. If I had thought about it I think that even back then I would have realised that he wasn't inviting me for my conversational skills or my sparkling repartee.

Marvin paid the bill, I thanked him for the tea, and we all stood together. A tourist was taking a photograph of her husband and for a moment Marvin was clearly in the frame.

'Move!' hissed Sheila.

Marvin jumped and looked startled. 'What's up?'

'You were nearly in that woman's photograph,' she said, hustling her husband away from danger. 'And the husband has a very cheap hair cut and is wearing a terrible jumper.'

We left the Café de la Paix together. Outside, standing on the pavement, we said our goodbyes and Sheila explained to me how to find their apartment. We walked a few yards in the direction of the Hotel Scribe. Marvin and Sheila were heading for the taxi rank.

Suddenly I realised that Marvin had slowed. I looked back and watched in astonishment as he sprinkled coins on the pavement.

'What on earth is he doing?' I asked Sheila.

'Because we live in Monaco he doesn't pay any tax,' explained Sheila quietly. An old woman stooped down and started picking up some of the coins. Two small boys joined her. 'It's Marvin's way of giving money to the people who really need it. He says he's adding tiny moments of joy to otherwise largely joyless lives.'

'How often does he do this?' I asked Sheila.

'Every time he comes out of a shop, a hotel or a café with change in his pocket,' explained Sheila.

At the corner of the rue Scribe we waited. Marvin caught us up. He was grinning broadly and looked very happy.

'Paying taxes never made me smile,' he said.

We parted. They climbed into a taxi and I waved them goodbye.

Chapter 21

Claudette took great delight in showing me the Paris that the tourists know and an even greater delight in showing me the Paris that most tourists miss.

To start with she insisted that I see the most famous parts of Paris. We took the lift up the Tour Eiffel and had an absurdly expensive lunch (paid for by her ever generous husband) at the restaurant on the first floor. One morning, before the tourists were up and about, we rode up and down the Seine in an almost empty *bateau mouche*. We visited Napoleon's tomb and marvelled at the pikes, muskets and armour in the military museum which fills acres of Les Invalides. We queued in the Louvre to see the Mona Lisa and the Venus de Milo. We marvelled at Sacre Coeur, walked around Montmartre and we sat arm in arm while a long-haired art student with an engaging smile, armed only with a grey sketching pad and two sticks of chalk – one black and one white – sketched us sitting together. We then made him do it all again so that we would have a portrait each. He rolled the portraits into tight tubes and fastened them with thin, blue rubber bands. When it started to rain we slipped into a *boulangerie* and bought an armful of croissants so that we could use the paper bags to keep our drawings dry. When the rain stopped we fed the croissants to sparrows and pigeons in a tiny park.

When we had visited all the well known tourist haunts Claudette started taking me to less well known parts of Paris.

Once, she took me down the rue du Chat Qui Peche (named, so she told me, after a cat who used to fish in the cellars when the River Seine was high).

'It is,' she said with the sort of inverted pride that Americans would never understand, 'the narrowest and shortest street in the world.' In the whole street there was only one tiny window. There were no doors.

From there we walked across the river, past Notre Dame and the offices wherein Inspector Maigret would have worked if he had been more than a figment of George Simenon's imagination, past the thousand year old Hotel Dieu and north to the Palais Royale. We bought two baguettes, ripe Camembert cheese and a bottle of heavy red wine from a delicatessen and had a picnic on a wooden bench.

'I love eating out of doors,' I said. Pigeons and sparrows were clambering over my shoes, searching for crumbs from the flaky, cheese filled baguette I was eating. 'Food seems to taste so much better.' I paused to crumble a piece of bread and toss it to a nervous sparrow who was too shy to join the mêlée. 'I think that I enjoy a simple picnic more than I would enjoy the most expensive restaurant meal.'

'My first husband used to say that a lot – when we first started courting,' said Claudette. 'It was one of the things about him that I really liked. Sadly, when he had more money he changed his mind.'

I looked at her and frowned. 'Your first husband?'

'Yes. My first.'

'How many have you had?'

'Too many.'

'What happened to your first marriage?'

'We married very young; far too young. It was a disaster. It all happened a long time ago. He was desperately keen on sport. We were together for two years but it seemed a lot longer at the time. In retrospect I think I spent six months sailing, six months watching rugby, six months watching soccer and six months making teas and washing his team's kit.'

'He didn't play golf?'

'Actually, golf was just about the only game he didn't play. He thought it was élitist.'

'And rugby and sailing aren't?

She shrugged. 'Rugby was his favourite game. Until he was thrown out of the club.'

'Your husband was thrown out of a rugby club?'

'Yes.'

'What on earth for?'

'For drinking and womanising.'

I couldn't help laughing. 'I'm sorry,' I said. 'But was your husband really thrown out of a rugby club for drinking and womanising?'

'He did a great deal of both and was sometimes too tired and too drunk to play. The only sport he was really fond of involved just two players, you see. And the other players did not much like him.'

'Why not?'

'He was too good-looking. Men felt instinctively that he was a threat to them. They were jealous of him.' She stopped and thought for a moment. 'Women were attracted to him,' she said. 'But they did not like him much, either. They did not trust him.'

'How did you meet him?'

'A sort of friend got us together. We were both alone and she thought we would be good for one another. It was a blind date. I never consciously blamed the friend but I realised the other day that I haven't ever seen her since that marriage ended.'

'What happened in the end? Was it very painful?'

'He went off with one of the other player's wives. A big, blonde girl. It was a relief rather than painful. He went in such a rush that he left his diaries behind. Since the age of fifteen he had been keeping a diary. He'd always claimed it was private because it contained his innermost, most spiritual thoughts but I discovered that it was merely a detailed record of his sexual conquests.'

'You read his diary?'

'Oh yes,' said Claudette. She laughed. 'I feel a little bit ashamed perhaps. But not too bad. Compared to what he did to me it was nothing. And reading the diary made me feel a little better. Everything was in there. I found that on the day when he first persuaded me into bed he had already been with a girl he'd met on the Metro. And I discovered that he had sex with two of the bridesmaids at our wedding. He did it with my cousin in the car park, up against the Bentley we'd hired for the day, and with a girl whose name he never knew in the gents' toilets. There were eleven volumes of sexual history. He had enormous stamina. If he'd been able to direct those energies into some other activity he would have made quite a name for himself.'

'And afterwards?'

'I vowed never to marry another man who had football socks to wash. And so I married a lawyer called Jean-Paul whose idea of strenuous physical activity was walking from a taxi to the front door of his office.'

'How long did that last?'

'Nine months. One evening we were at his sister's house in the Dordogne. His sister, Leonora, is sweet but a little neurotic. She is very shy. We still keep in touch. Every day life scares her half to death. She is a little unstable and unpredictable. Once, when she made a cake, she put all her pills into it and then handed around slices of the cake at a dinner party. Several people were quite ill afterwards. After that I was careful not to eat anything at her house. When I was invited to dinner I used to eat only white bread rolls, reasoning that she was unlikely to have poisoned those. Leonora will not touch any food that is not coloured. She believes that it is the colour which gives food its goodness.'

'Because it was a warm summer evening we had all gone out onto the patio and the paved area around the swimming pool. The swimming pool was shaped like a piano. I never knew why but I assumed that at least one previous owner of the house had been a pianist. I thought it very tasteless. And so, to be fair, did Jean-Paul.'

'Leonora started dancing. She had had far too much to drink – as she always did because she had a little problem with her drinking – and because she was wearing very high heeled shoes she slipped and fell into the swimming pool. She screamed and started thrashing around and it was quite clear that she was in trouble. I was upstairs fetching a jumper when I heard the scream. I looked out of the window and could see my husband standing about six feet away from her. I shouted at him to jump into the pool and save his sister but he refused. He actually refused! And do you know what his excuse was?'

I shook my head.

'He pointed out that he was wearing his new suit – beautiful brown silk – and that the water would ruin it if he jumped into the pool.'

'I shouted at him and told him that he could remove the jacket but he said that if he did that the trousers would still be affected and the suit would be ruined anyway.'

'I fell out of love with him there and then. There we were, standing on the edge of this pool and he was refusing to jump in and save his sister who was drowning. And why? Because the water would spoil his suit!'

'What happened to Leonora?'

'Another guest jumped in and saved her.'

'But you fell out of love with Jean-Paul?'

'It was such a selfish and terrible thing to do,' said Claudette. 'I could never forget and never forgive him.' She shook her head at the memory of it. 'But that is enough of me and my men. Tell me about you and your women.'

I did not know what to say to this. The truth was that the silence said it all.

'Have you ever had a serious girlfriend?'

'Oh yes.' I replied, with fake confidence.

'More than one?'

'Oh certainly.'

'But you don't have a girlfriend now?'

'No. Not at the moment.'

'Tell me about the last one?'

'Well. She was very sophisticated. Very beautiful. Very kind.' I paused.

'...and?'

'And she was very gentle but also very strong.'

'Gentle but strong?'

'Yes.'

'And very sweet.' I hesitated. 'But not too sweet. Also very sexy.'

Claudette reached across the table, put her hand on mine and smiled. 'You will find your love,' she said. 'One day you will find her. You are very young and you have all the time in the world. But when you find her do not expect too much of her.'

I looked at her and knew that she knew that what I had told her had not been the truth.

'The woman you have in your mind is a dream. Just a dream. But no real woman can be your dream.' She paused. 'You've never had a girlfriend, have you?'

'No. How did you know that...she did not exist...that I have had no girlfriend?'

'You describe the woman all men dream of wanting. It is the woman they believe they want; the fantasy, the dream. It is the same with women.'

'Yes?'

'Oh yes. Women want a man who is understanding. Soft and gentle like a woman. But although he is soft he must also be confident and secure. But not arrogant. He must be a tough, rough guy in bed but he must be never cruel or thoughtless. He has to be generous with his time and his money but at the same time he must respect her independence.'

'It sounds an impossible dream.' I said quietly. 'How could any man live up to that?'

'Exactly,' smiled Claudette. She paused for a long moment. 'Exactly. The dream man is unreal and unattainable and unliveable with because he has none of those endearing imperfections which make a man loveable and charming.' She paused. 'Do you like the movies?'

'Yes. Very much.'

'I love the movies,' she said. 'But if you think back to the great days of the cinema – the black and white greats – you will realise that the stars all had something which set them apart from the good actors and good actresses.'

I waited.

'They all had imperfections which made them endearingly human,' explained Claudette. 'Humphrey Bogart, Cary Grant, Clark Gable, Errol Flynn, Marilyn Monroe, Greta Garbo, Claudette Colbert – all of them were so much themselves that it was all they could ever be. They pretended to be other people but we always knew that they were simply pretending. They had so much charisma that they could only ever be themselves. The great stars are loved by both men and women – they are so full of magic that they can be a lover to one and a friend to the other. On the other hand the really great actors disappear into the roles they play. They are too good at their work to become stars. While actors become the person they are pretending to be the stars always look the same and play the same character in all their movies. But we do not love the great actors, we love the stars. And we love the stars because they are simply themselves. We love their charming imperfections. It is the same in life. When we fall in love we fall in love with the imperfections. If you are for ever searching for the dream you will never fall in love.'

And slowly, very slowly, I thought I began to understand.

'The understanding is in the not knowing,' said Claudette. 'You cannot know until you know what you do not know. And you cannot understand until you know that you cannot possibly ever understand. Only when you know what you do not know will you begin to understand.'

I stared at her.

'Your grandfather?'

'No. That was me.' She laughed. 'Take no notice,' she said. She picked up her packet of cigarettes. 'Take no notice of me. I am just a crazy, middle-aged woman who takes strange young men to the theatre so that she can embarrass her husband.' She took a cigarette out of the packet and put it into her mouth. She then handed me her lighter. 'Light my cigarette,' she told me.

'No,' I said, flicking the lighter and lighting her cigarette. 'You are not crazy. Well, yes, I suppose you may be crazy, in a way. But it is a craziness I think I understand.' I paused and thought for a moment.

'I will tell you one last thing today,' Claudette said, inhaling deeply. 'About a friend of mine called Irene. She swore that she would only ever go with the man of her dreams. She swore she would wait until she met her perfect man. She was very beautiful. And rich. And she had many suitors. But she rejected all of them. Many were good, kind, courageous men. One or two would have made wonderful husbands. But she was so intent on waiting for her perfect man to arrive that she did not give any of these men a chance. She had created, in her mind, a symbol of male perfection. And no man could live up to her dream. One man might have some small physical imperfection. He might, perhaps, be an inch too short or have too long a nose. Another man might be too quick tempered. A third might lack ambition and drive. No man is perfect. No man could match her dream. And so she is now 49, still unmarried, still untouched. She now lives alone with her dream.'

'So you are saying that I should not be too choosy?'

'No, no, no! No, no no! Of course you should be choosy. Every man and every woman should be choosy. But when you fall in love you should not confuse the man or woman you love with the man or woman of your dreams. When you fall in love it will be with the frailties and imperfections. For it is the frailties and imperfections – and the weaknesses – which make us who we are.'

And at last I understood. Or, at least, I thought I did.

I looked at her and sighed. 'I know that I do not understand and I understand that I do not know,' I said. I felt embarrassed before I'd finished the sentence. It sounded like one of those would-be clever Zen sayings. But Claudette laughed and clapped her hands in delight. 'You have it!' she said.

On the pavement outside she kissed me on the cheek and then climbed into a taxi. As the taxi disappeared she turned and I could see her face through the back window. She waved and blew me a kiss. I stood still and watched until the taxi had completely disappeared. And then I stood still and watched where it had been.

As I walked back to the hotel I tried to work out what I'd meant.

Chapter 22

Marvin and Sheila Brown had an apartment overlooking the Parc de Monceau. It was an imposing place in which to have an apartment. I didn't know whether they owned the apartment, had rented the apartment or just borrowed it from a friend.

An elderly woman concierge took my name, telephoned the apartment, obtained permission for me to enter the building and ushered me into a glass and iron *ascenseur*. It was far too complicated and beautiful a contraption to describe as a 'lift' or even an 'elevator'. Their apartment was on the third floor. As I rang the door bell, feeling terribly out of place, I couldn't help wondering why on earth these rich people from Monaco had invited me to dinner. I was much younger than they were, much poorer and knew nothing or no one that could possibly be of interest to them. Looking back I realise that if I had not been so young and naive I would have not accepted their invitation.

Sheila took my coat and hung it in a closet in the hallway, murmured something about having to deal with a crisis in the kitchen, and after showing me into a spacious, light living room disappeared again. The room was enormous in every dimension and had huge windows over looking the park. I knew nothing whatsoever about the prices of real estate in Paris but you didn't have to be a property speculator to realise that this was an expensive apartment.

Marvin was sitting on a bright yellow sofa, surrounded by papers, files and notebooks.

'Do you know anything about the stock market?' he asked me, as I entered.

I admitted that I knew nothing whatsoever about the stock market.

'Which way do you think the market is going to go?' he asked me.

'I have no idea,' I confessed. 'I don't know anything about it.'

'Let's make it easier,' said Marvin. 'Coca Cola. The company not the drink. Do you think the price of the stock is going to go up or down today? Or will it just stay the same.'

I just stared at him. I had no idea what to say.

'You have three choices,' said Marvin. 'It can go up, it can go down or it can stay where it is.'

'I don't know,' I said.

'Take a guess.'

I had no idea why Marvin was asking me this. 'Up,' I replied, for no reason at all.

Marvin picked up the telephone, dialled, spoke to someone and bought $10,000 worth of shares in Coca Cola.

'Why did you do that?' I asked him, horrified.

He just grinned at me, and levered himself to his feet. 'Wanna drink?'

'Er...,' I began, not sure what to ask for.

'You'd better have a Coke since you're one of the owners now,' he said.

'I don't have $10,000,' I said, nervously. 'I can't pay you back. What if the share price falls?'

Marvin held up a hand. 'Don't worry about it, son,' he said. He disappeared from the room.

I walked over to the window and looked out. There was a small balcony running the whole length of the room. Upon it stood a white metal table, three white metal chairs and several large pots full of plants. The park was small, neat and well kept. The building in which Marvin and Sheila had their apartment had a small garden, equally neat and well kept, which backed onto the park and was separated from it by huge, black painted, iron railings which were overgrown with ivy. There was a gate in the railings which led into the park. The brass handle shone in the remains of the day's sunshine.

'There are fourteen types of chaos in that kitchen,' murmured Marvin, handing me a glass of cola. He himself had what looked like a whisky. 'We have a maid called Louisa who comes in every day to tidy up, clean, take the washing to the laundry and so on. And we have a woman called Olivia who comes in to cook. They can't stand each other at the best of the times and at the moment they're having another one of their great rows. I have no idea what this one is about. Sheila is in there trying to stop them killing one another with our steak knives.'

'Do you think I should go?' I asked, rather nervously. I looked for somewhere to put my glass so that I could escape quickly and quietly. Marvin was a kind host but I really didn't feel as though I belonged.

'No, no!' said Marvin. 'Sheila will sort it all out. She's wonderful with these people.' I didn't know whether he was referring to French people in particular or to servants in general. 'I'll bet you whatever you like that she sorts it out within five minutes.'

I didn't know whether the bet was intended to be serious so I said nothing.

'Do you want to take the bet?' he asked me.

'I don't have any money,' I admitted.

'You must have a franc,' insisted Marvin.

I put my hand into my trouser pocket. I had a franc. But not much more. I showed the coin to Marvin. He nodded, pulled back the jacket sleeve on his left arm and showed me his watch. It was gold and looked ridiculously expensive. 'I'll bet my watch against your franc,' he said. 'It's a Patek Philippe. Worth $20,000.' He peered at it. 'Five minutes,' he said. 'OK?'

'OK,' I agreed.

'Sheila and I have been together a long time now,' he said. 'I met her in a chocolate shop near to The Ritz, where I was living at the time. She was still at school, on a weekend trip to Paris with her school. She was in the shop buying a box of chocolates for her mother but she didn't realise that the prices were for empty boxes.

They sold the chocolates individually at absurdly expensive prices. She was embarrassed when she realised this and I asked her to let me help her out. She bought the empty box and I bought the chocolates to go in it. That evening I took her and two friends to the Moulin Rouge and the next day she escaped from her teachers and spent the day with me at my hotel.'

I sipped at my cola and listened to him.

'She went back home the next day and when she finished school three months later she came back to me in Paris instead of going to University. We've been together ever since.'

'That's a beautiful, romantic story,' I told him.

Marvin leant closer to me. 'Don't tell Sheila I told you how we met,' he murmured. 'She gets embarrassed.'

'What does she get embarrassed about?' asked Sheila, who had entered the room unseen and unheard by either of us.

Marvin and I both turned round.

'Nothing, dear,' said Marvin, lying badly.

'You were telling him the chocolate box story, weren't you?'

'It's a good story,' insisted Marvin. 'And it's true.'

'It's a lovely story,' I added.

'It's embarrassing,' muttered Sheila. But I could tell that she wasn't really cross.

'Have you brokered peace in the kitchen?' asked Marvin.

'At a price,' said Sheila. 'Olivia can be very difficult. I have never known anyone jump to conclusions so quickly, to be so convinced that she is so right and yet to be so utterly, so fundamentally wrong. In the end I promised them both a bonus if they would just shut up and work together. Dinner will be ready in fifteen minutes.' She stood still and silent for a moment. 'I'm not entirely sure that they don't stage these little scenes just for me,' she said.

'Why on earth would they do that?' asked Marvin.

'Because they know I'll pay them a bonus,' said Sheila.

Marvin grinned, put his arm around her and kissed her. 'Then just pay them the bonus before they cause trouble,' he said.

'No!' said Sheila. She turned to me. 'Marvin thinks every problem on this earth can be solved or prevented with money,' she said.

'Most can,' said Marvin. He pulled up his left sleeve to expose his watch. 'Three minutes,' he said, showing me the time. I nodded, took a franc out of my pocket and handed it to him.

'Oh, you're not taking money off our guest!' said Sheila, horrified.

'Just a franc,' said Marvin.

'You have to watch him,' said Sheila to me. 'He's always gambling. He told you a story about me so I'll tell you a story about him. Do you know how he first got rich?'

Marvin, clearly knowing what was coming, laughed.

'No,' I said.

'Marvin was 24 years old. He and four other men were playing Monopoly at a hotel in New York,' said Sheila. 'They were playing Monopoly for real. They'd changed the board and named the squares after properties they actually owned. And instead of toy money they were using real money.'

'To get into the game I had $15,000 I'd borrowed from my boss,' said Marvin. 'The others were all multi-millionaires. One of them was oil rich. One had made his fortune out of silver. One was a real-estate operator. And the other guy was a casino owner.'

'And your boss didn't know about the loan,' said Sheila.

'That's true,' admitted Marvin, without shame. 'But he got it back and never knew about it so he was happy enough. I wanted to be rich. It was my best chance to get what I wanted. Some men are led by dreams – most are led by inertia. I took the initiative and made things happen for me. I'm not ashamed of that.'

'They were playing the game for real,' explained Sheila. 'The cash, the properties – everything. Marvin didn't own any property so he bet an office block in Chicago and a theatre in New York which he claimed he owned.'

'What happened?' I asked, incredulously.

'Marvin won everything,' said Sheila. 'He cleared them out.'

'$17 million in one game of Monopoly,' said Marvin. He paused and smiled his cheeky, boyish smile. 'And in those days $17 million was a hell of a lot of money.'

'What would have happened if you'd lost?' I asked him, aghast.

'For two years I woke up at night having nightmares about that,' admitted Marvin. 'The real-estate guy was 'connected' and it turned out later that the casino owner was playing with more of the Mob's money than his own. They were good about it; they regarded it as a debt of honour and paid up, but the guy I'd played with disappeared. Years later I heard that he was helping to hold up an Expressway in Detroit.'

'Oh, that's horrid,' shuddered Sheila. 'I wish you wouldn't tell people that.' She turned to me. 'Do you like the view?' she asked.

'It's beautiful,' I said. I looked around. 'It's a very luxurious apartment.'

'Better than where you're staying?' asked Sheila.

I laughed. 'It isn't luxurious like this.'

'That's twice you've used the word 'luxury',' said Marvin. 'Luxury is something you don't need, don't want and can't afford.' He waved a hand around the apartment. 'I need this, I want it and I can afford it. So it's not a luxury.' He put his head to one side, rather like a sparrow. 'Actually,' he said, 'luxury is an attitude more than anything else. It isn't expensive luggage, overpriced clothes or a large apartment. Real luxury is having the freedom to be what you want to be, where and when you want to be it, and to do what you want to do with your life. That's real freedom.' He paused. 'That's what I call real luxury.'

I thought about what he said for a moment. 'You're right,' I said. 'But for most of us that sort of luxury is utterly unattainable. We have to be content with nibbling at the other sort of luxury occasionally. And it's easier – and probably less stressful – to dream about expensive clothes and cars and apartments than it is to dream about your definition of luxury.'

'Are you doing what you want to do?' Sheila asked me.

'I was supposed to be at medical school,' I told her. 'But...'

'That's not an answer to the question,' interrupted Sheila. 'Are you doing what you want to do?'

'Some of the time,' I said, rather defensively and not a little uncomfortably.

Just then the cook appeared in the doorway. She did not speak but coughed rather loudly. We all turned.

'The meal,' the cook said. 'She is ready.'

I followed Sheila and Marvin into the dining room, a slightly smaller room than the living room but with just as high a ceiling and just as luxuriously furnished. When I noticed that there were only three place settings I asked what had happened to Archie. Sheila explained that he had had to go back to America. I never saw him again, though I am sure that I twice saw Fifi standing in a shop doorway in the rue St. Denis.

The food was simple and well cooked. As we ate Marvin kept me entertained with astonishing stories of his life. Afterwards we drank coffee in the living room. There were no liqueurs and no cigars and I was relieved rather than disappointed.

After we had eaten we returned to the living room and drank coffee, brewed by the cook and served by the maid.

'Oh, just a minute, before you go, let's see what happened to your share holding,' said Marvin. He looked at his watch. (The one that had so nearly become mine). 'The New York Stock Exchange will be closing in five minutes.' He picked up the telephone and dialled a number from memory.

Sheila fetched my coat and then she and I stood and waited while he spoke. From the kitchen I could hear the sound of a noisy argument. Sheila's brokered peace appeared to have broken down.

'You made $75,' said Marvin, after he had put down the telephone. 'What's that in toy town money?' he asked Sheila.

'Around 375 French Francs,' said Sheila. She turned to me. 'He's supposed to be a financial genius,' she said. 'But he still can't remember that there are five francs to the dollar.'

Marvin took out his wallet, removed four 100 franc notes and handed them to me.

'I can't take this!' I told him.

'I just gave you your first lesson in finance,' said Marvin. 'There are tens of thousands, probably millions, of investors and professional investment advisers who think they know whether Coca Cola shares are going to go up or down. You know nothing. But you beat most of them tonight. When you've got money and someone tells you that such and such a share is going up or going down remember what happened here today.'

'I can't take it,' I told him, trying to give him back the notes.

'Of course you can,' insisted Marvin. 'It's money you made on the stock market.'

With genuine reluctance I put the notes into my pocket. 'I should be paying you for the lesson,' I told him.

'You should,' said Marvin. 'And one day maybe you will.' He thought of something. 'Here's something else for you to remember,' he said. 'Whenever you sell something – and can think of a valid reason why you should be selling it – there is someone out there who can think of a valid reason for buying what you're selling. All you have to decide is who is wrong.' He grinned at me, pleased with himself. I tried to look interested, though to be honest I was not. At the time I thought the advice he was giving was boring and rather stupid. Nevertheless I wrote it all down when I got back to my hotel room that evening.

I kissed Sheila, shook hands with Marvin, walked back through the streets of Paris and went back to my hotel room.

The next morning, out of curiosity, I checked out the price of Coca Cola shares in a copy of an American newspaper which I purchased from a street vendor.

Coca Cola shares had gone down – not up – in price.

After that I thought that I perhaps understood Marvin a little better.

Marvin and Sheila were very rich and had all the freedom in the world.

But I realised that they were also rather lonely.

Chapter 23

I met Marvin and Sheila quite often after that; sometimes in unexpected places.

One day I met them in a café in Montmartre.

Marvin liked the seediness of the area around the Moulin Rouge and often went there to a cheap tourist café on the Place Clichy.

There were two billiard tables in a dimly lit back room and sometimes he played a game or two of billiards. Occasionally, Marvin would hustle a couple of the locals. He would pretend to be an ignorant American who didn't know which end of the cue to hold and would walk out an hour later with a pocket full of bills.

'Do you like our apartment?' he asked me.

'Yes, of course I do,' I answered. I was used to him suddenly changing the subject, and suddenly asking deeply invasive questions.

'By comparison the place where you're staying is pretty rough isn't it?'

'Yes.'

'Does that worry you?'

'No. Not really. If I could afford to stay somewhere better I would. But...' I shrugged my shoulders.

Marvin slapped me on the shoulder. 'Wise man' he said. 'Keep your needs and your wants below your achievements and you'll always be rich and happy.'

Puzzled, I looked at him. 'I thought needs and wants were much the same thing,' I said.

'Completely different,' said Marvin, shaking his head. 'I need a roof over my head. But I want silk sheets and room service. Do you see the difference?'

I admitted that I did.

'I can give you two tips about money,' he said. 'First, don't ever worry about what other people have. Just be content with what you have and make sure that you get what you deserve. Do you understand what I mean?'

'Not entirely,' I admitted.

'A chap I know works for a television company. He reads the news. He's always moaning about the fact that he earns less than two of the guys he knows at other TV stations. It really eats him up. Now this guy gets paid a small fortune. All he has to do is to be able to sit down and to read at the same time. It's hardly demanding work. Approximately 99% of the population could do his job just as well as he can. But instead of feeling grateful for his lot in life he chews himself up over the fact that he earns a few thousand dollars less than these other two punks. Now do you see what I mean?'

'Yes.'

Marvin waved a finger. 'Good lesson,' he said. 'Remember it. Worry about what you're getting, not about what the other guy is getting. Learn to be content with what you're getting and let the other guy worry about what he's getting.'

I smiled and nodded.

'Second lesson,' said Marvin. 'As soon as you start earning put some cash away in a freedom fund. Don't touch it. Leave it there. Build it up. That's the secret of happiness.'

'What on earth is a 'freedom fund'?'

'A pile of cash that enables you to say 'no' when someone wants you to do something you don't want to do,' said Marvin. 'If you've got a 'freedom fund' you can always walk away from anything you don't want to do.' Marvin wagged a finger at me and grinned. 'That's real freedom,' he said. 'You can't be free unless you've got a 'freedom fund'.' He leant closer. 'And do you know something really curious?' he said. 'When you've got a 'freedom fund', and other people know you've got one, you hardly ever have to say 'no'.'

'What else are you intending to do with your time?' asked Sheila.

'I'm writing a novel,' I said. 'I started it a little while ago.'

'Oh how wonderful!' said Sheila. 'Will you base any characters on us?'

'Of course.'

Chapter 24

When I arrived at the café Claudette was already sitting there.

'I'm sorry,' I said. 'Am I late?'

'No,' she said. 'I was early. I just had to get out of the apartment,' said Claudette. 'I could not stay there one minute longer.' She was drinking vodka. 'We have a friend of my husband's staying with us.' It always surprised me when Claudette mentioned her husband. I sometimes forgot that she lived with him. I also conveniently forgot that she still loved him. 'He is an artist and a very pretentious one. We put him into the big attic room because he said he wanted to do some work. It is a beautiful airy room with wonderful light. This morning there was a huge row. He has been working on a collage which he had been putting together on the floor – twigs, bits of paper, leaves and all sorts of dead and dried flowers and grasses. Madame Thenaud who cleans the house for us went into his room yesterday when he was out, swept up his work of art and threw it all away. She put it all out with the rubbish – in with the old bits of cabbage and bone. He did not get in last night until after three in the morning. He stumbled into bed drunk and didn't see what had happened until he got up for breakfast this morning. When he realised that his great work of art had been stolen he came down the stairs quite naked screaming and shouting for the police. It took me ten minutes to quieten him down enough to find out what had happened.' She laughed. 'I know I should be more understanding,' she said. 'But it was truly

very funny. He has a skinny white body and a very small thing.'
She laughed again and finished her vodka. 'Enough!' she cried.
'You cannot walk on tiptoes all your life.'

I looked at her. 'Your grandfather?'

'My grandfather,' she agreed. She emptied her vodka glass.
'Now.' she said firmly. 'Have you ever been to Père Lachaise?'

I shook my head. 'I've never even heard of him,' I admitted.

'It's a place not a him,' explained Claudette. 'A cemetery.
Today, I will take you there,' she announced, firmly. 'We will put
flowers on my grandmother's grave.'

We took a taxi to Père Lachaise and bought flowers at a
shop near the cemetery gate. We spent half an hour and, I suspect,
a small fortune in the florist's shop. Claudette spoke quickly
and with a resigned look on her face to a portly and rather bad-
tempered looking assistant. 'I told her that I thought it would be
impossible for her to find me two dozen yellow roses,' Claudette
whispered to me, as the woman disappeared into the back of the
shop. 'The first word a French baby learns is 'Non'. The first full
sentence is 'It is not possible.' So if I had asked if the woman had
two dozen yellow roses she would have taken great delight in saying 'Non'. But because I put the question the other way it is now
her joy to disappoint me by finding the roses. Being contrary will
enable her to retain face but it will mean that I get the flowers I
want.'

Moments later the assistant reappeared clutching a huge
vase filled with yellow roses. Claudette carefully picked out
two dozen. And then she had them wrapped into a huge and
impressive looking bouquet.

I had only ever been to two cemeteries in Britain but I had
driven past a few and to me they had all looked much the same.
Sad, neat rows of grey headstones stretching as far as the eye
could see. I did not expect Père Lachaise to be any different, or to
be in the slightest bit romantic.

I was wrong. Very wrong. Père Lachaise was like nothing I
had ever seen before. And in its unique way it was one of the most
romantic places I had ever visited.

'Is this just for French people?' I asked.

'It is for the people of Paris. The people who lived and died here. They did not have to be French.' She pulled a face and shrugged. 'People make too much fuss of nationality. Where you were born does not matter as much as who you are and what you are.' She paused in front of a tramp, sleeping on the pavement, and opened her bag and her purse. I expected her to take out a few coins. Instead she took out a large note, folded it and gently slipped it into his inside jacket pocket. The tramp did not even stir. 'The most notorious German did not come from Germany. He came from Austria. Napolean, the most famous Frenchman of all time was a Corsican.' She paused. 'Actually,' she said, 'lots of famous Frenchmen weren't French at all. Georges Simenon, the inventor of Maigret was born in Belgium. Picasso was born in Spain. Would it have really made any difference if General de Gaulle had been born in Portugal?'

We put the flowers on Claudette's grandmother's grave and knelt together while Claudette said a prayer. After we had left the graveside I looked back to see two youths picking up the bouquet, still in its cellophane wrapper. I started to run towards them but Claudette stopped me.

'It doesn't matter,' she called, with a smile.

'But they are stealing your grandmother's flowers.'

'She does not need them,' said Claudette, with unarguable logic. 'A tree with no branches does not need a trunk.'

'But...'

'It is only the giving that matters,' explained Claudette, with a smile. 'The rest is irrelevant. We brought my grandmother flowers because it made me feel good. Choosing the roses and putting them on her grave made me remember how much she enjoyed that colour. She always wore something yellow. Every day of her life. What does it matter if the flowers now go to bring some happiness to another person? The only reason for them to continue to be there is to impress other people but what does it matter what others think? The giving was the moment – why should we care about the views of people we don't know?'

She could see that I still did not understand.

'Do you ever go to church and light a candle for a friend or relative who has passed on?'

'No. I'm not Catholic.'

'You do not have to be Catholic,' she said. 'You should do it sometime. You will find, I think, that it will give you a moment of grace. But when you light a candle it is the thought not the deed which counts. It does not matter if the candle goes out a minute later. In spirit, once it is lit that candle never goes out.'

I suddenly remembered something from my childhood. I nodded.

'You understand?'

'Yes. I think so.'

'You have thought of something?'

'Yes. Just a silly thought.' I felt embarrassed.

'Tell me.'

'No, no. It was just something silly. Childish.'

She put her arm around mine and looked up at me, expectantly.

'I just remembered making a sandcastle when I was a boy,' I said. 'I thought it was the best sandcastle in the world. And when I had finished it I stood and watched as the sea came in and destroyed it. For a while I tried to build walls to protect it. But I could see there was no point. I was bound to lose. So I stood and watched the castle disappear. And in a way that made it pure and complete. There was a beginning and an end to the moment and that made it strangely perfect. No critics. No one else even saw it. I think I remembered that moment because before I never really understood it.'

Claudette squeezed my arm and we walked on through Père Lachaise in the growing winter gloom.

We sat in a café opposite to the florist's. The café was small, dark, full of atmosphere and patronised largely by students. Nearly everyone wore black and had shoulder length hair. (I knew that it was a café for intellectuals when I visited the subterranean *pissoir* and read the graffiti. 'Gertrude Stein was here, here, here' was my favourite.)

'This is a nice café,' said Claudette. 'I always come here

when I visit grandmother. At ten o'clock every morning one of the waiters fetches a blind man from his apartment two hundred yards away. At ten every evening another waiter takes the blind man back home. They have done this for nearly twenty years. And the blind man buys just one or maybe two glasses of wine all day and eats nothing but a sandwich for his lunch.'

'Let me try to order,' I begged Claudette. When the waiter came I spoke, slowly and with some difficulty, in French. 'I suppose it would be impossible to have a pot of tea for two?'

The waiter grinned at me. 'It would not be at all impossible,' he said in perfect English, and disappeared into the kitchen.

Claudette smiled.

'You see', I said, 'I am learning.'

'You are a good student,' she replied.

'Does your husband ever come here with you?' I asked her.

'Oh no,' said Claudette. 'Never. He never does anything useful or practical. And he is very lazy. I had to go away to Lyon to look after my mother last year,' she said. 'She'd had an operation and I was away from home for three weeks. When I got back to Paris the sink was full of dirty crockery and cutlery. He had used up every plate, every cup and every knife, fork and spoon in the apartment. They were disgusting. The food was dried...ugh. He had even gone out to the store nearby and bought another dozen plates and another dozen cups and more spoons and so on. They too were all dirty and in the sink. When both the sinks were full he had finally run out of things to use he had started eating all his meals in cafés.'

'What did you do?'

'I got a huge rubbish sack and threw away every piece of crockery and cutlery. I made him go out to the shop and buy new ones.'

I laughed. 'What did he say?'

'He did as he was told. He knew he had been naughty.'

'You make him sound like a child.'

'He is not like a child. He is a child.'

Chapter 25

I was beginning to feel more and more like a Parisian and less and less like a tourist. Although I still spoke very poor French I was learning to know my way around the city. I had my favourite seats in a dozen cafés including Deux Magots, Le Dome and the Café Flore. I was beginning to find my way through the maze of arcades, alleyways and passageways which criss-cross the city.

I was learning a little about life too. I was learning something about myself (mostly about how much I did not know or understand). But, most of all, I was learning a great deal about Parisian cafés.

Good cafés are serene and time stands still the moment you enter through the door. The world, and all its hideous technicolour problems, must stay outside. You can see (and do) just about anything in a Parisian café.

Walking to the Café Napoleon, one of my favourite Parisian cafés, I strode a little faster than usual in order to help work off the calories of a long and leisurely picnic lunch in the Jardin de Luxembourg. I was due to meet Claudette later.

When I arrived I shook hands with the waiter and apologised for being slightly out of breath. Cool and immaculate in his black suit and crisp white pinafore he looked at me sternly. 'You shouldn't hurry!' he told me. He nodded towards the street outside, alive with bustling pedestrians and horn-tooting motorists. 'Relax and enjoy the passing show.'

I took his advice, ordered a Ricard, and sat down to enjoy another afternoon which I might otherwise have wasted in fruitful endeavour. I had the notebook with me in which I was writing my novel. I thought I might later manage to complete a few more pages while I waited for Claudette.

I sipped my Ricard and watched the raindrops racing one another down the window pane. The pavement outside was thick with fashion designers, fashion journalists and models scurrying from theatre to hotel to couture house. The traffic was terrible and the only way to get about quickly was on foot. Everywhere I looked, expensive hair styles were being protected underneath huge umbrellas.

I sat that day and watched a real life drama unfold in front of my eyes.

When they arrived in the café they had clearly just met. He was about 45 and a Professor at an American university. She was about 20 and a student at a local college. He wore jeans and a sweater and had an impish smile. She wore a short skirt and a mohair jumper and had long legs and short blonde hair. They ate, drank and talked. They talked mostly about her boyfriend. They agreed that he was a heel and that she should leave him.

I ordered another drink. Sat, watched and listened. At five o'clock the waiters changed shifts. I paid the one going off duty and ordered a pot of tea and a sandwich from the waiter starting his shift.

They drank coffee, they smoked cigarettes. He lent her his lighter. When she handed it back their fingers touched. He held her hand. Their heads fell closer and their voices dropped. He joked a little, she giggled a lot. Her face and voice were both full of 'yes'. By six they had kissed and were sitting side by side. He had his arm around her waist. He told her he had to catch a flight back to America. He promised to telephone. By seven he had asked her to go back to America with him. By eight she had agreed to leave college, buy a plane ticket and go back with him. He confessed he was married but told her the marriage was over and that he would get a divorce. She promised to wait for him. By nine they were trying to decide where to live. She wanted a cottage in the country; somewhere with a log fire and a small stream. He wanted an apartment in town. They argued a little. By one in the morning the argument had built into a row. He took his arm from around her waist and they moved apart. At half past ten she stood up, tears running down her cheeks, and told him she never wanted to see him again. She left. He ordered brandy. A complete romance from start to finish. In one evening. No need for lawyers, no time for recriminations.

Only in Paris, I thought.

'There is a telephone call for you, sir,' murmured the waiter quietly. 'At the desk.'

I followed him to the desk, assuming and hoping that the caller would be Claudette. When the receptionist handed me the receiver I was delighted to find that Claudette was on the other end.

'I'm so sorry, my dear,' she said. 'I could not get away tonight.'

'Are you OK?' I asked.

'I'm fine. But Gerard – my husband – had one of his crises today. He insisted that he was not going to perform tonight. His manager, his agent and the director of the play were all here. He was threatening to leave the house, the city and the country. He said he was going to fly to China. I have no idea why. Sometimes I think he is completely mad. I had to persuade him to stay.'

'You succeeded?'

'Eventually.' Claudette sounded tired. 'I had to go to the theatre with him.'

'Good.'

'I'm sorry,' said Claudette. 'I was so very much looking forward to seeing you.'

'Me too.'

She must have been alone in the room for she blew me a kiss. I blew one back and told her that I loved her.

'Please don't say that,' she said.

'But it's true,' I said. 'Do you love me?'

'I will see you on Friday.'

'Say that you love me.'

'Don't be so silly.'

'Say it.'

'Someone may hear.'

'Say it or I will never put the telephone down and the manageress will call the police and have me arrested. I will plead insanity and you will have to find a doctor before they will let me out.'

Claudette sighed. 'I love you.'

'I love you too.'

The line went dead. I thanked the telephonist, paid my bill and walked back to my hotel.

I had never before told a woman that I loved her. Equally importantly, no woman had ever told me that she loved me.

Chapter 26

I plucked up courage one day to ask Marvin why he never made any attempt to speak French. It seemed strange to me that an obviously intelligent man who had spent several decades of his life living in French speaking countries appeared unable to utter a single word of French. Only once had I ever heard him speak any French at all. 'Mercy bow coup', he had once said, with a big smile to a waiter.

'I tried for several years,' he explained. 'I bought books and I went to three language schools.' But in the end I decided that there's no point in trying to learn French unless you're prepared to invest enough time to become very good at it.'

'The trouble is,' explained Marvin, 'that the French love criticising foreigners who try to speak their language. However hard I tried they would always delight in making me feel like a fool. If you pronounce a word one way they take great pleasure in pretending not to understand and then take great delight in telling you how it should be pronounced. Then, if you remember and try to use what you now think is the correct pronunciation they pretend not to understand and then tell you that you should have pronounced it the way you were pronouncing it in the first place.'

'And, if I thought I had understood a few sentences, the person I was speaking to would slip in a difficult word, a proverb or a few words of French argot just to make me realise how little I really understood.'

'They do this because the words the average Frenchman loves to hear most are *je ne comprends pas*. He regards this confession of ignorance as a licence to treat you like a complete idiot.'

I smiled.

'So,' said Marvin. 'I have discovered that speaking English gives me the edge. Best of all it enables me to treat the French as stupid for not speaking English.' He grinned at me.

'But you do understand some French?' I asked him.

'I understand a bit more than anyone thinks I do,' said Marvin, with a wink.

'I suppose that can be quite an advantage?'

Marvin just grinned at me.

Chapter 27

Theresa Wurtz was my second student. I did not know it at the time but she would turn out to be my only other student, apart from Jules.

We met at a café near her apartment. I carried a copy of *The Times*. She wore a lime green skirt, with a split which very nearly reached her waist and a white lace trimmed blouse which had a very low cut neck. She was wearing pink shoes with five inch heels. Her hair was perfect, her make-up immaculate, her nails freshly manicured and she smelt strongly of very expensive perfume. She terrified the life out of me.

'Hello,' she said. Her smile widened by another centimetre. She could have given a politician lessons in smiling.

There was another pause, plenty long enough for Leo Tolstoy to have tossed off one of those thick, two volume novels and probably cut the lawn as well.

'Do you like art?' she asked. 'Art is the most important thing in the world, don't you agree? So many people waste their lives. They collect postage stamps, listen to Elvis Presley, try to grow the biggest dahlias in their neighbourhood, practise aromatherapy or spend their weekends putting the spots on the trains.'

'Putting spots on trains?' I said, more than a trifle confused.

'I once went out with an English man who did this for his pleasure,' said Theresa, acknowledging with a scornful facial expression that it seemed to her an odd thing for a grown man to do. 'Every Saturday morning he would put on his anorak, make himself a flask of tea and head for the local railway station with his battered old notebook. There he would write down the numbers of all the trains he saw. A grown man! Can you believe such a thing?'

'Ah,' I said, rather relieved and understanding. 'He was a trainspotter.'

'Exactly!' said Theresa, pleased that I had understood at last. 'He put the spots on the trains. All these people – the stamp collector, the dahlia grower, the train spotter – are avoiding contact with the most important thing in life. Eventually they discover that these things do not matter one little damn. But by then, pfui, they are dead and they have wasted their lives on them.' She looked up at me. 'I am not driving down that particular street again!' she said, emphatically. 'Once smitten twice shy!' I said nothing.

'Paris is full of exciting art this week,' she said, breathless with excitement. 'Would you like to come and see some with me? You can give me my lesson as we look and listen and educate ourselves in the arts.'

Feigning enthusiasm I said I would.

'Wonderful!' said Theresa. She took hold of my arm as though anxious to anchor herself to something dull, solid and stable and dragged me towards the door. Maybe she was worried that I might be so overcome with excitement that I would run away. I wasn't overcome with excitement but I certainly wanted to run away. Indeed, I kept trying to think of ways to escape.

'We are this week spoiled for choices. We have a choice between a ballet, an exhibition of *lavage* and *repassage* at the Comedie Française and a display of brassières,' said Theresa as we clattered down the stairs. The stairs were too narrow for us to walk side by side and so Theresa led and I followed. 'Or maybe we could be greedy and go to all three!' she said.

'Aren't there any painting exhibitions?' I asked, hesitantly and trying hard to hide my disappointment. 'Or photography exhibitions?'

Theresa, paused for a moment, looked up at me, made a

rude snorting noise and screwed up her face. 'Those are not real arts,' she said, dismissively. 'If we see a photograph which is particularly realistic we say it is like a painting. If we see a good painting we will say it looks like a photograph. How can this be pure art? When you see a pair of shoes you do not say that they look like a hat or a pair of gloves, do you?'

Slightly confused I agreed with her. It seemed easier than trying to argue. Indeed, it seemed easier than trying to understand her. 'Tell me more about them,' I said. I harboured slight reservations about the exhibition which sounded about as much fun as a visit to the local launderette.

'The theme of the ballet is very modern,' said Theresa. 'The planet is dying and only a small group of human beings have survived. Before leaving earth on board a rocket they dance on their own soil for one last time. A friend of mine who saw it said it was both moving and poignant.'

'And the exhibition at the Comedie Française?' I asked, thinking that it couldn't possibly be less promising than the ballet which, despite her friend's approval, sounded even less attractive than the idea of watching someone else's washing go round and round.

'It is an exhibition of *lavage et repassage*,' said Theresa. She thought hard for a moment, searching for the English words. 'Washing and ironing,' she said at last, though I had already recognised the words. 'Have you heard of such a thing before?' I admitted that I had not. 'It is so original,' she said delightedly. 'And as a bonus there is a display of ironing provided by an expert ironer from the Comedie Française.'

I laughed, thinking that Theresa was joking. My laughter did not go down well for, sadly for both of us, she wasn't. 'So shall we go to the washing and ironing exhibition?' she asked, when she had recovered. 'It is close enough to walk.'

'OK.' I said. It occurred to me that the ironing display might perhaps be some sort of comedy. But, then again, Theresa did not seem to be over endowed with a sense of humour.

'Good,' said Theresa. 'I adore clothes, don't you?' she said, with a big sigh.

Tactfully, I agreed that without clothes life would be much the poorer and that we would, at the very least, suffer from fearful goose bumps and constantly face charges of indecent exposure.

'Ballet is good as far as it goes but it is clothes designers who are the only real artists left in our modern world,' said Theresa, ignoring the traffic streaming by and leaping out into the middle of the road. 'I am a shoe designer by instinct. That is where my true talents lie,' she called over her shoulder. 'When I have found the money I need I will open a shoe shop. I will call it The Shoepermarket.' Nervously, I hurried after her, miraculously managing to avoid the traffic and catching up with her just as she reached the safety of the opposite pavement. Two children on roller skates missed us by inches and reminded me that safety, like most things, is always relative. Being on the pavement might have been safer than crossing the road but it was still a lot less safe than staying in bed.

'If none of us wore clothes the authorities would have to repeal all the laws relating to indecent exposure, wouldn't they?'

Theresa looked at me quizzically.

'Clothes are important,' I said, keen to make some sort of contribution to the conversation. 'If there weren't any clothes the police would patrol in the nude and the judges would also be in the nude. They could hardly try someone for wandering around in the nude if they weren't wearing any clothes themselves, could they?'

Theresa looked at me with new respect.

'Have you designed any shoes?' I asked her.

'Of course,' she said. 'I have been designing shoes and lingerie since I was six.'

I looked down at her feet. 'Did you design those?' I asked. I had never really thought about people designing shoes. I had always rather supposed that shoe manufacturers simply grabbed a piece of material, tossed it onto a shoe making machine and picked the completed shoes out of the hopper at the other end of the conveyor belt. Apart from making sure that the heel was at the back and the toe at the front I had never really thought there was anything about a shoe that required much in the way of creative input. If I had thought about it at all I would have probably imagined that the extent of artistic input was sitting down in a dark room with a bottle of stout and struggling to decide whether to make the brown shoes on Mondays and Thursdays and the black ones on Tuesdays, Wednesdays and Fridays or the black ones on Mondays, Tuesdays and Wednesdays and the brown ones on Thursdays and Fridays.

'Good heavens, no!' cried Theresa, looking down with a visible shudder. 'Actually none of my designs have yet been made into shoes,' she admitted, somehow succeeding in making it clear by the tone of her voice that this was a reflection on the shoe manufacturing industry rather than her shoe designing skills. 'The world of fashion is a closed shop. Only those who are already established get an opportunity to display their skills to the full. I am putting my best feet forward but without success.'

'That's very unfair,' I said.

'I am also a bra designer,' she told me.

I looked at her in astonishment. As with shoes I had not realised that there was much opportunity here for designers to make their mark.

'I believe that the designer of brassières has a unique opportunity to bring together and offer up the essence of woman-hood,' said Theresa. 'The brassière is a synonym for all that is good and honest in our world.'

I looked at her and tried to look convinced.

'When we have finished with the laundry display we shall go to the exhibition of the bras, yes? It is in the Marais.'

Chapter 28

We watched the ironing and we looked at the bras. Then we had coffee and walked. To my relief, Theresa decided that we should leave the ballet for another day.

Half way down a narrow passageway she stopped suddenly. Since she was holding my hand at the time I stopped too. I was not particularly surprised to see that we had stopped outside a shoe shop.

'Look at those!' said my companion. She spoke quietly, in a reverential whisper, as though we had been in church, and pointed to something in the window. I followed her arm, her hand and her finger expecting to find myself looking at something exceptional; a pair of Fabergé eggs, perhaps. Instead I found myself looking at a pair of black shoes. Each shoe had a heel, a toe and a space inside to put a foot. Neither individually nor collectively did they look exceptional.

'Are they not truly beautiful?' she demanded, still in a whisper.

'Very nice,' I agreed. I looked to see if there was a price. There wasn't. 'Are you going to try them on?'

Theresa looked at me. 'Are you sure?'

I looked at her, puzzled. It seemed an odd thing to say. 'Why not?' I asked her.

She stood on tiptoes and kissed me on the cheek. 'You are too kind,' she said.

I suddenly went cold as I realised that Theresa seemed to have assumed that I was offering to buy her the shoes. Before I could think of a way to replace this misapprehension with the truth Theresa headed for the shop doorway, dragging me behind her. I could only hope (and it was a forlorn hope) that the absence of a price tag on the shoes did not bode too badly.

If I see a decent looking Harris Tweed sports jacket in a shop window I can pretty well guarantee that when I totter in and enquire whether or not they have the item in my size the assistant will wander off, hunt around in the stock room for twenty minutes or so and then return, invariably in a rather bad temper, and tell me that they don't have my size in the item in which I have expressed an interest but that they can manage something twice the price in a purple silk in a similar sort of size.

Naturally, however, they had the shoes which had caught Theresa's eye in her size. Indeed, the very shoes in the window fitted her as though they had been made for her.

'Would you like me to fit these little bows at the backs of the shoes?' asked the assistant, when Theresa had expressed her approval and confirmed that, as an alternative to paying off the Mexican national debt, we would be purchasing the shoes. The assistant spoke perfect English. She showed Theresa two tiny little black bows.

'Oh yes, how wonderful!' said Theresa. 'They are divine. They absolutely make the shoes!'

The assistant dutifully fitted the two little black bows to the backs of the shoes. 'Would you like some insoles?' asked the assistant. She held up a packet containing something which looked remarkably like a pair of cheap insoles – the sort which are marketed to people who have smelly feet and sensitive neighbours. 'We do recommend these very special insoles to all our customers,' she said. 'They are impregnated with diotixism crystals which may reduce internal wear and extend the life of a shoe by up to 12.4 hours.'

'Oh yes, I think so,' said Theresa. She turned to me. 'Don't you agree, my darling? It would be silly not to look after a pair of shoes as beautiful as these are.'

I nodded, as it is the custom of well brought up men to do under these circumstances, and reached for my wallet, hoping that we could conclude the transaction and escape from the shop before the assistant had any more bright ideas. But it was not to be. The assistant was a very fountain of good ideas. All of them expensive.

'You will want the non-slip soles, of course,' said the assistant. She held up a pair of rubber non-slip soles for us to examine and then, before we had chance to demur, slipped them dextrously into the shoe box.

'And a tube of our special nutrient polish? It is patented, prepared in our laboratories in the Loire and specially prepared to feed the leather on these shoes.'

'Oh yes.'

I felt safe in assuming that any shoe polish patented and prepared in laboratories in the Loire would cost rather more than the ordinary run-of-the-mill polish I was accustomed to ladling onto my brogues. Circumstances would, in due course, confirm that my assumption was an accurate one.

'And naturally you would like one of our patented applicators.'

'Oh yes, thank you.'

'We also have these beautiful silk stockings in stock,' continued the assistant, now apparently anxious to off-load the entire stock of the shop. 'They have a delightful motif at the back of the calf which will draw attention to madam's beautiful legs and which will, at the same time, highlight the bows at the back of madam's shoes.' She took a pack of the aforementioned stockings from a rack behind her and held it expectantly above the shoes (and their added bows), the uniquely patented polish, the non-slip soles, the special applicator and, of course, the ridiculously over-priced inner soles.

Theresa looked at me, expectantly.

'Of course,' I agreed wearily, almost too exhausted to care. Penury was beckoning. The assistant added the stockings to the expensive looking leaning tower of consumables balanced on the counter next to the shop till.

'And would madam like a new bag to match her new shoes?'

asked the assistant, pointing to a far corner of the shop where there was a display of handbags. Henry Ford would have been delighted. They had every colour under the sun as long as you wanted black. I looked at my watch and said I had to go soon.

The assistant added up the purchases and gave me the bill. Ashen faced I handed over the requisite number of notes and, in return, received a huge, fancy carrier bag. Just a few minutes before my wallet had been reassuringly plump. Now it was as skinny as a fashion model.

'You speak very good English,' I told the assistant, perhaps rather patronisingly.

'Thank you,' she replied drily. 'I'm from Cirencester.'

Shortly afterwards Theresa hailed a taxi. She thanked me and left.

Only when she'd gone did I realise that she hadn't paid for the lesson. I also realised that even if she had paid I would have still have been considerably out of pocket.

I never saw her again.

Chapter 29

Claudette and I were sitting in a park at the back of Les Invalides watching tourists coming to pay their respects to Napoleon Bonaparte.

'He was a great man, you know,' said Claudette. 'A very considerate and thoughtful man.'

I watched two pigeons fighting over a small piece of bread.

'Have you noticed how the roads of France have trees planted along the edges?'

I said I had.

'Napoleon started that,' said Claudette. 'He planted the trees so that his army would have shade when they were marching.' She looked at me, with pride. 'That shows forward planning and confidence, does it not?'

I agreed that it did.

A sparrow swooped down, picked up the bread and flew away. For a few moments the pigeons did not realise what had happened. They carried on fighting over the bread which had gone.

'Has your friend Jules fixed you up with any more women?' asked Claudette.

'He has,' I admitted, feeling rather embarrassed.

'Were they terribly pretty?'

'No.'

'Were any of them prettier than me?'

'No. Certainly not.'

'Good.'

'Do you have any more students?'

'Just one. But it wasn't very successful, from my point of view.'

'A man or a woman?'

'A woman.'

'Ah. Did you do something interesting together?'

'She took me to an exhibition. Actually, we went to two exhibitions.'

'Two exhibitions? You see, Paris is full of exhibitions. It is a very artistic city. To which exhibitions did she take you?'

'The first was an exhibition of washing and ironing,' I told Claudette. She looked at me. For a moment she tried not to laugh. Then she laughed. 'I'm sorry,' she apologised. 'Was it fascinating?'

'Oh absolutely,' I said. 'We watched a woman wash some clothes by hand. And then she ironed two shirts and a nightdress.'

'She ironed two shirts?'

'She was quite slow but very thorough.'

Claudette covered her mouth and struggled to suppress a laugh. 'It must have been, er...'

'Very boring?' I said, helpfully.

'Oh no, I'm sure it wasn't.'

'It was. It was very boring.'

'Yes. Well I suppose it might have been quite boring.'

I sighed. 'No. It was not quite boring, it was very boring. To be honest it was probably the most boring thing I've ever seen.'

'And the other exhibition?'

'Ah, well that, I confess, wasn't quite so boring.'

'No?'

'No. It was an exhibition of bras.'

'Bras?'

'Bras.'

'The thing a woman wears to, er...,' Claudette hesitated. She made a supporting gesture with her hands in front of her body. 'For her breasts? *Le soutien-gorge*?'

'That's right,' I agreed.

'An exhibition of bras?'

'A whole exhibition of bras.'

'Just bras?'

'Just bras.'

'How, er, absolutely unusual. Was that her idea?'

'She wants to be a bra designer.'

'Ah. A woman of hidden talents.'

'Yes.'

'I've never met a bra designer. Not knowingly anyway.'

'I can't imagine there can be too many of them around.'

'Actually,' said Claudette, 'I never really thought of bras as being designed at all. Isn't that silly? I mean, they obviously are designed by someone. But I suppose I just rather thought that they just sort of, well got made, in some sort of natural way without too much interference from designers.'

'Like shoes?'

'Like shoes.'

'There were some very strange bras in the exhibition.'

'What sort of things?'

'Well, they had a bra that was supposed to be the biggest in the world. I seem to remember that it belonged to an Italian woman who was married to a Mafia mobster.'

'I hope they washed it before they put it on display.'

'I'm sure they did.' I said. 'There was also a bra with taps on and a bra fitted with candle holders.'

'These I have not seen in the shops.'

'No, I suppose not.'

'And do you think that going to the bra exhibition was the starting point for a beautiful friendship?'

'No. I don't think so. Not really.'

'Oh,' said Claudette. 'What a pity.' She grinned at me.

'You're pleased that it was a disaster, aren't you?'

'No, of course I'm not,' said Claudette. 'I'm very sorry for you.' She laughed out loud. 'She took you to a display of ironing? And to an exhibition of bras?'

'Yes.'

Claudette laughed so much that the people at the next table turned round and stared at us.

'These things happen to me,' I said.

'It could have happened to anyone,' said Claudette. 'You just happened to be in the wrong place at the right time.'

'But it didn't happen to anyone,' I pointed out. 'It happened to me.' I paused and scratched my head thoughtfully. 'Odd things always seem to happen to me.'

'Then you should become a writer,' said Claudette. 'You would have a permanent supply of material for your stories.'

'I have started a book,' I confessed.

We sat in silence for a while. Just long enough for Rembrandt to have knocked off a couple of paintings and filled in his annual tax forms.

'You did not tell me.'

'I felt embarrassed. Do you think I could be a writer?'

There was another short silence. This was shorter. Van Gogh would have been pushed to paint a small bunch of sunflowers.

'Can you write?' asked Claudette.

I thought about it.

'I don't know.'

'Then there is only one thing for it,' said Claudette.

'What's that?'

'You must keep trying,' she said. 'And you must remember that disappointment is the mustard that makes success taste better.'

'Grandfather?'

'Of course.'

We sat in silence again.

'Did you know that Napoleon designed the Italian flag?' she asked me.

I admitted that I had not known this.

Chapter 30

Every time Jules tried to fix me up with one of his spare dates I tried to avoid the obligation.

But he usually won.

Isabella Petiet was one of the women I met on his behalf.

I arrived in the area close to her apartment three quarters of an hour early and found the café where I was supposed to meet her. It was called Le Petit Zinc. In Paris there is always a convenient café to sit in and it is often called Le Petit Zinc.

The café was full when I arrived but as I walked in an elderly man and his wife got up. He was wearing a blue raincoat and a blue beret. She was wearing a pale blue raincoat and a rain hood. Before they left it was she who took out her purse and counted coins into the saucer. At the doorway she fussed over him, making sure that his scarf was properly wrapped around his neck and that his coat was properly buttoned. The old man did not seem to mind being mothered. I got the impression that if he had ever objected to the fussing it must have been a long time ago. I sat down and ordered a small beer.

As soon as I sat down I realised, to my annoyance, that there were two women sitting at the table in front of me. They were involved in an earnest and quite noisy conversation.

The waiter had delivered my beer and I had taken the first sip when a man suddenly collapsed onto the chair opposite me, putting a cup of coffee onto the table with something of a clatter. He then quickly dropped a folded newspaper and a black leather notebook onto the table beside the coffee cup. I looked up. The newcomer, who had dropped so many of his possessions onto what I had already considered to be my table, was a man who seemed to be in his forties or fifties. He was tall, slightly overweight and had a mass of thick, grey, shoulder length hair. He also had amazingly piercing, pale blue eyes. He leant across the table and said something to me in French. Naturally, I did not understand. He then switched to English. 'Do you mind if I am sat at your table?' he whispered.

Being English I lied and told him that I did not mind.

'I am fascinated by the conversation of these two women,' whispered the newcomer, using his right hand to indicate the two women sitting behind him.

I stared at him, surprised at his strange confession.

'You mean you want to eavesdrop?' I whispered back.

'Absolutely.'

'But isn't that rude?'

'Of course, it is very rude,' he shrugged. 'But I am a writer. And I could not properly hear them from where I was sitting.' He leant back, opened his notebook, took a pen from his pocket, held a finger to his lips to tell me to be quiet, and started writing. He did not seem to be in the slightest bit embarrassed. I sipped my beer, watched him and wondered whether or not I should say something. To eavesdrop casually was one thing, but to do it deliberately, cold-bloodedly, seemed different. What would I say? And to whom? I quickly decided to say nothing. Instead, I too found myself eavesdropping on the two women. They talked incessantly about a man they both knew and whom they both claimed to despise. 'He is,' said one, 'very mean-spirited. If he was drowning and you threw him a lifebelt he would sue you if the water splashed into his eyes.' Throughout their conversation they did nothing but disparage this man; each, in turn, seeming determined to think up an ever more outrageous anecdote about him than the other.

'Jean Laconte,' said the writer, when the two women had disappeared. He closed his notebook, stuffed it into his jacket pocket, grinned at me and held his hand out across the table.

I shook his hand and told him my name. 'Do you do that sort of thing often?' I asked him. 'Listen to other people's conversations?'

'Oh yes,' Jean admitted, without embarrassment. 'You will be amazed at what you hear in cafés. Especially when there are Americans around. They either do not care about the world knowing their business or else they assume that no one within earshot can speak English. They never stop talking. It doesn't matter to them whether or not they have anything worth saying.'

'What do you do with it all?' I asked him, nodding in the direction of the notebook.

'I will use a phrase here, a sentence there,' explained the writer. 'Those two women were, of course, madly in love with the man about whom they were talking so energetically. Each was intending to persuade her rival that the object of her desire was utterly unworthy of her.'

'Do you think either of them succeeded?'

'Of course not. They both simply succeeded in convincing themselves of their love for this man.'

'What do you write?'

'For money, I write scripts for the television', he replied. 'For what the Americans call 'soap operas', and for situation comedies. Sometimes I write novels which, sadly, do not sell very well. At the moment I am writing a book about the street people of Paris.'

I was terribly impressed to meet a real life writer; far too impressed by the fact that he had written books to be concerned by the fact that they did not sell very well. I did not dare tell him that I had recently started to write a book of my own. I asked him to tell me about the people in the book he was writing.

'Today,' began Jean, clearly happy to talk about his work-in-progress, 'I have been talking to a wonderful artist from Nigeria. Like everyone else I know him as Kookie but that's not his real name. He is a pavement artist and you can see him at work every day on the Grand Boulevards.'

I had seen Kookie, though I'd never known his name. 'The huge black man who draws those fantastic chalk pictures of the countryside?'

'That's the guy! In the summer he sometimes takes a week to finish a drawing. The French very much appreciate art and hardly anyone ever walks over his drawings – even at night. I once saw a police car screech to a halt because a drunken tourist was dancing on one of Kookie's pictures. The police took him in their car and released him several miles away where he could do little harm.'

'It seems a great shame that Kookie's drawings are all so temporary,' I said. 'Even if people don't walk on them the wind and the rain must eventually mean that they disappear. Perhaps if your book makes him famous someone will take his work seriously. Maybe a gallery owner or collector will give him some money so that he can draw or paint on proper canvases.'

Jean smiled and shook his head. 'Believe me, there is no chance of that happening,' he told me.

I looked at him, puzzled. 'Why not?'

'Three years ago Kookie was an odd job man working in a nunnery,' said Jean. 'He was the only man there and he used to do all the heavy, manual work. He used to do kitchen work for them – peeling potatoes and so on – and he used to help keep their garden tidy. He did the digging and the sweeping and he cleared their ditches and pruned their trees. In return they gave him a room over the garage, fed him and gave him an allowance of a few francs a week. He spent virtually all his money on paper, canvas, paints and chalks because his great love was drawing, sketching and painting. He used to work hard every morning from seven until noon and then work for a couple of hours every evening, helping to prepare the evening meal and washing up the dishes afterwards. In between, his time was his own and he spent virtually every hour drawing and painting. It was, in his own words, the happiest time of his life. And then it all went wrong for him.'

'What happened?'

'One day a visitor to the nunnery saw him painting in the garden. The visitor just happened to be the wife of a rich American collector. She asked to see his other work, rushed home to tell her husband about her amazing find, and within a month Kookie was in New York. He was fêted. They threw special parties for him. There was an exhibition of his work at a local museum and one of the New York galleries organised a one man show. His paintings sold for huge sums.'

'It hardly sounds as if everything had gone wrong for him!'

'Oh, but it had. Kookie was terribly unhappy. He felt like a fish out of the sea. He was surrounded by people but he felt lonely. He was being paid huge sums of money to paint but he couldn't paint.'

'So, what happened? He obviously came back to Paris.'

'He came back to Paris but the nuns didn't want him back. They'd found another handyman. And besides they thought that he would have been contaminated by his trip to New York. They thought he would have lost his innocence. And so now Kookie is a street artist. And he's happy again. He's happy that no one can buy any of his pictures. He earns his living drawing. He has a room in a tiny hotel somewhere in Montparnasse. If anyone stops and makes too much fuss of his work he just picks up his chalks and walks away.'

'But he's a fantastic artist!'

'I agree. And now he's happy because he's unknown and undiscovered again.' Jean scratched his chin. 'And because he's happy, his paintings are fantastic – daring and provocative. He knows that if someone hangs his work in a gallery, and pays him a fortune for what he does, then he'll be unhappy and his work will suffer. His art is built on happiness and his happiness is built on a certain amount of suffering and struggling.'

'What an extraordinary story!'

'It is. But Kookie is by no means the only extraordinary person out on the streets. Most people just walk by. They never look and ask themselves how these people came to be doing what they do. They forget that some of the most creative work is done on the streets – by artists, musicians and so on. They forget that it is when the greats are unknown and struggling that they often produce their most exciting and most dramatic work.' He called to the waiter. 'Can I buy you a drink?' he asked me. 'Another beer, perhaps?'

I looked at my watch. 'No, thanks,' I said. 'I have a date in twenty minutes. And I don't want to turn up reeking of alcohol.'

'Your girlfriend?'

'Not exactly.' I explained, as briefly as I could, why I was meeting a woman I had never met and about whom I knew nothing.

'I did this thing once,' said the writer. 'I was lonely, I met a woman through an advertisement in a newspaper.'

'What happened?' I asked. 'Was it a good experience?'

'It was an experience,' he said. 'Good?' he pulled a face. 'I do not know if it was good. As a writer it was good. As a man it was not so good. She was a hypochondriac. She was married to a doctor. You would have thought that for her that it would have been a marriage in heaven but she was jealous. She complained that he spent too much of his time listening to other people's problems and not enough time listening to hers. She wanted to have an affair.'

'Did you?'

'Of course I did. It would have been – what is the word – ungallant?' I nodded. 'Ungallant to say 'no' to a woman in need.' He paused and frowned as he remembered. 'But it was not a happy time,' he said, sadly. 'She complained all the time – even when we made love. Once I spent three hours with her in a hotel near the Gare du Lyon. During that time she had three different types of cancer, two heart attacks and a neurological disease. I have never known such a woman.'

'How long did the affair last?'

'Two, possibly three, months,' said Monsieur Laconte. 'It was as much as I could cope with. I sent her back to her husband.' He laughed. 'I think the poor fellow knew she was having an affair but I also do not think he minded.'

He looked at his watch. 'Now you must go,' he said. 'It is not good for a man to keep a woman waiting. But you will meet me another time and tell me about your adventures?'

I agreed to meet him for lunch later in the week. He left.

I paid my bill and moments later I heard a voice behind me.

'You are the one who replied to my advertisement?'

Chapter 31

I turned round. The voice had come from a plump, blonde woman. I had no idea how old she was. She was wearing a stylish black trouser suit and a diaphanous white blouse. Underneath the white blouse she wore a black bra. Her fingernails were painted black, presumably to match her trouser suit, but her toenails (which poked out of the toeless black shoes she was wearing) were painted fire engine red. She sat down opposite me.

'Er, yes,' I lied, feeling terribly guilty. 'How on earth did you know that I spoke English?'

'Everything about you is English,' answered the woman with a rather superior smile. 'Your hair, your jacket, your trousers...,' she waved a hand around in a careless but stylish and unmistakeably Gallic way. 'Absolutely everything!' She stood back and stared at me thoughtfully. 'You have a very strong face,' she said. 'You should have been an actor.'

'How do you know I'm not?'

'Pfui!' said Isabella, with a laugh and a wave of the hand. 'You are no actor!' She made the statement as though the very idea was so far-fetched that it amused her. She looked me up and down as though I were a car and she was considering making an offer. 'But you are young and not looking too badly. And you are a little different. I always think that the men who reply to these type of advertisements are a bit sad and desperate. Do not you?'

I couldn't help noticing that Isabella looked nothing much like the photograph she had sent to Jules.

'Well, not really...,' I began, rather shocked to be thought of as sad and desperate before our date had even started. I wondered why Isabella bothered to put advertisements in the papers if she thought she was only going to attract sad and desperate men.

'Shall we go?' asked Isabella. 'This is a dreary café.'

I got up. She got up. We left.

'Last week I went out with a civil servant from the Ministry of Agriculture,' she told me as we walked away from the café. 'He was very fat and had bad breath. He offered me money to go with him for the weekending.'

'Really?'

'But it wasn't very much,' she told me. 'He said he would pay all the expenses and give me one hundred francs for every day I spent with him. It was an insult. I would not go with a man for so little. Besides, he wanted to take me to Orléans. Who wants to go to Orléans?'

I started to say something but Isabella continued.

'If a man wishes to give me a nice present that is very acceptable,' she told me. 'But I do not like fat people. If you had been fat I would have shown you the politeness and told you that I had a headache. Look at that woman,' said Isabella, pointing to a woman on the other side of the street who was waddling along, struggling with her shopping bags. 'She is so fat. How can anyone allow themselves to get so fat.' She shivered, in seemingly genuine disgust. 'Have you noticed that fat people have absolutely no sense of their own bodies? They come too close to you in shops and they bump into people. In a city it's worse because people who live in cities lose their feeling for their private space. Fat people should be banned from cities and made to live in the country.'

'We speak only the English tonight?'

'Yes,' I said, relieved. 'That suits me fine.'

'I want to improve my English,' said Isabella. 'She is not as good as I am wishing.'

'You speak very good English,' I told her.

'And you are not badly speaking the English,' said Isabella. 'You need to work on your accent and your pronunciation are a little weakly. However, on the whole you speak quite nice the

English although the rung of your grammar has a not so good about it. Why did you answer my advertisement?'

I wasn't sure what to say but it didn't matter, Isabella wasn't expecting a response. 'On my next advertisement I think I will say that I am a little younger,' she said. 'What are you thinking?'

I tried to think of a reply but I needn't have bothered. Isabella was not as keen on listening as she was on talking. 'Did you think I would be as young and beautiful as I am?' she demanded.

I did not have the experience to know how to answer that question but at least I was aware of my inexperience. Instead of answering I tried to look wise. That wasn't easy either.

'Maybe in my next ad I will say I am like a film star,' she said, who was far too self-obsessed to notice whether or not I was looking wise or pulling silly faces. 'Do you think I am looking like a film star?'

'Oh absolutely.'

'Which one?' From the unexpected silence and the quizzical look on her face I got the impression that it was a question Isabella wanted answering. Fortunately, she was incapable of leaving a silence, even a short one, unfilled.

'Marilyn Monroe? In the film Some Like It Hot?'

To be honest I thought she looked more like Jack Lemmon in drag but I decided not to share that with her. 'You look exceptional!' I told her.

My meaningless and rather bland response seemed to please her. She smiled at me coquettishly. 'I will then say in my next advertisement that I am looking like the sporting image of Marilyn Monroe,' she said. 'You are a very sexy man,' she purred, managing to fill that short sentence with a dictionary of meaning.

'Did you enjoy the photograph I have sent?' she asked.

'Yes,' I said. 'You look very beautiful.'

'Oh, it is not me on the photograph,' she said. 'It is my daughter Karina. She looks very much like me. I did not have a photograph of myself so I had some copies made of a good photograph of her. It is quite impossible to tell us apart.'

I murmured something that I hoped might sound appropriate.

'I have met some very famous men in my life,' she told me. 'Last week I met a famous American musician,' she told me proudly. 'I went to his hotel. Afterwards I sat in the theatre and watched him perform. I saw thousands of women screaming for him and felt very proud. Of all the women there he had chosen me for himself.'

'How did you meet him?' I asked.

'A friend of mine works for his record company,' Isabella explained. 'She knows that he likes women with some experience. It was very exciting to be in the theatre and know that just an hour earlier I had been in his bed.'

'Do you believe in God?' she asked, suddenly and utterly unexpectedly. She speeded up, slipping with surprising agility around a woman with a pram. Her heels click-clacked on the pavement.

'I'm not sure,' I said.

'You must!' she said. 'Oh you must. I cannot go with a man who does not have faith.'

'Well...' I began.

'Good!' said Isabella, though I wasn't quite sure what she was pleased about. 'And your politics. Are you hanging to the left or the right?'

I had to try hard not to laugh at this. Instead of replying I simply smiled and hoped it looked enigmatic.

'I am a middle person; very much to the right of the left,' she told me. 'As young people we should be a little to the left. But as man and woman of the world we should be hanging more to the right side. Don't you agree?'

I agreed.

Isabella stopped and I stopped too. 'This is my coach!' she announced proudly, indicating a tiny, white Renault. It had dents in the bonnet, the boot, all the doors I could see and even the roof. One front headlamp was broken and neither of the wing mirrors had any glass in them.

'You like my little coach, yes?' she asked. She opened the driver's door and climbed into the car.

'It's, er, lovely,' I told her, getting in beside her, though I did not see how Isabella was going to move the car which seemed to me to be hemmed in by the vehicles in front and behind it.

'She is perfect for Paris,' said Isabella. 'And she has a glassy look.'

I tried to work it out. 'A glassy look?' I said, slightly bewildered.

'That touch of glass!' explained Isabella, clearly slightly exasperated at having found the only Englishman alive who hadn't heard the phrase before. 'You English! Hrmph!' she said, with what I was learning to recognise as ubiquitous Gallic arrogance. 'You can't even speak your own language improperly.'

She put the tiny car into gear, pressed her right foot flat to the floor and accelerated into the car in front which lurched forward a few inches. Looking through the windscreen I could see the whole row of cars in front of us shake with the impact. Isabella then slammed the car into reverse and drove into the car behind. She did this until she had created enough space to manoeuvre her tiny car out of its now much enlarged space. Once out onto the road she put her right foot down and drove at full speed down the centre of the road, for all the world as though she were driving some tiny racing car fixed in some invisible slot. 'Do you have a car?' she asked, having to shout above the whine of the complaining engine. She changed gear only when it seemed that the engine would explode. 'No, I'm afraid not,' I said, as she careered around a corner at full speed. Clearly no one had introduced her to the notion that the brake could be used for anything other than halting the vehicle once it had reached its final destination. I sat alongside, gripping the dashboard in front of me with one hand and the handle on the side of the door with the other. I had by now worked out what she meant by 'glassy', but it seemed a little late to tell her that I understood, and a little discourteous to tell her that she'd got a 'g' mixed up with a 'c' so I said nothing. The French, I had already learnt, like to think that they can speak everyone else's language perfectly but that no one can speak theirs at all.

'This is the cat's knees, no?' She paused for a moment and looked at me, with a coquettish flutter of her long eyelashes. And then she frowned. 'Or is it the bee's whiskers you say?' She shrugged, as though it was of no consequence.

'You like to drive fast?' I wheezed, as we hurtled between two buses with centimetres to spare on either side. She had dowsed herself in a noxious perfume which smelt as though it had been created out of some sort of toxic waste and it clearly contained at least one chemical to which I was allergic.

'But of course,' she replied. 'It is the best way. But only when there is no traffic. Today the roads are too busy to drive fast and so I must go slowly.'

I watched in horror as people leapt out of the way as we shot across a pedestrian crossing. An elderly couple, a woman with a small child and a man with a briefcase all threw themselves onto the pavement. 'These people are so dangerous!' she said, taking both hands off the steering wheel and waving them about. 'I do not lead my car on the *trottoir*. Why do they walk themselves on the road?' She waved a finger pointedly at her rear view mirror but I doubted if the pedestrians would have seen it. I suspect that they were too busy picking themselves up off the pavement, and well out of the way of the next homicidal motorist, to be concerned with what Isabella was doing with her right index finger.

'What baggage do you brought to our relationship?' asked Isabella.

I looked at her, confused.

'All peoples bring baggage into a relationship,' she said. 'This is another word for your vocabulary,' she added. 'There is the physical baggage – the furniture, the crockery, the cutlery, the towelling, that is all brought by the women – and there is the baggage of the emotions which is brought by all the sexes.' She looked at me to see if I had understood. I hadn't, and it obviously showed.

'Your past relationships with women,' explained Isabella. 'Your hang-outs.'

'Ah,' I said, thinking I probably understood. 'No, I don't have any hang-ups.'

'Hang-outs,' said Isabella, correcting me. 'Not hang-ups. That is for the shirts and the trousers. Hang-outs is the emotions baggaging.'

'No hang-outs,' I said. Isabella was not a woman many people disagreed with. I certainly wasn't one. It occurred to me to mention that the pedestrians concerned had been merely trying to cross the road at an authorised crossing place but I kept quiet about that too.

'That is good,' said Isabella. 'I have several husbands but they have left me with no baggages.'

I started to say that I thought this was a good thing.

'My last husband was a fast driver,' said Isabella, interrupting me. 'He was a very horny man.'

'Very horny?'

'*Mais oui.* He never took his fingers off the horn.' To illustrate her point Isabella pressed two fingers onto her horn. A small Citroen van in front of us swerved to the right and collided with a parked BMW. A man carrying a baguette fell off his bicycle. 'He said it was the safest way to drive,' explained Isabella. She took her fingers off her horn and waved a finger scornfully at a taxi driver who had the temerity to pull out in front of her. 'He was an idiot,' she said.

'I think he thought it was his right of way,' I explained, referring to the taxi driver. The traffic lights were green for him and red for us, so it was understandable.

'Not that one,' said Isabella impatiently. 'My husband! He was a good driver but a complete fool. I am glad to be rid of him.' Without slowing down at all she turned left. We went round the corner on two wheels. There was much squealing of tyres. A hubcap came off and rolled past us. I watched, horrified, as it bounced over a kerb and disappeared down an alleyway. 'But he was very good in bed too,' she remembered, ignoring the hubcap and the avalanche of magazines, newspapers, maps, packets of sweets and miscellaneous papers which cascaded from one side of the dashboard to the other as we rounded the corner and then straightened up again. I clung to the door handle to stop myself falling on top of Isabella. Some of the maps and papers skidded onto the floor. 'We were married for three years and we made the loving every single night,' she told me proudly. 'Even when we were divorcing he came to my apartment and we had sex at least once a day. We did it once in the lift going up to my lawyer's office.'

'So why on earth did you get divorced?' I asked.

She snorted. 'He was a man to have sex with not a man to marry,' she explained, slamming on the brakes and skidding to a halt in the middle of the road. 'He is not trustworthy enough for use as a husband. He has the roving eyes. He works for a car manufacturer and drives rally cars. For a month he has been driving all over Africa. He drives through deserts and forests and mountains; across rivers and rocks. He finishes the rally without crashing once. But when he comes back to Paris, on the first morning he is here he sees a pretty girl on the boulevard Haussman; he drives onto the back of a bus and breaks his leg.'

Without warning she put the car into reverse and shot backwards. I turned my head and could see that we were aiming for a small parking space. The space looked to me to be at least a foot shorter than the car. This, however, was clearly not something Isabella was prepared to regard as an impediment. I winced as she crunched the back of her tiny car into the car behind us and winced again as she crunched the front bumper into the car in front of us. Eventually, after a good deal of crunching of metal, much wincing by me and much changing of gears and pulling on the steering wheel by Isabella the intrepid motorist managed to cram her now rather shorter car into the now rather larger space. 'There!' she said, triumphantly. 'A perfect fit.' And indeed it was. When I got out of the car and stood, shaking and wheezing, on the pavement I could see that there was not one centimetre of space between Isabella's car and either the car in front or the car behind.

'Now we eat!' cried Isabella, abandoning her car and marching off.

'Aren't you going to lock the car?' I called, walking after her. I had a suspicion that she had left the keys in the car.

'There is nothing in it to steal,' she answered, over her shoulder. 'And who would steal it?' she demanded. 'In front of it there is a new Mercedes. Two cars behind there is a new Jaguar. Across the road I saw a Ferrari and a Bentley. There are expensive motor cars everywhere. Who will be stealing my little car?' I hurried to catch up with her. She walked almost as quickly as she drove.

I looked back at her small, squashed Renault, crammed tightly into its bespoke parking space. 'I suppose you're right,' I agreed.

'We are going to a traditional little French restaurant,' she said. 'You will like it.'

'I'm sure I will,' I agreed.

'You will pay, no?'

'Er, oh yes,' I agreed.

'Good,' said Isabella. She wagged a finger at me. 'I should have put that in my advertisement,' she said, as though it was my fault that she had forgotten to do so. 'That the man will pay for the meals. I will make a note of that in the mind. It is good life for a woman. If she meets a man every night she never need pay for food.' She smiled at me, as though expecting me to share her happiness. 'But you must know that I will not sleep with you tonight,' she warned me. 'If we get on well then tonight you may kiss me. On the second date I will let you touch the bosoms. And on the third date we will have some sleep together. But not before.'

I felt myself blushing. 'I wasn't, er, expecting...' I began, not quite knowing exactly what I wasn't expecting.

'I think it is best to be clear about this things,' explained Isabella. 'Maybe in my next advertisement I will put my rules.'

'Your rules?'

'Kissing, touching of the bosoms and then sleeping on the third date,' she explained, as though to an idiot.

'Maybe that would be a good idea,' I agreed.

'I am not a prude but a woman must have standards,' she said. 'My sister is a prude. My sister once refused to get into a lift with two strange men she did not knowing well because she said the lift was too small and body contact would be unavoidable.'

By now we had reached the restaurant. We went in. Isabella spoke to the waiter, who knew her and spoke to her by name, and we were taken straight to a table by the window. We both chose and ordered items from the menu. Isabella ordered some wine. I desperately added up the cost of the items we had ordered and hoped I could afford the bill.

The meal was not a great success. The food was not particularly well cooked and the service was slow and rather too intrusive and flamboyant for my taste. Isabella never stopped talking, except to stuff food into her mouth. She did this speedily. Chewing food she did not regard as incompatible with speech. She talked about anything and everything. Sentences poured from her, often accompanied by small portions of partly digested food. Often there was no link between one sentence and the next.

'I have an idea that would make the French army the best in the world,' she told me at one point. She leant forward across the table. 'I have written to the President about it,' she said. 'We should employ only tiny soldiers,' she said. 'That is my plan. Only the soldiers who are small or very small.'

'Right,' I said, having no idea what she was talking about.

'It makes good sense, does it not?' she said. 'The small soldiers will be far less likely to be hit by bullets than the bigger soldiers!'

I agreed that there was much good sense in this apparently novel idea.

Occasionally she asked me trick questions, intended, presumably, to test me.

'If you were going with another woman and you met me would you go out with me?' she suddenly asked.

I thought about this for a while.

'No.' I said, having no idea whether this was, or was not, the right answer.

'Good,' she said, patting my hand. 'That is the right answer.'

Eventually, the waiter brought our coffee. And then, to my enormous relief, he brought the bill, which I found I could afford to pay. The ordeal over, we walked to the door and stood on the pavement outside the café. Isabella put her arms around my neck, thanked me politely for dinner, and kissed me on the lips. She did this as though she was conveying upon me a great honour; as though she was ennobling me in thanks for my services to my country.

The kiss, which lasted just a couple of seconds, did absolutely nothing for me.

'That is your thank you for a quite good evening,' said Isabella, taking her arms from around my neck and stepping back. 'You are a quite pleasant young man. You have good teeth and hair and you are quite tall enough.'

I instinctively knew that there was a 'but' coming very soon.

'You have quite good English and you are a little bit interesting as a companion,' she told me. I felt like a student receiving an end of term report. I still knew that there was a 'but' coming very soon. I was not to be disappointed.

'But you do not excite me,' said Isabella, bluntly. 'I do not feel a great urge to take you to my bed.'

'Oh,' I said, feeling more relief than disappointment. I tried not to show this relief and, indeed, tried to look disappointed.

'You are perhaps the right age, though maybe a little old, but I am looking for someone better looking and with more muscles,' said Isabella. 'Your nose is not quite right and you do not have the jaw line which I like. Plus your clothes are not very expensive and you do not have a car of your own. I think I am looking for someone who is richer than you are.' She started walking in the direction of her car.

'That would not be difficult,' I told her. 'I am quite poor, I'm afraid.'

'What do you do for a vocation?' she asked. It was the first time in the evening that she had asked me anything or shown any interest in my life.

'I'm working part time as a teacher,' I said.

'You see,' she said. 'You will not make big money teaching. You should make for yourself a career. A banker, a lawyer or a doctor.'

'I have a university place to study medicine,' I told her.

She brightened considerably at this. 'That is very interesting,' she said. 'I wish I had known earlier. I would have told you about my illnesses. You would have been greatly interested. For example, yesterday I ate something which disagreed with me.'

I was tempted to say that I was surprised that any food had

had the temerity to disagree with her. But I did not have the courage to turn the thought into words.

'If you are going to be a doctor you will become rich quite soon?'

'Oh, I don't think so,' I said. 'I have a long training ahead of me.'

'But I have never known a poor doctor,' said Isabella. 'I will perhaps give you another chance. We will have dinner again and I will see if perhaps you make my blood boil after all. Then, maybe, we meet again in a few years time when you are nearly finished your studies?'

'That's very kind of you,' I said.

'I give you my telephone number,' said Isabella. She opened her handbag and took out a diary with a pencil attached to it. She wrote her telephone number on a page at at the back of the diary, added a lipstick kiss, tore out the page and handed it to me. 'I do not want to live a life with any regrets. I always say 'yes' when 'no' might sometimes be less risky. A 'yes' may sometimes be dangerous but it is also often more profitable and more fun, do you not agree?'

I agreed.

'You ring me when you can see me again. And you come, pick me out and take me again up for dinner. You will know my apartment building easily and remember it for there is the huge pair of brassy knockers right on the doorway. I will look forward to it and will break almost any date for you.' She looked at me. 'If things go well with us, young Monsieur le Docteur, I will let you touch me a little. After all, even if there is some time to wait it will be our second date together and you remember my rules. You give me the telephone. But not on Tuesdays or Thursdays.'

'Not Tuesdays or Thursdays,' I repeated.

'On those days I have my self-confidence training course,' she said proudly.

'You are on a self-confidence training course?' I said. I was astonished. I had never met anyone who seemed less in need of self-confidence training.

'I am the lecturer,' she told me, indignantly. We were by

now standing beside her little white Renault. 'Shall I give you a lift?' she asked. 'Where from are you going?'

'No, it's OK, thanks,' I told her. 'I think I would like a walk.' I paused. 'Unless you want me to see you home?'

She laughed. 'You are so sweet a boy! No, I will see myself home safely,' she said. Then she put her head to one side, as though thinking. 'Maybe you are being clever. Maybe you think that perhaps if you see me home I will invite you in because you are going to become a doctor and you will get more than a cup of coffee?'

'No, no, not at all!' I said hastily.

'Are you sure?' she asked me, lowering her head and looking at me through her upper eyelashes. 'I think you fancy me a lot don't you?'

'Oh no...,' I started to say. 'Well, yes, of course I do. I am sorry. It probably is better if I walk.'

'You walk off your urges!' laughed Isabella. 'Tonight is not your night. I am seeing my last husband in an hour at my apartment and he would not be pleased to see you there. But another time — who knows?'

She climbed into her car, started the engine and looked up once at me. She waved. I waved back. And then I walked away. Behind me I could hear her little white Renault banging against the two cars on either side of it. I walked quickly and turned a corner so that she would not drive past me. I did not want to see her again. I passed a rubbish bin on the pavement, paused for a moment, ripped the page she had torn out of her diary into tiny pieces and tossed the pieces in amongst the rubbish.

Chapter 32

My finances were in a rather delicate condition. If they had been a coat they would have been too threadbare to donate to a jumble sale.

I sat in La Rhumerie twice a week looking forward to my time with Jules for two quite different reasons. I enjoyed Jules' company very much. But I also needed the envelope he gave me at the start of each evening. Sometimes I felt guilty about the fact that we talked more like friends than teacher and student. But the guilt did not stop me taking the money; partly because I knew that the cash came from Jules' father, an exceedingly wealthy man who reputedly regarded it as money well spent, and partly by the fact that hunger is an even more potent driving force than guilt.

Jules was never predictable; always full of surprises.

'Do you mind coming for a walk?' he asked one day.

It was a gloriously sunny day; the first really warm day of summer and the café proprietors had removed their screens, opening up their terraces so that customers could sit, eat and drink in the fresh air.

'Let's go down to the river,' he suggested.

There was something about him that told me that he was troubled and I knew, when we left La Rhumerie, that he had something important to tell me.

'It appears that it is time for me to be settled up,' said Jules, with a grand sigh. 'It is time for me to find a woman who wears sensible underwear, wants babies and stretch marks, who knows where to buy the best duvets and who worries me about the price of soap powder.'

I stared at him. This did not sound like the Jules I had grown to know.

'Maybe it is the time,' said Jules. 'The day before yesterday,' he confided, 'I had a terrible experience. It was, perhaps, the omen.' He paused and shuddered before regaining his composure and continuing. 'I have been seeing the widow once a week for a month,' he said. 'She was married to the gourmand. A man who was a member of a club where men ate the rare and expensive animals. They used to buy them from all other the world. When he died he left nothing. He had spent all their money on these indecent feasts. It was terrible. So do you know what the widow did?'

Having absolutely no idea what the widow had done I shook my head.

'She sold his body for a big sum to the gourmand dining club of which he had been the member. And they ate him up with blackcurrant sauce and a sprig or two of parsley.'

'They ate him!' I asked, horrified.

'Every last inch of him. And I believe that he was a big man.' insisted Jules. 'So, afterwards his widow put an advertisement in the magazine and I responded. Sometimes I have found older widows to be entertaining and grateful. They do not expect too much but they are pleased when they are treated as women. Two days ago she decided that it was the time for us to go to the bedroom. She took me to her apartment in the 15th *arrondissment* – a horrid little backstreet to which I would not normally go and where there are hardly ever any taxis. I sat down on the sofa and drank some whisky while she went into the bedroom to prepare herself for our romance. When she reappeared nearly forty minutes later I did not recognise her. Without her elastic underthings she was twice the size she had been earlier. And she had taken off her hair.' He closed his eyes and shook his head.

'You had no idea about this?'

'None!' insisted Jules.

'So, what did you do?'

'I did my duty,' said Jules. 'Of course, I did my duty. I am a gentleman. I could do nothing else. I told her that there are many stars in the sky but that even if they were all together they would not have the sparkle and brightness of her eyes.'

'She had nice eyes then?'

'No. She had cataracts and without the spectacles she was quite blind.' He shivered, as though cold. 'It was terrible. It was like a nightmare.'

For a while we both walked in silence, lost in our respective thoughts.

'When I was young I was reckless with my life,' Jules continued at last. 'Now, in my middle years it is time for me to be more cautious and to value my life.' He stopped, thought for a moment and then brightened. 'Of course, when I am old I will be reckless again because then I will have so little to lose and I will have had a good life.'

'In your middle years?' I said. 'What has happened? You are not in your middle years!'

'Oh yes I am,' he replied, sadly. 'Yesterday I had an anniversary.'

'A birthday?'

'I am another age. Is that what I mean?'

'Yes.'

'Then I was having a birthday,' he agreed. He clapped me on the back. 'You see, you teach me such good English.'

'How old are you?'

'I am 22,' he replied.

'That isn't old!'

'Maybe not to you and to me,' agreed Jules. 'But yesterday, after dinner, my father called me into his study for what he called a little talking. He told me that it is now time for me to begin to settle up a bit.'

'I thought your father...'

'Oh yes. But he has trouble at his heart. His doctor has told him he cannot now even have second-hand excitements.' Jules shrugged and pulled a face. 'It is serious. So, sadly, that is it for me. Now I must become a sensible and responsible man of business, with a plump wife, a golf club membership, a sensible motor car, and small children so that my father can see the next generation at play before he has the big attack of the heart.'

'So what has happened?'

'My father has told me that I must leave the university and take up a place at his business. I must learn the trade so that I can be ready to take over when he is....' Jules waved a hand to complete the sentence.

'When?'

'Soon. Now. Tomorrow. This week.' Jules shrugged. 'He wants me too to find myself a wife. A good, solid, sensible woman who can give him the bouncy grandchildren and bake the big apple pies.'

'Do you have anyone in mind?'

'I do not myself know Parisian women who can bake pies of any sort,' said Jules. 'They would not want the pastry under their fingernails. But my mother has found someone for me.'

I could hardly believe what I was hearing. 'An arranged marriage?'

'A daughter of another businessman,' explained Jules. 'Her father and my father have property together. It will be a – what is the word – an alliance. It is perhaps more of a merger rather than a marriage.'

'Do you know her? Have you met her?'

'Oh yes,' laughed Jules. 'I have known her since we both children. She lives with her parents near where my parents live. She is plain and plump and has the good hips. I am confident that she will bear me many strong children.'

'And your parents and her parents have arranged a wedding?'

'Oh yes. It was all fixed yesterday. Myself I would not be bothering with a wedding,' said Jules. 'A wedding, like any contract, is a waste of time. The people who wish to become married should only say to one another that they will be kind. That is all. The priest should say: 'Will you treat this woman as you would wish yourself to be treated?' And the man would say: 'Yes'. And the priest would turn to the woman and ask the same question and she would say: 'Yes'. He would say: 'Do you promise to be kind to one another?' They would both say 'yes'. And then everyone would go eat, drink and dance and the couple would go off on their holiday together.'

'Honeymoon.'

'Honeymoon? What is that?'

'When a newly married couple go on holiday it is called a honeymoon.'

'Ah. That is for us a *lune de miel* or a *voyage de noces*,' said Jules.

'You seem to be taking all this very well,' I said to him.

He looked at me, surprised. 'In what way do you mean?'

'It's just that I think you are so free,' I told him. 'And yet you are ready to give up your life for your father.'

'Of course,' said Jules. 'There are two civilisations in France,' he explained. 'There is the civilisation which is based on cafés and boutiques and good food and wine. That is a very free and Roman civilisation. Self-indulgent. And there is, side by side, another civilisation – more Greek – in which the rules are all that matters. We can enjoy ourselves better than the Italians but we can be even more bureaucratic and pompous than the Germans,' said Jules. 'France is wildly over governed. We love administrators. We love being told what to do. Of course, although we pretend to do as we are told we still do what we want. We have the feathered costumes of the showgirls at the Moulin Rouge but we also have the formal gilded architecture at the Opera House. They go together very well. It is the same country and the same people. I have enjoyed my time with the feathered costumes. Now it is my time to play my stern part among the gilded architecture. The fancy ties and jackets will be put away and I will wear the dull ties and the smart suits.'

Something he had said stuck in my mind. 'You say the French pretend to do as they are told,' I said. 'How will that affect your marriage?'

'Oh, I will be a typical French husband,' said Jules with a laugh. 'I will be a loyal and faithful husband to my wife and a loyal and faithful lover to my mistresses.'

I stared at him, horrified. 'You mean that you will get married knowing that you intend to take a mistress?'

Jules laughed at me. 'You are shocked!'

'Of course!'

'Do not be my friend but perhaps what is good for the French goose would not do for the English gander.'

We stopped at a café overlooking the River Seine and with a splendid view of Notre Dame.

'Let's have a drink,' said Jules.

We found a table near the window, sat down and ordered drinks from a stern looking waiter in a heavily starched snow white apron.

'You realise now my friend,' said Jules, 'that this must be our last lesson.' He put his hands on my shoulders and looked me straight in the eyes. 'You have been a good teacher and an even better friend,' he said. 'I will miss you very much. But I hope we can still see one another when I come to Paris?'

Amazingly, it had still not occurred to me that I would be losing my one and only student. 'I'll miss you,' I told him and meant it. 'My life will not be the same without you.' I meant that too.

He put his arms around me and gave me a bear hug. 'Let's have a drink,' he said.

We sat in the café at the bottom of St. Michel, drinking Ricard and watching the tourists scurry by. It was starting to rain and many were draped in plastic raincoats or carrying small umbrellas. Just a few hundred yards away stood Notre Dame, imposing and grand.

We sat there together, silent, alone with our own thoughts.

Chapter 33

'Are you ready, Jean?' demanded the newcomer, a short, almost round, man. He was slightly over five foot tall, wrinkled and very hairy. He had a straggly grey beard and shoulder length grey hair and wore an army combat jacket and a pair of scruffy, faded blue jeans. The jacket had at least a dozen pockets. All of them were bulging. He had a huge, heavy looking camera bag slung over one shoulder and an expensive but slightly battered Leica camera slung around his neck. He was carrying a collapsible tripod.

'Do you want a drink?' Jean asked the newcomer.

'I want to get some shots done before it rains.' He replied. He seemed rather bad-tempered.

'OK,' said Jean, with a sigh. He slid off his bar stool with surprising grace and introduced us. The photographer, he told me, was called Johnny. The two of them were collaborating on a book about the street people of Paris.

'This city is crammed to the boundary with fascinating people,' Jean told me. 'More or less at random I picked out twenty five. I've done the interviews and written essays about them all. Now Johnny is going to take the photographs.'

'The photographs are what people will buy the book for,' said Johnny, who struck me as a rather gloomy little fellow. Unlike Jean he didn't look like a man who got a lot of fun out of life. I wondered how the two of them had got together.

I tried to pay for the two glasses of *vin chaud* we had drunk together but Jean beat me to it by the simple expedient of dropping a note onto the bar counter and indicating, with a wave of the hand that had dropped the note, that the barman could keep the change. We followed Johnny out of the café and onto the street. Encumbered with fat and cameras, Johnny walked like a woman wearing a hobble skirt. The temperature had dropped noticeably in the short space of time since I had first entered the café. The warm spell had ended far too soon; and an unseasonal chill was clinging to the Paris streets.

'Who am I photographing tonight?' asked Johnny, stopping for a moment.

'Paul,' said Jean, overtaking him, leading the way and setting off at quite a surprisingly fast pace. I ran for a few paces and walked alongside him. Johnny, mumbling inaudible complaints, hobbled along behind us. 'Paul is a clown,' Jean explained to me. 'He works a patch of pavement just a few hundred yards from here. Up until three years ago he worked as a civil servant in the French Treasury. He lived for the moment – and the next cocktail party. All he knew for certain was that he had got to get somewhere, and that he had to get there quickly. Sadly, this ambition was slightly complicated by the fact that he had no idea where he was heading or what he was doing with his life – or why. Then one day, much to the astonishment of absolutely everyone he knew, he resigned and bought himself a clown costume and one of those old-fashioned music machines that operates when you turn the handle round.'

'He'd never done any clowning before?'

'Never.'

'Is he married? Does he have a family? What was their reaction?'

'He's married. Two children. One is a lawyer and the other a doctor. His wife stuck with him and they're closer now than they ever were. She brings him sandwiches and a flask for his lunch and in the winter pops out with hot soup and hot coffee every couple of hours. Four months ago he had really bad flu and couldn't get out of his bed. His wife put on the clown costume and took over his patch for him for six days.'

'And the kids? What do they think of their dad?'

'They've totally disowned him,' said Jean flatly. 'One of them – an exceptionally mean-spirited son called Alphonse, who is, you will probably not be surprised to hear, the lawyer – has an office nearby. Every morning and every evening he walks several hundred yards out of his way simply to avoid passing his father.'

'How sad. Paul sounds a fascinating character,'

'Thankfully, Paris is full of people like Paul,' said Jean, pausing to buy an evening newspaper from a wizened old man who appeared to be wearing at least three overcoats. He handed the vendor a twenty franc note and waved a hand when the man reached into his pocket to find the change.

'I buy a newspaper from that chap almost every day,' continued Jean. 'Every time I buy a paper from him I give him a twenty franc note. He always offers to give me the change and I always tell him to keep it. The day he doesn't offer to give me the change is the day I stop letting him keep it – and the day I start buying my newspaper from someone else.'

'Is he in your book?' I asked, resisting the temptation to look back.

'Yes, of course,' replied Jean.

'He hasn't always been a newspaper seller?'

'He was a doctor for twenty five years. Then, about eleven years ago, he performed an illegal abortion for a friend of his daughter. The authorities found out and he lost his licence to practise. His wife and daughter left him and he went bankrupt six months later. He now lives in a hostel in Montmartre.'

Jean told me that the streets of Paris were well stocked with such individuals.

We approached a grey-bearded man with a wooden sandwich board strapped around his neck.

'What does that say?' I asked Jean, nodding towards the sign on the sandwich board.

'He's warning us that the end of the world is coming very shortly and that we must pray to try to avert disaster,' said Jean. 'Thanks for the new warning!' he said to the sandwich board holder, stuffing a handful of coins into the man's hand.

'A capitalistic pessimist,' said Jean as we walked on. 'A pragmatic Nostradamus. He's been standing there predicting the end of the world for as long as I've been living in Paris. He changes the date on his placard every few months and if you challenge him about the fact that the world hasn't ended he replies that it was only thanks to the power of prayer.'

'Who else is in your book?' I asked, a minute or so later.

'A toy seller who used to be a pop singer,' replied Jean instantly. 'A thirty-year-old former professional golfer who sells Eiffel Tower keyrings in the Tuileries gardens – and a street photographer from Chartres who has been working the same tourist patch outside one of the big hotels for forty nine years.'

I looked at him, slightly puzzled. 'Did you say a golfer who sells keyrings? He really used to be a golfer?'

'Quite a good one. He worked hard at his game but he didn't have the natural talent. I spoke to a sports writer I know who told me that he used to work harder than anyone on the tour.'

'Not fair, is it?'

Jean grinned at me, as though charmed by my innocence.

'When I lived in America in the 1950s I knew two guys who played golf professionally. One of the guys had an enormous natural talent. He could hit a golf ball any way he wanted. He could put a draw or a fade on a ball as easily as you and I could take the club out of the bag. Do you play?'

I admitted that I didn't.

'Doesn't matter,' said Jean, with a wave of the hand. 'The other guy had very little natural talent but he was a worker. He used to practise until his hands bled. When they started bleeding he would send his caddy off to fetch plasters and bandages. Then, when his hands were plastered and bandaged he would start again.'

'He would be up at dawn practising and he'd be out there on the practice range long after everyone else had gone home. At the end of a four day tournament he'd be on the practice range when all the other professionals were already on their way back home. His caddies hated the work. He used to pay them twice as much as everyone else but they never lasted more than three or four months.'

'Because I knew these two guys quite well I used to travel to tournaments to watch them play. And do you know what always surprised me most?'

I shook my head.

'The guy who worked hard had virtually no fans,' said Jean. 'But the guy with the talent was always surrounded by a massive entourage of fans and hangers on. People loved his talent and they wanted to be around him. He excited and thrilled people. And because of that the sponsors threw huge amounts of money at him. I always felt sorry for the guy who had to work for his success,' said Jean. 'It always seemed to me strange that people would have more respect for the guy who succeeds simply because he has natural talent than for the guy who succeeds because he works hard.'

We walked for a while in silence.

'So he gave up golf and now sells keyrings.'

'And he tells me that he's happier now than he's been for years,' said Jean.

'They all sound remarkable people,' I told him.

'I got the idea for a book when I overheard two social workers talking about Paul in a café across the road from his usual patch. They spoke about him very patronisingly and described him as one of society's dull failures. It seemed to me that Paul is more useful to society in one day than those social workers are in a lifetime. When you haven't got anything to do for an hour so just sit in a café and watch him. He puts smiles on thousands of faces every day. How many people have jobs which do that? These people affect our lives in small but definable ways and I think it's the little things that really make the difference.'

'Do you really think so? That the little things do make a difference?'

'Absolutely,' said Jean. 'We're all dependent upon one another and the world is far smaller than you might think it is. Let me tell you a true story. A woman I know is married to a very rich man. They live in a very elegant town house in the Place des Vosges – where Victor Hugo had an apartment. I don't know how he made his money and it doesn't matter. She has led a bizarre and unnatural life. She's so used to being waited on that I don't think she's ever opened a door in her life. She was having an affair with the foreign minister of – you don't need to know that – and one evening two months ago, he was in Paris and they had a date to meet at his hotel for dinner and a little indoor exercise. But she broke a fingernail. I can't imagine what she was doing to break a nail but she did. She telephones her beauty salon and the girl who looks after her nails is away with her boyfriend in Cannes. Now my friend is not a woman to go out of the house with a broken fingernail so she cancelled the date and the foreign minister, in a very bad mood and feeling extremely randy, went to a rather seedy club in Montmartre where he duly got himself arrested when the police swooped on the place, raided it, found several pounds of cocaine and picked up everyone in it on drug related charges. As it happened, the minister knew nothing about the drugs but the arrest led to the newspapers taking a hard look at his life and finding out that he and two other Ministers of his country were mixed up in some sort of arms deal with the Russians. There was an outcry, the ministers were all forced to resign, the opposition called for an election and rioting in the capital led to the government being overthrown and a military dictatorship taking over.'

I stared at him.

'So, there you are,' said Jean. 'A woman breaks a fingernail and as a direct consequence a government falls.'

'Is that all true?' I asked him.

'Of course!' said Jean.

'Is Johnny photographing all the street people?' I asked, reverting to the original subject.

Jean turned and nodded. 'Johnny is a grumbler,' he admitted. 'He himself readily admits that he always manages to find something to moan about. Whingeing is his great joy in life. It's what he lives for. But who cares? He's a bloody good photographer and that's what he's here for. He gets better pictures with that battered old Leica of his than most of the youngsters can get with bags full of fancy Japanese equipment. I've known him for him years.'

A few minutes later we arrived at the piece of typically broad Parisian pavement where Paul, the former civil servant, worked and earned his living. Wearing the usual clown make-up – white face and huge red lips – and dressed in a checked, baggy suit, oversized shoes with flapping soles and an absurd hat with a massive artificial sunflower attached to the crown Paul was imitating the walks of pedestrians passing by. Judging by the hat full of coins standing on the pavement in front of his old-fashioned, wind-up music machine, business had been going quite well.

Jean waited until Paul had finished mimicking the overweight waddle of a humourless American, dressed in ghastly tight lime green pants and a white, red and blue checked jacket, and then introduced first Johnny, and then me.

'The Americans are easy prey,' said Paul, rather apologetically, speaking to me. 'You do not mind my joking on the American?'

I shook my head. 'Certainly not!'

'I can tell you are not American,' he said. 'You are not fat enough to be American. But sometimes the English they like the Americans.'

I reassured him.

'I enjoy taking the mickey from out of the Americans,' confessed the clown. He spoke good English with a Maurice Chevalier accent. Through the make-up I could see that he had remarkably twinkly eyes and it was difficult to imagine him dressed in a grey suit and white shirt and sitting behind a desk in some grey office full of dull and worthy French bureaucrats. 'The Americans are pompous people who think they own the world because they gave us Coca Cola. They wander around Europe so unaware of everything around them that they do not realise that they are despised, sneered at and disliked. They talk loudly and often but say so very little worth listening to. Mimicking them is good business because everyone can recognise the Americans and everyone dislikes them.' He removed the hat on his head and winked at two elderly women who had tossed a handful of coins into his other hat on the pavement. A small boy in short trousers, balancing with the natural ease of a child on roller skates, added a single coin to Paul's wages for the day. The boy stared in awe at Paul for a moment, grinned with delight when Paul tousled his hair with a white gloved hand, and then rolled gracefully back to where his parents, who had given him the coin, were standing waiting for him. The boy, watching carefully, clung to his father's leg and half hid.

'Are you having a good day?' asked Jean.

'Not bad,' said Paul. He banged his hands together and stamped his feet on the pavement. 'It's cold enough for people to feel sorry for me but not so cold that they won't take their gloves off to find some coins for my hat.' He laughed. It was a wonderful, throaty chuckle.

As he talked, Johnny was already working, circling his prey like a tiger; silently and deliberately taking single photographs.

'Do you want a drink?' Jean asked me. 'I could do with a nice hot wine.'

I said I wouldn't mind a glass of something warm.

'Do you want a drink, Paul?' Jean asked.

Paul smiled and the flower in his button hole lit up.

'*Vin chaud?*' suggested Jean.

'That'll do very nicely,' said Paul, with a grin. The grin, like the chuckle, was infectious. I was surprised to find just how good I felt in his company.

We headed for the nearest café – about ten yards away. I was rapidly learning that one of the wonders of Paris is that you are rarely more than half a minute's walk away from a café and a glass of something cheering.

'Psst,' said Paul, loudly. He mouthed the word 'Americans' and nodded towards the next table. I turned my head. Two young Americans had entered the café just ahead of us. He was in his mid-twenties, tall and already grossly obese. She was two or three years younger, almost as tall as him and not yet as plump as she would become. They both wore denim jackets with American flags stitched onto the breast pockets.

'I want two Cokes and two turkey rolls,' shouted the American to the solitary waiter, who was standing at the back of the café.

'Do you hear me?' called the young American impatiently.

The waiter walked over to the Americans' table and pulled out his order pad and pencil.

'Two Cokes and two turkey rolls,' said the American. He shouted the instructions as though he thought the waiter to be deaf, stupid or both.

The waiter looked puzzled.

'Tur-key,' said the American. 'Like chicken.'

The waiter glowered at him, put his pad and pencil away and disappeared. The American sneered and said something I did not catch to his companion. She snorted unpleasantly.

Jean ordered three glasses of *vin chaud* from the barman, a miserable looking Algerian in a dirty white overall, who poked his head through a hatch behind him and passed the order on to some invisible kitchen worker. 'What about Johnny?' I asked Jean.

'Johnny doesn't drink when he's working,' said Jean. 'Not any more. He and I once worked together for a week in Cornwall, England,' said Jean. 'I can't remember the story we were on but while we were there we decided to go for a walk along the cliffs. We took a few half bottles of whisky to keep out the cold. By the time we got to where we were heading – a small fishing village where there was a village pub which had won prizes for its fish stew – I was fairly merry and Johnny was pretty well plastered.'

'There was a pretty young barmaid in the pub and Johnny, being a bit of ladies' man in those days, started chatting her up. He told her he was a professional photographer, showed her his camera and offered to take some portrait shots of her.'

'She, being a simple country girl, was thrilled at the idea of having her picture taken by a hotshot professional photographer – especially when Johnny told her that in the month before he'd photographed Elizabeth Taylor, Princess Margaret and half of the Beatles. She was over the moon.'

'Meanwhile, we carried on drinking. We were on expenses and with the paper's money we bought a couple of bottles of pretty decent claret that the landlord had tucked away and then moved onto a bottle of very good brandy he sold us for a song.'

'When the pub closed for the afternoon the barmaid went home, changed, and came back in her best frock. Johnny then proceeded to shoot a couple of rolls of film. She kept her best frock on for the first roll but he talked her out of it for the second.'

'We tottered back to our hotel that evening and we were both smashed. Johnny had, however, given the barmaid our hotel telephone number and the next day, inevitably perhaps, she was on the phone wanting to know when she could see her photographs.'

'Johnny took the rolls of film into the local newspaper office and asked the picture editor to do him a rush job which – being impressed to meet such a well-known photographer – he duly organised.'

'Sadly, when we got the prints back we discovered that Johnny, being plastered, had managed to cut off the barmaid's head in every single picture. He didn't have one decent picture of her – not one. Johnny was mortified. He was so embarrassed that he got a taxi and went back over and did another shoot stone cold sober. I didn't go with him – I had to interview someone – and when he got back he told me that the girl – whom we had both thought was the most beautiful creature we'd ever seen was in reality one of the ugliest broads he had ever seen let alone photographed. He said it took him three hours to take one picture that made her look half way presentable. Since then he's never touched alcohol when he's been working.'

At this point the miserable looking barman finally appeared with three glasses of *vin chaud*. He seemed to have been trained in surliness and presented them to us as though he was doing us a favour. This time I managed to persuade Jean to let me pay.

As we sat there, quietly sipping, Johnny continued to take photographs of Paul.

'This isn't turkey!' complained the American, who had just taken a bite out of his roll. 'It's chicken.'

The waiter sauntered over to his table.

'This is chicken,' said the American, lifting up the top of the roll and showing the offending meat to the waiter.

'Yes, it is chicken,' said the waiter.

'I don't want chicken,' said the American. 'I want turkey.'

'I do not know this 'turkey',' said the waiter. 'You said 'chicken'. I bring you chicken.'

'I'm not paying for this,' snarled the American. He and his companion stood up.

'You pay or I call the police,' said the waiter, circling the table so that he stood between the American and the doorway.

'Do you know who my father is?' asked the young American.

'No,' replied the waiter, without hesitation. 'Do you?'

The young American seemed slightly shaken by this. As an observer I was impressed. I can think of sharp and witty put downs but I always think of them a day or two too late.

'Actually I think perhaps I knew your mother well,' said the waiter. 'Maybe I am your father!' He thought for a moment. 'Or perhaps I know the dog.' He stared closely at the American. 'Yes. You have the look of the Dobermann about you. I remember your mother always liked big dogs.'

The American backed away a little. 'My father is a very important real estate operator,' he said. He now sounded more nervous and less confident. 'He plays golf with an American senator.'

The waiter picked the bill up off the table and held it right under the American's nose. 'I do not care who is your father,' he hissed. Without looking down he picked a knife up off the table. 'Pay the bill or I cut off your nose.' He sounded very serious.

The pale American looked at the bill, pulled out his wallet and took out two notes. He handed the notes to the waiter who reached into the leather pouch at his waist and threw some coins onto the table. The American looked at them, thought about picking them up, changed his mind and walked out, closely followed by his companion.

'He would not have done it,' said Paul.

We looked at him.

'He was bluffing,' said Paul. 'He would not have cut off the young American's nose. I eat here often. The knives are not sharp enough to cut off a nose.' He grinned and laughed out loud.

It was approaching midnight when Johnny finally announced that he had taken enough photographs. We said goodbye to Paul, whose wife had arrived to help him push his old-fashioned music player (it was on wheels) back home, and started to walk back towards where Johnny had parked his car.

It suddenly occurred to me that although I seemed still to

be able to walk I was quite drunk. Jean, who had drunk twice as much, was decidedly wobbly and was grinning at everyone.

Johnny opened his car, climbed in, started the engine and drove off with a perfunctory wave. He was not a particularly sociable sort of fellow. We had not, I realised, exchanged one word all evening.

'He carries a lot of burdens on his shoulder,' said Jean in explanation.

Just then revellers who had been celebrating poured out onto the pavement from a café. They were waving balloons and streamers and bottles of wine and had clearly been having a very good time. They invited us to join them.

'Goodnight,' I said to Jean, thinking that this was probably a good moment to go back to my hotel and get some sleep.

'Aren't you going to join the party?' asked Jean, who had already acquired a balloon, a paper hat and an opened bottle of wine. 'There are plenty of women!'

I told him I thought I would go back to my hotel.

'You are meeting someone?'

'No.'

'Are you in love?'

I felt myself blushing. 'There is someone I like very much,' I admitted.

'A woman?'

'Yes, of course.'

'There is no 'of course' about it.' He paused and looked at me carefully. 'She is married?'

Startled I looked at him. For a while I did not speak. 'Yes,' I admitted. 'How did you know?'

'If she was not married you would be in love. But because she is married you are denying it to yourself.' He smiled. 'It is impossible for you to be in Paris for all this time and not to be in love. Am I not right about all this?'

'I suppose so,' I admitted.

'Make sure she knows how you feel about her.'

I did not say anything.

'When I was your age I was very much in love,' said Jean. 'I was a student and for a while so was she. She had tuberculosis and had to leave college. Her parents were very rich – they had a huge house on the avenue Victor Hugo – and they sent her away to a sanatorium in Switzerland. They did not approve of me and so they were happy to send her as far away as they could.'

'We wrote to each other and declared our love but I did not dare visit her and she did not dare encourage me to do so. We were both frightened of her father. I told her that I would make my fortune and come back for her. I dreamt of driving up to her parent's house in my Mercedes and receiving her father's blessing. I told her I would write no more until I could come back and claim her as my wife. She promised to wait for me.'

He did not speak again for a minute or two.

'What happened?' I asked him, gently.

'It took me two years to buy the Mercedes. I wrote a screenplay and sold it for a lot of money,' said Jean. 'I drove up to the house on the Avenue Victor Hugo in my Mercedes, rang the doorbell and demanded to see Sophie. I was totally confident. I thought that even if she had forgotten me and married someone else I would be able to persuade her to come with me.'

'Was she there?'

Jean lowered his eyes and his voice. 'No.' he said. 'She was not there. Her mother told me that she was with her grandmother. I said I would go to see her at her grandmother's. The mother then explained that she was with her grandmother at Père Lachaise. She was dead.'

I did not know what to say. I said nothing.

'She had died five months after my last letter to her,' said Jean. 'Her mother wanted to know why I had stopped writing, why I had made no effort to see Sophie.'

'I'm sorry,' I said.

'It was the biggest mistake of my life,' said Jean. 'I should have run away with her. I should have married her. If I had known how ill she was I would have married her immediately.'

I said nothing but walked to a telephone booth at the back of the café. When I got back Jean looked up at me.

'I rang her,' I told him. 'I arranged to see her tonight.'

Chapter 34

'I am twenty years older than you are,' said Claudette quietly. 'Probably much more.'

'What has that got to do with anything?' I asked her. 'I am not in love with you because of your age. I am in love with you because...,' I hesitated. 'I love you.'

'No, no, please don't say that,' said Claudette, backing away from the table as though to put as much distance as possible between us. 'I'm too old for you.'

'What on earth does age matter?' I demanded, feeling desperately frustrated.

'Age makes too much difference,' said Claudette. 'To everything. You don't understand. You can't. Being old takes up so much time. The less time you have left the more time you have to spend just to say alive. Every morning I have to do the exercises for my back and for my neck, and there are the stretching exercises too. I have to decorate my nails, and I have to take my vitamins and my garlic and my other tablets. I take twelve tablets and capsules every morning. Do you know how long it takes to swallow twelve tablets and capsules?'

I shook my head.

'Twenty minutes! I spend twenty minutes a day swallowing tablets to help me live longer. Sometimes I think that I am spending more time than I am saving.' She thought for a moment, and shrugged before continuing. 'I have to moisturise my skin – which takes another twenty minutes – and floss my teeth and medicate my gums with a toothpaste which my dentist recommends. There are calories to be counted, even at breakfast, and I have to do my eye exercises. The older I get the longer it takes to put on my make-up. I go to exercise classes three times a week for my heart and visit the hairdresser and the trichologist twice a week.' She sighed, rather sadly. 'Perhaps it is all a waste of time. You can wind up your watch but the hours will still pass at the same rate.'

I didn't know whether this was one of her grandfather's sayings or not. I didn't ask.

'I will probably be dead in twenty years,' continued Claudette. 'Just as you are beginning your life. For you to be in love with me would be crazy.'

'That's madness,' I told her. 'Women live longer than men. You will live until you are 100 at least. When you are 100 I will be 80. And then the difference in our ages will be irrelevant.'

'No,' said Claudette quietly, shaking her head. 'No.'

'If we were both the same age and you were ill with some terrible disease you would not say that we could not marry because you might be dead in twenty, ten or five years,' I pointed out. 'All that matters is that I want to be with you.'

'But, sadly, it is not all that matters,' whispered Claudette. She spoke so softly that I hardly heard her. 'I have a husband,' she reminded me.

I looked at her, hardly daring to speak, hardly daring to ask the question I had to ask.

Eventually, I found the courage. 'Do you love him?' I asked her.

Claudette spoke but I did not hear what she said. 'Do you love him?' I asked her again.

This time she looked straight at me and spoke with exaggerated clarity. 'Yes.' she said.

I looked at her. There were tears in her eyes. 'I love him,' she said. 'I cannot leave him. He needs me.'

'I need you,' I said. Now there were tears in my eyes too.

'You are young and strong,' she said. 'You do not need me as much as he does.'

'He is strong,' I protested. 'Look at the way he treats you. He is terrible. He flaunts his mistress before you and everyone else.'

'He is an actor,' said Claudette, as though that explained everything. 'He is a child. He does not mean to hurt me.'

'I love you,' I told her. I could hardly see for tears.

'I love you too,' she said. 'I love you so very, very much. But if I go with you we will have no future. We are from different worlds. Different times.' She looked up at me, reached out and held my hand. 'Our love will be suffocated by my guilt and shame.'

For a while neither of us spoke.

'Can we be friends?' I asked her. I hardly recognised my own voice.

She shook her head. 'Please go,' she whispered. 'I do not have the strength to leave. Please go.' She gripped my hand tighter and then let go, gently pushing my hand away from her. She closed her eyes. Her cheeks were soaked and her mascara had run down almost to her chin.

I reached down deep into my soul and took hold of every piece of courage I could find there. I stood up, bent down and kissed her forehead. 'I don't believe you,' I said. 'I don't believe you love him.'

She looked up at me. For what seemed an eternity she did not speak. We just looked at one another. 'Do you remember the theatre we went to that first evening?'

'Of course.'

'There is a big, fashionable café next to the theatre. I can't remember the name. The Café du Theatre, I think. There is a party there tomorrow. After the performance. About eleven. Come and look. Do not speak to me. Do not approach me. Just look.' She looked into my eyes. 'You will come?'

'Yes. Of course.'

'You promise not to approach me? Not to speak to me?'

'Yes.'

'Say it. Say you promise.'

'I promise.'

'You will see me with him. You turn round, you go away.

And we never see one another again.'
    'I promise.'
    I walked away.
    I felt as though my life had ended.

Chapter 35

It was raining heavily that evening but nevertheless I walked to the theatre where Claudette's husband was starring. I wanted to be alone. I couldn't bear the thought of standing next to other people on a bus or on the Metro. Walking the deserted, wet pavements was exactly what I wanted.

The walk took me two hours and I had no umbrella; just my scarf and my beret. My jacket provided little protection. I was soaked by the time I got there.

The theatre performance had just finished. Word had spread that the actors would be attending a party in the café next door and the pavement outside the theatre was crowded with fans. A canvas awning had been erected so that the party guests from the theatre would not get wet. The gawping theatre-goers had spilt out into the road, where they stood, dripping wet and as patient as only true fans can be. The rain must have started after the theatre performance for many of the theatre-goers were dressed only in dresses or suits and had neither coats nor umbrellas to protect them. A few held newspapers or magazines above their heads in feeble attempts to protect themselves.

Whoever had arranged the party had paid the café owner to close his establishment to other customers and there were two huge bouncers standing on the pavement each side of the doorway, preventing gatecrashers and fans from getting inside. I pushed and jostled my way into position so that I would have a good view of the actors and the other guests as they walked from the theatre to the café.

I almost missed her.

She looked utterly amazing. She was wearing a simple, black, high neck, dress with long diaphanous sleeves. The dress reached down to the ground and dragged behind her slightly on the red carpet the organisers had lain down on the pavement. Her hair was piled high on top of her head and a single stream of tight curls cascaded down across each temple. She wore a stunning diamond necklace with matching earrings. She looked exactly what she was: the wife of one of France's most successful actors.

When I saw her I stepped back, trying to melt into the crowd so that she would not see me. She had her arm threaded through her husband's and they were walking side by side. They looked, I thought, like newlyweds; totally devoted to one another and very much in love. As they passed me I looked down to avert my eyes. But I don't think I need have bothered. Claudette did not even seem to see me. She was laughing at something her husband had said. Someone in the crowd shouted something, I don't know what it was, but he waved and shouted something back. Claudette lay her head against his shoulder proudly and affectionately. I did not, and do not, know how much of this was genuine and how much was for my benefit. Claudette would certainly have known that although she could not see me I would be there. Sometimes I comforted myself with the thought that the whole thing had been an act; performed solely to convince me that I should allow my love for her to fade and die. Perhaps.

I had seen more than enough. I turned away, fought my way through the crowd and walked back to my hotel, through the pouring rain; totally soaked and utterly broken-hearted. There was lightning and thunder as I walked and my tears added to the floods in the deserted streets. I didn't care a fig about the rain. Once you are wet through you can get no wetter. I cared only about what I had seen and about what I had lost.

The next morning I went to the Gare du Nord and bought a ticket to London. I went back to the hotel and wrote goodbye notes to everyone I knew. I didn't want to see anyone. In the notes

I explained that I had been called back to England in a hurry. Then I packed, gave the key to my room in to the receptionist for the last time, walked to the railway station and caught the evening boat train.

Chapter 36

At Calais I left the train from Paris and embarked upon the ferry which would take me back to England. I felt both miserable and excited. It seemed like a lifetime since I had first arrived in Paris. In fact it had been considerably less than a year.

When I had arrived, shy, diffident, gauche and nervous, I had felt as though I was watching rather than taking part in my own life. Now, leaving France I felt as though I had graduated and had become a player rather than a spectator. Oh, I was still very ignorant of the world. But I knew that there were many things I did not yet know. And I knew that I would not learn the most important lessons of my life at university.

On the boat I found a quiet seat on deck, at the stern, and took out the thick notebook in which I had written my first novel. I started to re-read my manuscript. It was a novel about a young man who leaves home to spend a year abroad. I knew nothing whatsoever about writing but I knew a good deal about the young man who had left home. The more I read the more it became apparent that my knowledge about the latter did not outweigh my ignorance about the former. The novel was ponderous and pompous. It was fearfully dull.

One by one I tore the pages out of the notebook, held them up in the air and let the wind take them. They fluttered behind us as we sped back to England, landing on the waves in our wake, floating for a moment or two and then sinking out of sight.

Eventually the whole book had gone and I was left with just the covers. I kept them as a souvenir.

I unfastened my suitcase, reached inside and took out the large, red notebook my mother had given me when I had announced that I was going to Paris.

I opened the notebook, which at her suggestion I had used as a diary, and started to read.

I remember that as I read it occurred to me that the diary of my personal springtime in Paris would be invaluable if I ever decided to write a book about my early days in the Queen of Cities.

Chapter 37

A couple of weeks later I arrived back at medical school for the autumn term of my first official year as a student. I still missed Claudette terribly. It would be some time before I did not dream of her, both during the day and at night.

But I would, I knew, be eternally grateful for my illness, and the opportunities it had given me.

One of the first people I met at medical school was William Bright-Perkins, the student with whom I had shared a room when I had made my first attempt to start to train to be a doctor.

'How are you?' William asked.

I told him I was fine.

'Pity you had to waste a year,' he said. 'Still, I guess you're in for a pretty easy time of it this year.'

I looked at him, puzzled.

'Why do you say that?'

'I expect you've been swotting away for the last year,' he said. 'That's certainly what I would have done.'

'I'm afraid I haven't,' I confessed.

'Then you'll probably wish you had,' he said ominously. 'You're in for a tough time. You'll regret wasting the year.'

He then spent twenty minutes telling me of some of the horrors which lay ahead of me. He told me about the anatomy classes he'd attended, the physiology books he'd read and the exams he'd passed.

'So,' he said when he had finished. 'That's what you've got ahead of you. Now are you sorry you'd didn't spend the year swotting?'

'No,' I told him honestly.

A year ago I would have undoubtedly been alarmed by what he had said. But now I wasn't in the slightest bit concerned.

'You haven't learned anything for the course?'

'I haven't learned anything for the course,' I agreed. 'But I know a great deal more now than I did when I left.'

William looked at me, clearly rather puzzled.

'So, what have you learned?' he asked. 'Oh,' he said, suddenly remembering where I'd been. 'I suppose you speak perfect French now. I guess that might be useful.'

'No. I'm afraid not. I still speak the school boy stuff. But I have learned quite a lot about me.'

He frowned. 'Bit of a waste of a year then wasn't it? That illness may not have killed you but it effectively cost you a year of your life. The way I look at it is this: if you lose a year from your studying life now, in the end you'll lose a year from your earning life. That little illness of yours will have cost you thousands in the end.'

That wasn't the way I looked at it at all. I felt sorry for William because he knew so little that he didn't know the importance of what I'd learned and what he hadn't.

I was absolutely certain that I'd learned far, far more during my months in Paris than I would have learned at university.

'No one sees the stars when the sun is at its brightest,' I said.

He frowned. 'What on earth does that mean?'

'It's just a saying my grandfather was fond of,' I told him. I looked at my watch. 'Sorry,' I said. 'I must fly. I've got my first lecture in three minutes.'

I left him standing there, looking very confused.

I don't know how long he stood there. I didn't look back.

Epilogue

When I decided to write this book I went to Paris and spent two months attempting to trace all the people I had met in 1963. I was surprisingly successful. Here is an update (correct as at 2002) on the people described in this book (in the order of their appearance).

William Bright-Perkins

After qualifying as a doctor, William specialised in radiology. He was one of the first students of his year to be appointed a hospital consultant. He married a nurse and after two years in the Middle East settled down at a hospital in the North of England. Tragically, he died in 1986 of cancer, leaving a widow and three small children. Two years later his widow married a local GP.

Sylvie Roland

Two years after I met her, Sylvie Roland married an American businessman and emigrated to Colorado. She and her husband now run a very successful mail order business selling health products. Sylvie has not been back to France for over thirty years. They have four children, none of whom speak a word of French.

Sylvestre Baptiste

Amazingly, at the start of the year 2002, Monsieur Baptiste was still manager of the same pharmacy in Paris. The store had changed hands four times since I'd worked there but Monsieur Baptiste had remained throughout these changes of ownership. When I worked there I thought of him as middle aged. He cannot, however, have been much more than in his mid to late twenties at the time.

Archie Trench

Archie Trench was arrested in 1972 for fraud. He served eight years in an American prison. After his release he travelled to Europe and started an agency providing American companies with European office facilities. He died in a car accident in 1989.

Marvin and Sheila Brown

Marvin died in 1981 after a long illness. Sheila still lives in the same apartment in Paris and now shares it with a young American woman called Kitty Kamber whom she met in 1988. They insisted on having their cook make me afternoon tea (cucumber sandwiches on brown bread) and Sheila wept when I left. She told me that Kitty is an artist and playwright whose talents have not yet been widely recognised. Marvin left a considerable fortune in trust to Sheila. She does not know where the money goes when she dies and so she saves every month so that she will have something to leave to Kitty, to whom she is clearly devoted. (I kept in touch with Marvin and Sheila until 1981, but lost contact with Sheila after Marvin died.)

John Tennyson

Less than a year after I left Paris, Mr Tennyson's wife caught him with a girl (not Natalie). He had been spotted by a friend of hers taking the girl into the George V hotel just off the Champs Elysée. The divorce crippled him financially and he had to sell the chain of pharmacies. But within five years he had bounced back and built up a chain of shops selling sex toys and erotic lingerie. His current wife (his fifth) is a stripper, who was rumoured to be just sixteen years old when they married. The Tennysons live in a five bedroom apartment in the Marais in central Paris.

James Whitechapel

The former language school proprietor retired in 1978 to a cottage in the Loire. His language school was never successful and lurched from one crisis to another. Mr Whitechapel's finances were saved when he inherited a sizeable sum from an aunt and it was this sum which enabled him to buy his cottage and retire. He died in the autumn of 1999, just months before I tried to get in touch with him.

Jules de Prony

Jules is still very happily married. He and his wife have a beautiful chateau which stands in 25 hectares of parkland just south of Paris. They have three children. The oldest (a boy) is a doctor, the middle child (a girl) got married and divorced, has no children, and is now training to be an architect. The youngest son, who was apparently regarded as a musical prodigy, now works in a Paris bank as a foreign securities trader. Jules runs the family business very successfully. We had a very pleasant lunch in a restaurant near to his office. He insisted that he has been totally faithful to his wife and has never had a mistress. Much to everyone's surprise (and delight) Jules' father, whom I never met, survived for another fifteen years after his retirement.

Claudette Foucault

Claudette and Gerard were divorced in 1974 after 23 years of marriage. Claudette is now married to an editor who works for a leading French magazine group. Together they have written several books on French architecture. Gerard, her actor husband, died of liver failure in 1983 and was buried in Père Lachaise. He left Claudette bankrupt. Claudette told me proudly that half the women in Paris turned out to mourn him. She looks, and acts, fifteen years younger than she is.

'You forgot all about me within three months, didn't you?' she said, when we met again (at the former Café Napoleon – now renamed).

'I never forgot about you, that's why I'm here,' I reminded her.

'But the love had evaporated within three months?' she persisted.

'Around that,' I smiled. Young love is very fickle.

'Puppy love for you,' she said. 'But not for me. Giving you up was the hardest and noblest thing I ever did. Getting over you took me twenty years.'

Anne-Marie

I never knew her surname and without it found it quite impossible to trace her.

Theresa Wurtz

Theresa is now married to a dentist with a practice in Marseilles. I telephoned her and discovered that they met when he was visiting Paris for a convention of orthodontists in 1972. Theresa still designs bras and shoes but has not yet had any of her designs accepted by a manufacturer. She told me that her husband has agreed to finance a small shop in Marseilles and she intends to have some of her designs hand-made so that they can be sold in the shop – which will, of course, be called 'The Shoepermarket'.

Jean Laconte

Jean married a divorcee, a paediatrician with a practice in Paris in 1968. He died in 1991 after a short illness. His widow told me that his book about Paris street people was never published. A string of publishers turned it down. Jean continued to write for television until his death. His widow did not know anything about the whereabouts of Johnny (the photographer with whom he was working when I met him).

Isabella Petiet

I could not trace Isabella. When I finally found the site of her apartment building I discovered there was an office building in its place. No one in the neighbourhood could tell me anything about her current whereabouts.

Also by Vernon Coleman

It's Never Too Late

Tony Davison is bored, tired and fed up with life. He has lost his job and his wife, and doesn't have much of a future. In despair, he sells his house and most of his belongings and sets off to Paris for a weekend holiday. But what started off as a quick holiday break soon turns into a once-in-a-lifetime experience.

It's Never Too Late tells the uplifting story of Tony's search for a new life and happiness in a new country. Full of the gentle humour and anecdotes which are so much the hallmark of Vernon Coleman's novels.

"Imagine that you feel like settling down in a comfortable armchair with an entertaining book – one that will keep your attention and combat the desire to nod off ... If this description fits you then you could do much worse than spoil yourself with this book. The author's style is both easy to read and makes you want to keep turning the pages – in fact I had to force myself to stop reading and put the book down. I am sure you will enjoy the book, which apart from anything else brings to life the atmosphere of Paris – so why not give it to a loved one or friend ... and promptly borrow it to read yourself!? Whatever you may decide, we have chosen this as our Book of the Month."
(Living France)

"*It's Never Too Late* is a light-hearted reversal of the ageing process." *(France Magazine)*

Price £14.95 (hardback)

Published by Chilton Designs
Order from Publishing House • Trinity Place • Barnstaple • Devon EX32 9HJ • England
Telephone 01271 328892 • Fax 01271 328768

Also by Vernon Coleman

Second Innings

The characters leap from the page as they draw you in to this tale of a young man (Biffo Brimstone) who overcomes the adversity of modern day living by, quite simply, running away! He leaves an unrewarding job, a shrewish and demanding wife and a couple of surly children and takes the next train out of the miserable suburban estate which has been his home for the past few years of his mundane life.

The train takes him to a part of the country he has never before visited, and the subsequent bus journey deposits him in the village of Fondling-under-Water. It is there that his new life begins.

"A piece of good old-fashioned escapism, an easy-to-follow plot; just right to relax with after a busy day ... you would be happy to lend it to your granny or anyone else's granny come to that. This author has the ability to create a distinctive 'mind's eye' picture of every character. The story would 'translate' into an excellent radio play." *(The Journal of the Cricket Society)*

"Settling down with Vernon Coleman's latest novel is one of the best restorative treatments I know for relieving the stresses and strains of modern living. Right from page one you can feel yourself unwind as you enjoy the antics of the wonderful array of characters and their exploits. Terrific reading for anyone." *(Lincolnshire Echo)*

Price £14.95 (hardback)

Published by Chilton Designs
Order from Publishing House • Trinity Place • Barnstaple • Devon EX32 9HJ • England
Telephone 01271 328892 • Fax 01271 328768

Also by Vernon Coleman

The Bilbury Chronicles

A young doctor arrives to begin work in the small village of Bilbury. This picturesque hamlet is home to some memorable characters who have many a tale to tell, and Vernon Coleman weaves together a superb story full of humour and anecdotes. The Bilbury books will transport you back to the days of old-fashioned, traditional village life where you never needed to lock your door, and when a helping hand was only ever a moment away. The first novel in the series.

"I am just putting pen to paper to say how very much I enjoyed *The Bilbury Chronicles*. I just can't wait to read the others."
(Mrs K., Cambs)

"...a real delight from cover to cover. As the first in a series it holds out the promise of entertaining things to come"
(Daily Examiner)

"The Bilbury novels are just what I've been looking for. They are a pleasure to read over and over again."
(Mrs C., Lancs)

Price £12.95 (hardback)

Published by Chilton Designs
Order from Publishing House • Trinity Place • Barnstaple • Devon EX32 9HJ • England
Telephone 01271 328892 • Fax 01271 328768

Also by Vernon Coleman

The Village Cricket Tour

This superb novel tells the story of a team of amateur cricketers who spend two weeks of their summer holidays on tour in the West Country. It proves to be a most eventful fortnight full of mishaps and adventures as the cricketers play their way around the picturesque coastline of Devon and Cornwall.

"The only word to describe (this book) is hilarious. It is the funniest book about cricket that I have ever read. In fact it is the funniest book I have read since *Three Men in a Boat*."
(Chronicle & Echo)

"I enjoyed it immensely. He has succeeded in writing a book that will entertain, a book that will amuse and warm the cockles of tired old hearts."
(Peter Tinniswood, Punch)

"His powers of observation combine with his penchant for brilliant word pictures to create a most delightful book ... a first class example of humorous adventures in the West Country"
(Sunday Independent)

"The Village Cricket Tour has provided me with much amusement and a great deal of pleasure."
(Mr A., Canada)

Price £12.95 (hardback)

Published by Chilton Designs
Order from Publishing House • Trinity Place • Barnstaple •
Devon EX32 9HJ • England
Telephone 01271 328892 • Fax 01271 328768

Also by Vernon Coleman

Mrs Caldicot's Cabbage War

Thelma Caldicot was married to her husband for thirty dull and boring years. The marriage could not have been described as fulfilling in any way, shape or form, but she stuck it out in her usual uncomplaining and subservient way. Then, one afternoon, two police officers knocked on her door to bring her some news that was to radically change her life.

Mrs Caldicot's Cabbage War is the poignant, warm and often funny story of an ordinary woman who, after being pushed around by other people for most of her life, finally decides to stand up for herself.

"Thank you so much for *Mrs Caldicot's Cabbage War*.
All your books are great."
(Mrs N., Surrey)

"... quite hilarious and my sort of reading."
(Mrs C., Darwen)

"A splendid relaxing read."
(Sunday Independent)

Price £12.95 (hardback)

Published by Chilton Designs
Order from Publishing House • Trinity Place • Barnstaple •
Devon EX32 9HJ • England
Telephone 01271 328892 • Fax 01271 328768

Also by Vernon Coleman

The Man Who Inherited a Golf Course

Trevor Dunkinfield, the hero of this novel, wakes up one morning to discover that he is the owner of his very own golf club – fairways, bunkers, clubhouse and all. This unexpected present lands in Trevor's lap as a result of a distant uncle's will which he discovers, to his dismay, contains several surprising clauses. To keep the club he must win an important match – and he's never played a round of golf in his life!

"This scenario is tailor-made for Vernon Coleman's light and amusing anecdotes about country life and pursuits. His fans will lap it up."
(Sunday Independent)

"Hugely enjoyable, in the best tradition of British comic writing."
(Evening Chronicle)

"Light hearted entertainment ... very readable."
(Golf World)

Price £12.95 (hardback)

Published by Chilton Designs
Order from Publishing House • Trinity Place • Barnstaple •
Devon EX32 9HJ • England
Telephone 01271 328892 • Fax 01271 328768

For a catalogue of Vernon Coleman's books
please write to:

Publishing House
Trinity Place
Barnstaple
Devon EX32 9HJ
England

Telephone	01271 328892
Fax	01271 328768

Outside the UK:

Telephone	+44 1271 328892
Fax	+44 1271 328768

Or visit our website:

www.vernoncoleman.com